Circle of

Lover's Sacrifice

Other books by R. A. Steffan

The Horse Mistress: Book 1
The Horse Mistress: Book 2
The Horse Mistress: Book 3
The Horse Mistress: Book 4
The Complete Horse Mistress Collection

The Lion Mistress: Book 1
The Lion Mistress: Book 2
The Lion Mistress: Book 3
The Complete Lion Mistress Collection

Antidote: Love and War, Book 1

The Queen's Musketeers: Book 1
The Queen's Musketeers: Book 2
The Queen's Musketeers: Book 3
The D'Artagnan Collection: Books 1-3
The Queen's Musketeers: Book 4

Sherlock Holmes & The Case of the Magnate's Son

Diamond Bar Apha Ranch
Diamond Bar Alpha 2: Angel & Vic
(with Jaelynn Woolf)

Circle of Blood Book Three:

Lover's Sacrifice

R. A. Steffan & Jaelynn Woolf

Circle of Blood Book Three: Lover's Sacrifice

Copyright 2018 by R. A. Steffan

All rights reserved. Printed in the United States of America. No part of this book may be used or reproduced in any manner whatsoever without written permission except in the case of brief quotations embedded in critical articles or reviews.

This book is a work of fiction. Names, characters, businesses, organizations, places, events and incidents either are the product of the author's imagination or are used fictitiously. Any resemblance to actual persons, living or dead, events, or locales is entirely coincidental.

For information, contact the author at http://www.rasteffan.com/contact/

Cover art by Deranged Doctor Design

First Edition: March 2018

INTRODUCTION

This book contains graphic violence and explicit sexual content. It is intended for a mature audience. While it is part of a series with an over-arching plot, it can be read as a standalone with a "happy ever after" ending for the two main characters, and a satisfying resolution of the storyline. If you don't intend to continue the series, you may wish to avoid the epilogue.

TABLE OF CONTENTS

One...1
Two..24
Three...40
Four...56
Five..74
Six..95
Seven...110
Eight..126
Nine...145
Ten...163
Eleven..181
Twelve...199
Thirteen..224
Fourteen...237
Fifteen...247
Sixteen..262
Seventeen...274
Epilogue..293

ONE

This really wasn't how Mason had expected to spend his Friday morning.

Endless piles of paperwork? Definitely. Arguing over the phone about continued funding for the clinic? Probably. Counseling sessions with some of the children under his care? Yep.

Staring down the barrel of an automatic weapon wielded by a twelve-year-old? Not so much.

The black muzzle of the AK-47 never wavered as it pointed at Mason's chest, held securely in the hands of a wild-eyed Haitian boy. The child appeared dwarfed by the high-powered assault rifle cradled against his scrawny shoulder, but Mason knew all too well how deadly he could be.

The MP escorting a small group of newly liberated child soldiers to Mason's rehabilitation clinic had turned his back for less than a second before the boy struck like a snake—yanking the weapon from his slackened grip and turning it on the people he no doubt saw as enemy captors.

Both Mason and the MP stood frozen in place. The MP's mouth was hanging open in surprise. No doubt the man had thought himself lucky to draw such a cushy posting in Port-au-Prince, guarding adolescents instead of fighting in the rebel-held villages out in the hinterlands.

2

More fool him.

As the physician in charge of the ragtag, under-funded *Center for the Rehabilitation of Underage Conscripts*, Mason knew exactly how hazardous the duty they were performing here could be. And if he survived the next few minutes, he would bloody well find out who had failed to adequately brief the hapless soldier standing next to him. At which point, he would rip that person a new orifice, Hippocratic Oath or no.

It was fairly obvious that the MP was going to be little help in defusing the situation, though Mason supposed it would have been worse if he'd decided to go all Rambo on the kid and do something fatally stupid.

Mason stood perfectly still, his hands hanging loose at his sides, trying to breathe calmly through the massive adrenaline dump coursing through his body. He recognized the hallmarks of the body's fight-or-flight response, though his detailed medical knowledge of the process did little to curb the wash of instinct that was trying to shut down his logical thinking ability just when he *seriously fucking needed it*.

His senses were heightened, strained to their utmost, taking in the oddly jarring sounds in the background of the tense scene. The happy shouts of children playing. The creak of palm trees swaying in the sea breeze. The smell of salt clinging to the air, buried beneath vehicle exhaust and decomposing garbage.

The way the matte black finish of the automatic weapon's barrel seemed to swallow the daylight.

Mason mentally shook himself, trying to force his focus back to the boy—to his body language and facial expression. Remaining calm was the key. Panic would only get him—and possibly a lot of other people in the immediate area—killed.

There was no cover to speak of in front of the clinic, and few options for outside assistance. Even if the wide-eyed child holding the rifle felt like letting Mason stroll around the corner for a moment to place a leisurely phone call on his mobile, calling the coppers in Port-au-Prince these days was about as effective a method of summoning help as picking up a random tin can from the street and shouting into it.

Face it, mate, he thought. *It's up to you to keep this thing from going tits-up.*

He took a slow, measured breath and let it out before speaking.

"Okay, let's just take a minute to calm down and talk," he began, his Aussie accent becoming more pronounced than usual, as it always seemed to when he was under stress. "You're in charge... you've got the gun. I promise you, you're perfectly safe here—"

The boy lifted the gun a fraction, his aim moving from Mason's chest to his head. "I might be safe, *blan*," he said, eyeing Mason's pale skin and obviously foreign mode of dress, "but *you* aren't. Have this soldier take me an' the others back where you found us, or I'll kill you." He bared white teeth. "Maybe I'll just kill you anyway, eh? What d'you think of that?"

Movement in the corner of his eye drew Mason's attention, and a face appeared at the screen door of the building next to him. *Bugger.*

"Joni," he said in a calm voice, speaking to the young nurse who was little more than a teenager herself, "why don't you take the rest of the children out the back way and go down to the beach for a bit?"

Their eyes locked, and he saw the same fear he was holding at bay reflected in her face. He forced a reassuring smile and jerked his head toward the back of the structure, silently imploring her to get herself and the other children to safety. With a clipped nod, she backed away from the door, and he could hear her issuing quiet instructions to the kids who had gathered at the front of the clinic for their mid-morning medications.

He turned his full attention back to the boy and steeled himself to try something that would either improve the situation... or escalate it.

"It's me you need to talk to," he said in the same conversational tone. "I'm the one in charge, here. Let's have a chat, just you and I." He flicked his eyes to the MP. "You—take our other guests inside, please, and help Joni."

The soldier looked at Mason like he was bent in the head. He might've even had a valid point about that. Still, Mason nodded toward the door, insistent.

He met the eyes of the half-dozen other children who had arrived with this group. "Go on—

please make yourselves at home. There are bottles of Coke chilling on ice in the corner of the front room. Help yourselves."

The other boys looked uncertainly at each other, but after a few moments of indecision, two of them wandered toward the door and peeked inside. Upon seeing the large red cooler sitting in the corner as promised, they went inside. The others followed.

"Go on," Mason told the MP, praying like hell that he wasn't making a deadly mistake.

With a final, uncertain nod, the man backed cautiously away until his hand brushed the doorknob. He opened the door and slipped through, closing it silently behind him. The AK-47 did not erupt into a deafening hail of gunfire, though its muzzle did begin to tremble almost imperceptibly.

Well, that's everyone except me out of harm's way, at least.

Letting the air flow silently from his lungs, Mason turned back towards the boy in front of him and tried to give him the same friendly smile he'd used to reassure Joni. It felt like the muscles in his face had frozen, though, and he didn't think he'd really pulled it off.

The child staring at him with bloodshot eyes did not react, simply gazing back with a sort of dull, distant anger. The only move he made was to readjust his grip on the powerful AK-47 clutched in his small hands. He shifted on his feet, standing in front of Mason in baggy cargo shorts and nothing else, save for the soiled green bandana tied around his head.

Mason didn't want to make any move that might startle or upset the boy, but, at the same time, this stalemate needed to end. The longer they stood out here, staring at each other with a high-powered weapon between them, the greater the likelihood that Mason would end up riddled with bullet wounds.

Moving slowly, Mason lowered himself into a crouch so that he was below eye level with the scared and angry boy. At the same time, he did a quick visual inspection, cataloging the child's condition with the eye of a physician.

Short, brittle hair. Bloodshot eyes, flat affect, dilated pupils. Probably under the influence of some sort of stimulant. Discharge from the eyes and nose. Chapped lips with sores in the corners of his mouth. Thin frame. Bloated belly. Multiple scars and marks from badly healed wounds. Partially healed gunshot wound to the upper right arm, from approximately six weeks ago. Cracked feet showing signs of advanced fungal infection.

"How old are you?" Mason asked, looking up at the boy.

The question seemed to startle him. He blinked several times, and a look of confusion crossed his features before they hardened back into flat anger. "I'm fifteen, *blan*. What do you care?"

Stunted growth due to emaciation.

"I bet you're a hell of a soldier," Mason said in lieu of an answer. "You overpowered that MP like it was nothing."

"I'm the best in my unit," the youth bragged, tipping his chin up as if daring Mason to dispute it.

"That's why you're gonna send me straight back, and the others, too."

"Okay, let's discuss that," Mason said easily. "My name's Dr. Walker, by the way. What's yours?"

There was a tiny hesitation. "They call me *San Silans*."

Silent Blood? Christ on a crutch.

For the thousandth time since arriving here, Mason mentally shook his head in disbelief over what was being done to Haiti's children during this long and bloody civil war.

"Sorry, San—my Creole is shit, as you can probably guess," he said, not completely truthfully. "What's your real name?"

He'd seen this before, many times, from other child soldiers receiving treatment at the clinic. Their captors would take them from their families—sometimes dragging them straight from the arms of screaming or dying relatives—and erase their pasts. They would brainwash the children, ranging in age from those who were barely more than toddlers to those in their teens, using a combination of drugs, intimidation, and rudimentary psychological techniques.

After a few weeks or months, the victims were utterly convinced that their loved ones had been killed and desecrated by "the enemy," and that to avenge them, they were honor bound to kill any government soldier who came into their sights without hesitation. The rebel unit was their new family, and the penalty for disloyal behavior was death at the hands of their fellow child soldiers.

8

The boy hesitated at Mason's question about his real name, a flash of something like unease crossing his features. "*My name is San Silans.*"

"It's just that *San Silans* is an unusual name," Mason pressed carefully. "Maybe there was something else you were called before people started calling you that?"

The kid pursed his lips together in a tight line, his knuckles tightening around the stock of the rifle. He stared hard at Mason, as if sizing him up — or perhaps trying to understand him. Mason returned the boy's gaze without blinking, purposely keeping his energy low and calm.

The moment stretched out like taffy, before Mason's captor dropped his eyes to the side, giving a bit of ground. Though he maintained his firm grip on the weapon, a fraction of the tension bled out of his shoulders.

"I used to be called Eniel," he muttered.

"Eniel," Mason repeated. "That's a traditional name in the south, isn't it? A good name. Strong, like you."

"Yes." Eniel still wasn't meeting his eyes.

"Well, Eniel, since you're here at the clinic, what can I do to help you?"

Eniel's eyes hardened. "I already told you, *blan*. You can send me back where I belong. I need to report to my commander. I won't stay here with you government scum."

Mason spread his hands in a gesture indicating harmlessness. "Eniel, mate — I'm Australian. I'm not a rebel *or* a government lackey. I'm just here to help pick up the pieces."

Eniel lifted the gun and jerked his chin toward it. "The stupid *kochon* I grabbed this from is government scum. You could smell it on him."

"And you ran him right off, so no need to worry about him right now," Mason said. "Eniel, we can't send you back to your commander. Your commander's the one who sent you here in the first place."

"Lies!" Eniel snapped, his voice rising.

Actually, that much was the complete truth. Mason and his contacts had been negotiating the release of child soldiers from rebel forces for months now. Public image was enough of a concern for the insurgents that they were willing to give up some of their low-value fighters in exchange for the goodwill it would garner.

Especially the ones who were already on the verge of physical or mental breakdown… though it would probably be better for Eniel not to hear about that part, just now.

"I'm afraid it's the truth," Mason countered. "Your commander was worried about you. He sent you here for medical help. That's a gunshot wound on your arm. It must be bothering you, even though you're such a good soldier that you hide it well. I could help you with that."

As if on cue, Eniel's body began to quiver. He sniffed hard, wiping mucus from his nose with the back of one arm. It smeared and glistened across his face as his eyes glittered in the bright sunlight. "He said I had to get in the truck with the others. He didn't say what would happen or where we were going."

Mason nodded in understanding. "And what did you think about that?"

Eniel raised and lowered one shoulder. The shaking in his body intensified, and he scowled at Mason, almost as if another personality had consumed him. "I thought maybe it was a test, or a mission." He pointed to the clinic building. "They are from the government; they are the people responsible for killing my family! I thought, maybe, this is a way for my commander to infiltrate the enemy, by sending me here to kill them!"

Mason knew better than to argue with him. He'd heard the same story many times before. It was common practice to tell young, impressionable children that the government had been the ones to kill their families. The rebel leaders instilled that hatred among their young soldiers early on to ensure total obedience. It would take them months, if not years, to undo the brainwashing most of these boys had sustained.

"Like I said," Mason began, "I'm not a part of your war. I just want to help you, like your commander intended when he ordered you to come here. So, when was the last time you ate? Are you hungry?"

At the mention of food, Eniel's gaze seemed to tighten on Mason's face. What had been dirty looks and constant scanning before, suddenly became almost dog-like hunger, focused and unmoving.

"Come on," Mason coaxed, keeping his tone calm and matter-of-fact. "We'll get you a meal and you can tell me a bit more about yourself."

The boy stayed completely still for several moments, staring at Mason's face.

Shite, I'm getting too old for this. My legs are going completely numb, Mason thought, as he tried to slowly shift positions to allow the blood flow to return to his tingling right foot.

Eniel's shoulders sagged and his grip softened on the AK-47. He grimaced, as if in physical pain. "You should be afraid of me. I have… done things. Terrible things."

Mason felt his heart ache, as it always did when the children at his clinic spoke about their past. All of them had been turned into monsters by the rebel kidnappers that forced them into the war, giving them weapons and brainwashing them until everything they used to believe was forgotten. Many of them had killed hundreds of people, mowed down opposing forces, or even killed other child soldiers in different militia units during the night for scraps of blanket or morsels of food.

It was likely that Eniel was no different, standing here in the bright sunlight with snot smeared across his face, pointing a high-powered weapon unerringly at Mason while looking so weak and malnourished that it was amazing he could even stand up.

Most people would look at Eniel and see a murderer. But Mason knew that he was merely seeing a weapon, fashioned and honed by adults who placed more value on winning a war than on the sanctity of childhood.

Ironically, the phrase "it's not your fault" was one of the surest ways to enrage a child soldier.

They hated hearing it, because it chipped away at their tenuous sense of control over their own lives. And yet, it was true. One did not blame a grenade for exploding and killing people. One blamed the person who pulled the pin and threw it.

Eniel was not to blame for the lives he had taken. Every day, Mason told himself that the rebel commanders at whose feet those deaths truly rested would pay eventually. At times like this, he almost wished he could personally extract that payment—but he knew that his place was here, healing the broken bodies and damaged souls of these, the most vulnerable victims of Haiti's relentless war against itself.

"Eniel," he said after a quiet moment, "lots of the young people here have done bad things. I still want to help you."

"Why?"

Mason had to gather himself for a moment before answering, "Because in this clinic, we don't leave anyone behind."

Eniel cocked his head at that, fidgeting, his thin fingers trembling around the stock of the gun. He shrugged one shoulder towards his ear several times, as if to displace an irksome fly. Shifting his weight back and forth, his gaze turned towards a gap between the buildings, where only a few palm trees blocked the view of the beach and stunning blue ocean.

Finally, Eniel looked at Mason and parted his chapped, raw lips. "I... I..."

Mason didn't move, just remained frozen in his position, a look of quiet expectation across his face.

"I left people behind," Eniel said in a rush. Wetness glistened in the corners of his eyes. "My friends…"

In a very soft voice, Mason replied, "Why don't you put the gun on the ground and tell me more about that."

Eniel gripped the gun harder for a second, pulling it towards his chest. A wild fear seemed to grip him, making him look eerily like a cornered animal. Mason remained still, his calm expression never wavering.

After a long moment, Eniel relaxed. Never taking his eyes off Mason, he lowered the gun slowly towards the ground. As soon as it was resting on the dirt path in front of the clinic, Mason carefully rose to his feet and gestured Eniel towards the steps.

Thank God for crisis intervention training.

The boy stood still and watched suspiciously as Mason crossed to the steps and sat down, his legs and feet still numb from his awkward, crouched position.

To further put the boy at ease, Mason made quite a show of removing one of his shoes and massaging life back into his foot. He guessed that Eniel would feel more comfortable moving nearer if he wasn't faced with uninterrupted eye contact.

To Mason's relief, the boy took a few faltering steps towards the stairs and lowered himself down against the railing, as far away from Mason as possible.

"Thank you, Eniel," Mason said. Out of the corner of his eye, he saw the boy chew on his lower lip thoughtfully. The gun lay abandoned in the dirt in front of them.

"Now... you were telling me about your friends?" he prompted, pulling his sock back on and brushing the sand and dirt off the fabric.

Eniel was silent for several moments before he spoke, watching Mason carefully adjust his shoe and retie the laces.

"We camped at night in a line, a long line of men and boys. Some had guns, some did not," Eniel began in a hoarse whisper. "My place was near the middle of the line."

Mason nodded to show he was listening, though he looked out through the palm trees dotting the landscape in front of the clinic. His fingers mindlessly found a stone stuck in the crack of the wooden stairs, and he pried at it with a fingernail just to give himself something to do while Eniel spoke.

"I could not sleep, so I stayed awake and watched the stars. The fire in the camp flickered, throwing many shadows. There was no noise except the wind in the grass and trees. Then, I heard screams from the far end of camp. I ran to them, but they were already gone. I raised the alarm, but it was too late. They disappeared."

"Other soldiers?"

"Other boys. Their sleeping places were empty, and their shoes left behind. This happened many times while we traveled, and even though we searched, we could never find them afterward. Never. They are gone… lost in the hills."

Mason breathed out slowly through his nose. *Must have been the government forces taking the boys in secret*, he mused. *But that doesn't make a lot of sense. If they were all sleeping except for a handful of lookouts, why not just capture the entire band of rebels, or kill them? Why just take a few?*

He shook his head, trying to clear his thoughts. He would never understand the ways of the military, and he knew better than to start raising questions that might embarrass the people who held the fate of his clinic in their hands.

Turning his attention back to Eniel, Mason tried to regain the thread of the conversation.

"It sounds like you did everything you could though, right? You kept watch, and you raised the alarm when you knew something had happened."

Eniel stared at his hands, which were cracked, scabbed, and dirty. He nodded, but a frown still marred his features. "James was lost," he said quietly.

"Who was James?" Mason asked.

The frown grew deeper. "My friend. We were together from the very beginning. He was very tall, so his place was near the end of the line. He was taken during the night and I never saw him again."

Eniel's shoulders trembled and he wiped his nose on his arm once more.

"I'm sorry Eniel, I lost a friend not so long ago myself," Mason said. It was true—one of his friends from uni had recently been killed in a suicide bombing in Sydney. Admittedly, the two of them hadn't been terribly close in the years since they'd both graduated and had gone on to different medical schools. Still, Mason knew that he needed to establish a rapport with Eniel, and this was one way to do that.

Eniel turned towards him with glittering eyes. "You did?"

"Yes, and it hurts me very much." Also not a lie. Bess had been like the sister he'd never had growing up. Thinking of her brilliant spark being extinguished during a pointless act of terror made him ache, even months later.

Eniel nodded and set his head down on his arms, which were propped up on his knees. "I am tired of fighting. So tired."

"You fought bravely for a long time. You deserve to rest now," Mason told him. "Think of it as military leave, if that helps."

Eniel snorted. "I was traded by my commander to the government, and they sent me here." He muttered something under his breath that Mason didn't understand, but by the tone of his voice, Mason guessed it was expletives.

"Yeah, I hear you, mate," he said. "It sucks balls when you're told what to do and have to obey sometimes."

"I am a *soldier*, not a child!"

Mason blinked at the sudden rage and anguish that filled Eniel's face, but he didn't back down. "You are both of those things. And soldiers are no strangers to obeying orders, as I imagine you know very well." He reached down and plucked a long strand of the pampas grass stubbornly clinging to life next to the steps. Absently, he weaved the grass leaf through his fingers.

The motion mesmerized Eniel, who watched with wide, unblinking eyes.

"Can I tell you what I want right now, and you tell me what you want?" Mason asked in a soft voice, still toying with the grass.

Eniel's lips parted, and it looked like exhaustion was crashing over him. Even so, he rallied enough to nod at Mason's request.

Mason nodded back. "Good. I want for you and I to go inside together, and check you out medically. We need to make sure you're okay; then you can eat and rest. Now, what do you want?"

Eniel jerked, as if taken by surprise. He glanced into Mason's face and then back towards the ground. "To forget."

Mason sighed quietly. "I'm afraid it's not quite that simple, Eniel—but I can promise you that the bad memories will start to fade, and things will get better with time."

For a second, Mason thought he could make out a tear trickling down the side of Eniel's face. It was wiped away so quickly that he couldn't be sure, though. He stood up slowly and watched as Eniel flinched, recoiling from him.

"It's okay," Mason said, "I'm just going to make this gun safe—that's all."

Eniel did not respond, but continued to watch with wary eyes as Mason carefully disarmed the weapon and pulled the strap over his shoulder, letting the rifle rest against his back. With the chamber empty and the magazine held securely in one hand, Mason walked past Eniel and pulled open the rickety screen door, which creaked loudly. He held the door open for the boy, who remained sitting on the front steps.

Eniel's gaze flickered back and forth between the packed dirt of the street and the front door several times, as if he was trying to make up his mind about something. Finally, he rose to his feet, his back straight, and walked into the clinic.

-o-o-o-

Many long, exhausting hours later, Mason sat down heavily at his desk, pushing aside the clutter of folders until he could power up the laptop he'd brought with him to Haiti. With the way things were in the capital these days, they didn't have the option of reliable cable or DSL internet service. Thankfully, Doctors Without Borders had provided him a satellite uplink to ensure he could remain connected to their agency and the outside world.

After carefully documenting the events of the day and sending an incident report to headquarters, Mason checked his watch.

He frowned at it. Where had the time gone? Christ… his brother Jack would be calling any minute.

Sure enough, within a matter of moments, an alert popped up on his screen that he had an incoming FaceTime request. He accepted it and smiled into the camera, his mood lightening immediately.

"Sitting at home on a Friday night again? You're getting old, Jack," he quipped.

"Greetings from Singapore, brother mine," Jack responded with a matching grin. "Age has its compensations, you know—we can't all dwell in the youth of our twenties forever."

Jackson Walker was only four years older than Mason was, in reality, but the disparity was still a running joke between them. He and Mason both shared their father's piercing blue eyes and light brown hair. At six-foot-two, Mason had a few inches on his brother, and he had been a bit more dedicated when it came to staying in shape after years of playing rugby.

"No, I suppose we can't," Mason agreed.

At twenty-nine, there were some days that he still felt invincible and on top of the world, but more and more of his nights were turning weary. Even if he had been living in a trendy first-world city somewhere, rather than the outskirts of the impoverished capital in civil-war-torn Haiti, he was beginning to feel like he wouldn't have been able to keep up much of a social life after the toll his job took on him.

He'd seen too much in the past few months. It felt sometimes as though he'd aged far beyond his years. These days, even the most studious of his peers were starting to seem shallow and vain to him, with their successful careers, posh houses, and expensive BMWs. Meanwhile, the horrors Mason had witnessed while volunteering in war-torn areas would be forever branded on his memories—and today, staring down the barrel of a gun held by a child who should have been playing ball in a schoolyard somewhere, was one of the days he was unlikely to forget.

Apparently, enough of this showed on his face to be obvious even over a pixelated video chat, because Jack sobered.

"Something happened, didn't it?" Jack asked, perceptive as ever. "Want to tell me what?"

Mason sighed. *Where to even begin?*

"Right, little brother. I don't like that expression *at all*. Start at the beginning," Jack said, as if reading his mind.

Mason shook his head and relayed a concise version of the day's events. "… and then I finally convinced him to come inside, where I got a nurse to help me with an examination. Let me tell you, *that* was a huge battle, all on its own. I don't know if this kid has ever seen a doctor before, but there were times he screamed hysterically at us about spirits and curses—all sorts of superstitious craziness. He's seriously emaciated, and he needed antibiotics for an infection in his lungs, but he fought like a madman when I tried to put in the IV."

Jack swore. "I don't know how you do it, Mason. I'd tear my hair out if I had to deal with things like that."

Mason cocked an eyebrow, dredging up a brief smile. "No shit. That's why you're an engineer."

"Exactly my point," Jack agreed. "I fix things that other people mess up, and design stuff that, ultimately, some crappy builder somewhere is going to end up changing without my permission so the whole system will fail to work. *You* deal with snotty noses, messed-up children, and having high-powered rifles pulled on you every other day. *I* deal with infuriating clients and impossible deadlines. Though I guess, when you look at it like that… it's practically the same thing, right?"

Mason snorted. "You always were the funny one."

"Damn right. The funny one… the good-looking one…"

"The modest one," Mason put in, still smiling. He sighed, sobering. "Really, though, they're *not* bad kids, Jack. This little guy isn't some spoiled brat. He's deeply traumatized, starving, hopped up on drugs, and brainwashed."

The humor drained from Jack's expression as well. "Jesus. I still can't wrap my brain around the idea of stealing kids to fight in a war. It's just… *sick*. I mean, how do they get them?"

"Depends on the kid," Mason answered, rubbing his tired eyes for a moment. "Depends on the family. Sometimes it's revenge kidnapping; sometimes they come in after a battle and take the survivors away. Sometimes it's just opportunity. They'll grab a kid who's walking alone."

Jack was uncharacteristically quiet for a moment. "Then they go to war and—"

His voice trailed away. Mason did not break the silence for a moment but eventually took a breath and said, "And they're soldiers. They carry out their orders and kill dozens, if not hundreds, of people over their years of captivity."

"And then they come to you."

Mason laughed—an ugly sound. "And then they come to me. The government realized that this was a tactic the rebels were using not long after the practice started. Whenever it's feasible, the youngest children in the rebel forces are captured by the government soldiers, rather than being killed. They're taken and matched with missing children reports, when possible."

"How often does that happen, though?"

"Rarely," Mason admitted. "Haiti is being torn apart at the seams. Any information from the smaller villages being held by the rebels is old, often inaccurate, or contains nothing useful. The rebels intercept most unencrypted messages, and they don't want the government to realize just how many children they're holding hostage."

Jack whistled behind his teeth and shook his head. "This is fucking depressing, Mason."

"You think?" Mason didn't even try to keep the bitterness from his voice.

"These kids are coming to you so messed up that they'll pull a gun on you and nearly kill you?"

Mason shook his head. "If you'd asked me a month ago, I would have scoffed and said it wasn't that bad. That sort of thing never used to happen. Don't get me wrong—these kids have problems. They're sick, half-starved, full of parasites, and emotionally traumatized. We have all the problems you would associate with that kind of thing—fighting, bad behavior, nightmares, and so forth. For the most part, though, once we get them weaned off the drugs, they're sweet and scared."

"If I'd asked you a month ago?" Jack echoed. "What changed in the last month?"

Darkness settled over Mason's heart like a pall, and a shudder rolled down his spine. He couldn't bring himself to look at the screen and see the concern in his brother's face. Nor could he banish the sense of evil that seemed to be creeping over him like black oil. In his mind's eye, he could see the same darkness covering all of Haiti, inciting bloodlust and insanity everywhere it went. It was like a heavy plume, billowing outwards across the land, blocking out all the beauty and light from the sky. A superstitious chill pierced his heart.

"Mason?" Jack pressed, concern in his voice. "What's changed?"

Mason looked directly into the camera at the top of his computer, his mouth dry and his voice hoarse. "Everything."

TWO

"Wait," Xander said, looking down at Oksana as though he wasn't sure he'd heard correctly. "You're telling me they pour perfectly good alcohol onto the *ground*? And they do this *on purpose*?"

Oksana blinked at him, even as Duchess let out a rather indelicate snort from her other side as the three of them walked down the street in Port-au-Prince.

"Xander," Oksana said, meeting his scandalized green gaze, "we're in the middle of a war-torn nation struggling under a yoke of poverty and corruption. I've just explained about the ceremony we're about to witness so that I can ask the vodou spirits—"

"The loa, yes," he interjected. "See, I was listening."

"So that I can ask the vodou loa for assistance in finding Bael's next vortex of chaos," she continued patiently. "And *this* is the part you're worried about?"

"When one is stuck in a war-torn, poverty-stricken land, one *drinks* the booze, Oksana. One does *not*," Xander said very slowly and clearly, "spill it onto the dirt. Now, I have as much cause as anyone to respect the vodou gods—"

"Sure he does. Just ask Madame Francine," Duchess interrupted dryly.

A smile of amusement tugged at the corners of Oksana's lips, almost despite herself. She and Duchess had both heard the account of Xander's rather humiliating run-in with the elderly New Orleans mambo in the days before he and Tré had called the rest of them to the Big Easy.

Xander raised a finger, leaning around Oksana to point it at Duchess without slowing his stride. "Excuse me," he began, "but you know full well that we do *not* speak of that incident. *Ever*. Now, as I was saying, Oksana, I have every reason to respect these loa you worship, but the booze thing is just plain wasteful. Shockingly so. You can't possibly expect me to approve of such a practice."

She rolled her eyes. "If the priest or priestess doesn't offer the loa food and drink, they won't come. Which would rather defeat the purpose of the exercise, don't you agree? If it makes you feel better, there will probably be people smoking ganja, and maybe taking mushrooms. Just… do please try to be discrete? This is my home, after all."

Duchess snorted again. "Xander is always discrete, *ma chérie*. Well, except for that one time in Tokyo. And the one in Brisbane. Oh, and Montreal. We mustn't forget Montreal…"

"Duchess," Xander said, "you know I adore you. But I'm not sure you're the one to throw stones when it comes to the quality of discretion. Does the term *glass houses* ring a bell?" He scowled.

"And I still have no memory of anything noteworthy ever happening in Brisbane."

"Yeah, you probably wouldn't," Oksana murmured under her breath, and smiled sweetly when his scowl turned on her. "Anyway, like I said, if you're hungry, you shouldn't have trouble finding someone suitable after the ceremony begins to wind down."

Honestly, it was no surprise that Xander was in search of a bit of chemically mediated oblivion — short-lived though it would be, given his vampire metabolism. Haiti was no holiday destination these days, but even compared to Port-au-Prince, all three of them had spent the last couple of months in hell.

In fact, their friends were still back in that abyss of suffering, where they had all spent the first days after the detonation of the suitcase nuke in Damascus pulling survivors from the rubble under cover of darkness. After that, rescue had turned to recovery, only for them to find that someone — or *something* — had been there before them.

The undead were rising *en masse* from the wreckage, spreading outward across Syria and into neighboring countries, to the accompaniment of growing hysteria from the human population. Tré, Snag, Eris, Della, and Trynn had stayed behind to monitor the situation and step in whenever doing so might make a difference without getting them all killed in the process.

Oksana had spoken to Eris after experiencing several odd dreams during the stolen hours of sleep she was able to catch here and there as they worked. Communications in the region were spotty at best, but the nightmares had started after she'd heard a snippet of a BBC newscast about reports of war crimes and a humanitarian crisis related to Haiti's current round of rebel insurrection.

Eris encouraged her to follow the strange pull that seemed to be drawing her back to her homeland, pointing out that, with as little as they truly understood about the war Bael was waging on the world, her dreamlike visions were as a valid an avenue for investigation as any other.

Tré listened to them both and agreed almost immediately, though he insisted she not go alone. Duchess had volunteered, and Xander had shrugged in easy agreement when Tré asked him to go along as well.

The cynical part of her—a part she tried to keep buried lest it swallow her whole—couldn't help noticing that their trio comprised three of the four of them who had not yet found their reincarnated mates. Given that Snag pretty much did whatever he wanted to do, no matter what Tré or anyone else said about it, it seemed fairly apparent that there had been some behind-the-scenes discussion between Tré and Eris about sending her, Xander, and Duchess away, specifically.

The rational corner of her mind knew that it made a sort of sense. Eris had found his mate Trynn during the disaster in Damascus, and it seemed highly unlikely that another of their reincarnated mates would just happen to be located in the same area. If she, Duchess, and Xander were traveling, moving around, it was more likely that they would stumble across one of the strange vortices of chaos that formed when a vampire drew close to his or her mate. It was simple statistics.

Unfortunately, the *less* rational part of Oksana's mind tended to shut down completely whenever she contemplated the idea of finding her beloved Augustin, reborn. In the most abstract sense, she understood that it was a thing that might happen someday.

In a more concrete sense, she couldn't really come to terms with what it would mean if she suddenly had to confront that part of her past. She knew the others thought of her as *the nice one*. The sweet one. Youngest, except for Xander. Well—also Della and Trynn, now that they'd been turned. She didn't think the rest of them understood that if she presented a lighter, happier demeanor to the outside world, it was only because she had cut free large swathes of her past and let them drift away, as a form of self defense against the memories.

Or, perhaps it would be more accurate to say that she'd buried those memories. There was an almost painful irony to that metaphor. She choked back a snort of bitter laughter that had nothing to do with humor.

Buried, indeed.

The scrape of her state-of-the-art Flex-Foot Cheetah prosthetic foot replacement against the gravel beneath her was the only sound for a few minutes as she and the others walked companionably down the road. The smell of the sea grew more pronounced as they entered an impoverished area of Port-au-Prince near the coastline, where former factory and warehouse sites had given way to slums, as the island's shaky economy grew ever weaker.

"You really believe this might help us learn something useful?" Xander asked.

She shrugged. "I don't know. Eris thinks it's worth a try. The older I get, the more I've come to believe that all religions hold facets and reflections of the truth of the Light and the Darkness. Haitians are closer to the spirit world than most; we always have been. And, once upon a time, the spirits seemed to favor me."

"Fair enough," Xander said. His eyes crinkled at the corners briefly as he added, "though I still think we should try to rescue some of that wasted alcohol."

Her laughter this time did not hold the same tinge of bitterness, so she let it come. She looped her arms through her companions', glad beyond measure that they were here with her.

-o-o-o-

The trio continued their journey toward the coast. The smell of salt water, fish, and garbage grew more pronounced as the breeze from the ocean stirred the dust around them. The houses became smaller and smaller until they were surrounded by mud-walled shanties with tin roofs. As the last light of evening gave way to night, children came running along dirt paths through the grass, shouting and laughing as they waved goodbye to each other and returned to their families. Women walked briskly along the road, carrying large pails and jugs of water after their last trip of the day to a nearby pump.

As they came to a crossroads that led down towards the ocean, Oksana jerked her thumb and gestured them on towards the right, following the mental map she carried in her memories.

"You really know your way around here," Xander murmured, the words escaping into the deepening darkness.

"It's my home," Oksana said simply. "Don't tell me you couldn't navigate London's twisting roads and alleys just as easily."

"Maybe so." Xander gave her another flicker of a smile and turned to Duchess. "Still, it's a good thing we have our own personal GPS unit to walk around with us. Who needs modern technology, eh?"

Duchess jerked her head around to look at him, as if he had startled her. "Hmm? Oh… yes. Quite right."

Her eyes wandered back to a small girl in a dirty pink dress who was crouched outside of a dilapidated shanty, staring at them with wide, hungry eyes. Duchess had practically made a life's work out of hiding her soft underbelly, but Oksana knew that the weeks spent dragging injured and dead children from radioactive wreckage in Damascus had left her friend raw and aching in a way that the rest of them could not fully appreciate.

They all had their particular demons to slay. And not *just* the real life demon that wanted them dead.

The sound of drums beating reached Oksana's sensitive ears. "We're getting close now," she said, hoping to draw her friend back to the present.

A couple of minutes later, they rounded a corner and the peristil came into view. It was a rough structure, mostly open on the sides, with a roof of mismatched lengths of tin supplemented with tattered blue plastic tarps.

She gestured. "Here we are."

Duchess stared at the unprepossessing ceremonial hall. "Are you sure this is the place?" she asked. "For some reason, I expected something a bit more... grand."

Oksana shrugged. "Yes, this is it."

"Your Catholic roots are showing, Duchess," Xander chided. "Religion isn't all cathedral spires and gold crucifixes, you know."

Duchess glowered at him, but then she appeared to shake herself free from her earlier distraction, giving Oksana's shoulder an apologetic squeeze. "I'm sorry, *ma petite*. That was crass of me. What can be found inside such a place is far more important than the roof and walls."

Oksana covered her hand to show she wasn't angry. "It's all right. For what it's worth, we have Catholic churches here, too. Though I imagine the gold has mostly been looted by now."

She led the others into the peristil, ignoring the suspicious looks thrown their way as people stared at her companions' pale skin. The three took up inconspicuous positions along the structure's only wall, next to the handful of wooden benches occupied by worshipers. The rough concrete blocks were cool at her back, in contrast to the stifling heat of so many human bodies packed close together in the humid Haitian night.

A group of men and women knelt in a circle around a flickering fire at the center of the peristil. A man with smooth skin the shade of burnished teak stood inside the circle, pacing back and forth, eyes closed, as he murmured unintelligible words under his breath.

The darkness outside had fallen fully over the city, and the only light in the peristil came from the ceremonial fire and the multitude of candles burning on the various altars set up to the loa. Some held food, some held bottles of drink, some held money, while others held more obscure items like cosmetics or jewelry. The scent of incense hung in the air.

Each spirit demanded a different offering, in accordance with their individual persona and eccentricities. Without the offering, they would not deign to enter the peristil and inhabit the body of one of the people present. The vodou religion was steeped in tradition, and while the sight of possessed worshipers might appear chaotic to an outsider, the beginning of a ceremony never deviated from established ritual.

The man at the center of the circle wore a flowing white shirt and loose trousers, with a vest covered in intricate beadwork of the African style. His hat, too, was covered in patterned beads, with a small plume of white feathers attached at the front.

He held a large beaded rattle with a bell attached at the bottom, which he shook in time with the drumbeats. The men and women in the circle started to chant, their voices rising and falling to the beat.

"That's the houngan," Oksana whispered, confident that her vampire companions would be able to hear. "He'll lead the ceremony, even though there may be several other priests and priestesses in the circle. The calabash rattle is called an asson. It's the mark of his station, and contains snake bones."

Her audience of two looked on with interest.

"I can feel it," Duchess said, keeping her voice low. "There's power in it, though I can't tell where it's coming from."

"Everything in the ceremony is meant to intensify the houngan's connection with the spirit world," Oksana replied. "That's the source of a houngan or mambo's power. Often, such a ceremony would take place outside, under the stars and near a focus of power such as an ancient tree. They must not want to attract attention tonight."

"After the reports we've heard of attacks on vodou practitioners in the city, you can't really blame them," Xander said, all his earlier flippancy gone without a trace.

"No," Oksana agreed. "It still troubles me, though. I've never known any houngan to be afraid of the night."

Sadly, the backlash against the old religion was not unexpected. Nor was it the first time it had happened. It seemed those Haitians who claimed to be the most progressive were often the most superstitious, at heart. Whenever strife came to the island, violence against vodou practitioners followed close on its heels as frightened people blamed vodou curses for their woes.

It was a running joke that Haiti was seventy percent Catholic, thirty percent Protestant, and one hundred percent vodou. The Christian population might dismiss the existence of the loa publicly—but privately, they believed in the spirits' power over their lives.

The ceremony continued, with those chanting in the circle calling on Papa Legba to open the gates to the spirit world so the loa could pass through. Afterward, each spirit was summoned individually with the proper form. Oksana heard Xander's quiet noise of disgust when the houngan laid out a geometric pattern on the dirt floor with cornmeal and poured a bottle of vodka over it.

When the bottle was empty, he straightened and raised his arms. His body began to shake and twitch, the drums intensifying as if to keep time with the movements of his body.

Without warning, memory rose up and drew Oksana into the past.

-o-o-o-

Standing in the bright sunlight, Oksana clutched her mother's hand as they approached the houngan. He sat in the dust at the side of the road, eyes closed—still as a statue.

Their master had sent Manman and the other women into town to gather supplies for a feast later that night. They were returning now, with heavy baskets and slings full of food tied to their backs. Even though Oksana could only count seven years, she was laden like all the others.

"This is how we used to do it in Africa, child," *her mother always whispered to her as she tied on the burden.*

Another woman in their group had spotted the houngan and insisted they stop to speak to him for a few moments. Oksana pressed closer to her mother in fear. She had never been to Africa, but she thought the man looked wild.

He's a lion-man, she thought, remembering the stories of the great maned beasts with their fangs and claws.

"Tamara," *Oksana's mother called to the woman approaching the houngan,* "there's no time. We need to get back."

"No one will ever know we stopped," *Tamara replied, brushing off her concerns.*

"Time," *the houngan said in a low, slow voice,* "makes fools of us all."

Tamara knelt in front of the seated man like a child before a teacher. "What can you tell us from the spirits?" *she asked, her voice low and respectful.*

The houngan did not answer, but closed his eyes and tilted his face towards the sun. A breeze whipped around them, stirring the dust and dirt into spirals on each side of the man. Oksana watched with wide eyes, mesmerized by the sight of the wind and the earth dancing together.

I want to fly someday, she mused, her eyes following the path of a leaf of dried grass floating back to the earth.

"Come to me, my pale-skinned child." The houngan commanded, ignoring Tamara.

Oksana jumped in surprise and turned towards the man, only to find him looking straight at her with eyes so dark they almost seemed black. A great stillness seemed to settle over the group, and Oksana tightened her hold on her mother's hand.

She hated being different – even though Manman's friends made much of her lighter skin, telling her she was beautiful and special because of it. She'd heard them whisper many times about Manman and the master, though she didn't understand exactly what they meant. Her skin did not look like the master's, which was pale pink, like all the other white people she'd seen.

Of course, Oksana's skin didn't look like her mother's, either. Her mother's skin was beautiful – dark as ebony.

"Do not be afraid, child," the houngan insisted, *motioning again for her to come closer.*

Oksana felt her mother release her hand and nudge her forward. She looked up into Manman's face and received a reassuring smile in return.

Several tentative steps brought her within a few feet of the man. She was still wary of getting too close. The houngan sat up straighter. He reached out a wrinkled hand and pressed his forefinger gently to the center of Oksana's forehead.

She felt a strange force pass through her, as if a chill wave had rolled over her body. She shivered and took a hasty step back, breaking contact with the houngan.

"You ask the wrong questions," the houngan said *in a strange tone, his gaze flickering to Tamara for a moment.*

"I'm sorry?" Tamara asked, confusion evident in her voice.

"You ask the wrong questions," he repeated, settling himself back. He rested his elbows on his knees and clasped his hands together in front of him.

"I still don't understand what you mean," she said.

"Just a moment ago," he replied after a lengthy pause, "you asked me 'what can you tell us from the spirits?'"

The houngan paused again, his head tilted to one side as he considered Oksana.

"The wrong question," he murmured.

The group of slaves stood in total silence as Oksana shifted her feet uncomfortably back and forth. She didn't like being the center of his focus as he stared at her in thoughtful contemplation.

"You should ask 'whom have the spirits sent to us?'"

As Oksana looked around at the adults standing in the sun, each and every set of eyes turned towards her. Their gazes felt heavier than the pack of food strapped to her back. The weight of their eyes might as well have been the weight of the world settling across her young shoulders.

-o-o-o-

A touch on her arm startled her. Duchess was looking at her with mild concern. "Are you still with us, *mon chou*? Something is happening inside the circle."

Oksana blinked and focused back on the houngan before her, instead of the one wrapped in ancient and hazy memory. He was being supported by two of the women. His eyes closed and his face transported as his body continued to shake.

"The spirits are here," she said quietly.

Other people were rising from the benches now, chanting along with the group in the circle, their bodies moving and swaying with the beat of the drums.

"They're possessing people?" Xander asked, looking around in interest.

"Yes," Oksana confirmed. She closed her eyes, reaching out to take in her surroundings, and then shook her head in frustration. "I can't feel them at all, though—only see their effects. I'd hoped, maybe…" The words trailed off.

"You'd hoped… what?" Xander asked, his attention firmly back on her.

She blew out a disappointed breath. "Ever since I was turned, the loa ignore me. My soul was too badly damaged, I think. I'd hoped, perhaps… with Bael drawing nearer… with our soulmates reappearing… that might have changed."

Duchess spoke, ever practical. "Maybe it's for the best. I'm not in any particular hurry to see you possessed, *ma chere*. If you have questions for these spirits, just ask one of *them*." She tilted her chin to indicate the houngan and several others who appeared to be lost in possession.

Oksana squared her shoulders. "Yes," she said, pushing away the old bitterness that threatened to rise. "You're right, of course."

The priest straightened away from the hands supporting him. He reeled for a moment as if he'd forgotten how to use his legs, but then his equilibrium returned.

"Two great realms are crushed together," he proclaimed. "They will bring chaos as the barriers crumble. The beast grows hungry. Upheaval will follow!"

Xander sharpened like a hawk sensing prey.

"Will it indeed?" Duchess asked, her perfect brows drawing together.

Oksana was already on the move, pressing through the dancing, chanting crowd, using her mental influence to clear a path for herself. She felt the others right behind her as she slipped through the last few people to reach the houngan.

"Please, you must tell us," she said, hoping that whichever loa currently inhabited the man was a sympathetic one, and not a trickster. "Is Bael coming here? What should we do?"

The houngan's eyes seemed to burn as he looked down at her from his advantage in height. His lips curled, and his voice was oddly deep and resonant as he replied with two words.

"*Get. Out.*"

THREE

Oksana only became aware that she'd staggered back a step when Duchess and Xander steadied her. The jolt of shock and pain at being ordered away from a peristil by a priest stole her voice for a moment.

She felt a prickle of power from her left as Xander bristled and stepped forward, standing half in front of her.

"Now just a *bleedin' minute*, mate—" he began, his tone low and menacing.

He was interrupted when two things happened simultaneously. A low rumble tickled at the edges of Oksana's awareness, and the houngan turned, addressing the crowd at large as he bellowed, "*Get. Out!*"

Duchess' hand clenched around Oksana's shoulder. "Can you feel that?" she asked; then she raised her voice, as well. "Earthquake! Everyone get outside!"

"*Shit*," Xander cursed, barely audible. He and Oksana added their voices to the call, ordering people outside in French and Creole.

To their credit, the people of Haiti were well acquainted with earthquakes. Despite the revelry of the dancing and drumming, it took only moments for the crowd to heed the cry and hurry into the street outside. The rumble grew into full-scale trembling just as the three vampires followed the last of the people from the peristil into the open.

Oksana steadied herself as the earth bucked and rolled in waves, relying on vampirically enhanced balance to overcome the disadvantage posed by her prosthesis. The pulses of energy as the earth's crust slipped against itself jarred her preternatural senses, making her clench her jaw against a wave of nausea.

Around her, people cried out in fear, more of Port-au-Prince's residents spilling onto the road rather than risk staying under a roof that might fall on their heads. The quaking went on for a little over a minute before subsiding, leaving Oksana feeling like she needed a moment to get her land-legs back.

She swallowed and looked around, her night vision allowing her to see her surroundings despite the lack of light. Many of the mud and plaster walls on the buildings around them were cracked, but none appeared demolished. Some of the mismatched tin from the peristil roof had come partially free from the rafters and was hanging over the edge of the roof. A couple of the wooden posts that supported the open-air structure were off-kilter, but had not snapped.

"It wasn't a bad one," she said aloud.

"Bad enough," Duchess replied. "It doesn't look like anyone here is hurt beyond cuts and grazes from falling down, though."

Xander's mouth was a grim line. "I need to get access to a data link. Find out if there's a tsunami warning for the area."

He pulled out a mobile and flicked the screen-lock. Oksana and Duchess followed suit.

"Nothing," Oksana said, unsurprised.

"The satellite phone is back at the hotel," Xander said. "But we're too close to the beach for comfort here."

"Right," Oksana agreed, and switched back to Creole. "Everyone! Get your families, grab whatever you need, and head for higher ground in case a big wave comes! Don't risk yourselves by staying here. Spend the night in the highest place you can find and come back when it's safe!"

There was muttering as the frightened people around them debated the merits of leaving their homes unprotected overnight, but several other people lifted their voices in support.

"She's right! Don't risk it…"

"Be quick and we'll all go together."

"Yes, let's do it."

Convinced that most of them, at least, would do the smart thing, Oksana gestured for her companions to follow her into the shadows where they could transform unseen into mist, and fly back to the hotel rather than waste time walking. As she turned to go, however, running footsteps approached.

The smell of sweat, antiseptic, and human fear teased Oksana's nostrils. The sound of a pounding heart driving blood through arteries in a frantic rush reached her ears an instant later. A young woman with dark skin and close-cropped black curls burst into their midst. As she clutched a stitch in her side with one hand, she began pointing urgently back up the road down which she had just come with the other.

"What is it?" Xander asked in French, moving forward to stand in front of her.

"Help us!" she gasped, taking huge, deep breaths. "Hurry, please! A roof collapsed and children are trapped inside!"

Duchess was off in the direction the girl had come from before the echo of the final word faded. Xander shot Oksana a dark look. They followed, keeping pace with the young woman, who ran as fast as she could even though she was still gasping for air and clutching her aching side.

Oksana took care on the uneven footing of the pockmarked dirt road, feeling the compressed power of her flexible Cheetah foot propel her effortlessly forward with every stride. She judged that their destination couldn't be far, given how quickly the girl had arrived after the trembler subsided. They were re-entering the area of abandoned warehouses and factories, some of which had obviously been turned to other purposes since the economic downturn.

One of those buildings had a collapsed wall, with the heavy roof lying over it in a twisted pile of wood and metal. Adults in medical scrubs scrambled over the scene with flashlights and kerosene lanterns, prying up pieces of tin and pulling bloody, crying children form the rubble.

"What can we do?" Duchess called, grabbing the arm of a woman trying to rush past with an armful of towels.

"The roof collapsed before we could get everyone out! We've got about fourteen children trapped inside," she snapped in reply, already pulling free to continue toward the building.

"We've got recent experience with search and rescue. We can help you get them out," Xander told her, as they followed her to the collapsed section.

Too right we've got recent experience, Oksana thought grimly. *I'm still finding bits of radioactive rubble in odd places after Damascus.*

They hurried after the woman, to a side of the building where the wall was leaning over. Soft whimpers could clearly be heard, coming from the dark gap beyond.

"Hello? Can you hear me?" Oksana called into the hole, which looked big enough for her to fit through. *Just.*

A strangled cry of fear emerged in response.

"Eniel!" A strong male voice came from behind Oksana, woven through with an Australian accent. "Hang on, Eniel. We can hear you. You're going to be all right!"

Oksana turned to see a man perhaps an inch or two taller than Xander, with intense blue eyes and tousled, light brown hair. He, too, was wearing scrubs, though they were dirt-smeared and bloodstained.

"We need to get him out quickly. I don't know how stable this section is," the man said in a low tone, not blinking at the sudden appearance of three strangers at the scene. It was obvious that his entire focus was on rescuing the trapped children, and everything else was secondary. "I was just trying to find some rope in hopes of feeding it through the gap to him and pulling him out," he continued, "but everything remotely useful seems to be buried."

Oksana felt an odd little jolt in her belly at the man's single-minded focus on the boy's safety. "Well," she told him, "it's a good thing you have someone small enough to squeeze through the gap, in that case."

Duchess' bright eyes landed on her, and the other vampire's brow furrowed. "Are you sure, *ma petite*? You and small spaces are not the best of friends. I might be able to fit."

Oksana looked at the gap again. Duchess was all voluptuous curves where Oksana was slender lines, and frankly, she doubted it would work. Before she could say so, the Australian spoke again.

"You're claustrophobic?" he asked. "If so, you shouldn't go. We'll find somebody else. Joni could probably get in. She's around here somewhere, I think—"

"No," Oksana said, cutting him off. "It's fine. I can handle it. Though I may need someone to help pull us out afterward if it's too tight for me to turn around inside."

And I may also need someone to give me a mental smack if my brain decides to go stupid on me—since I am, in fact, claustrophobic, she added silently.

On it, Xander assured.

Of course, said Duchess, adding, *Be careful, petite soeur.*

"Okay. I've got this," Oksana said. "Oh—and in case it's not self-evident," she added, glancing at the Aussie's arresting blue eyes, "Don't pull on the left foot when it comes time to drag me back out. It comes off."

The barest hint of humor touched the man's face, transforming it into something beautiful in the light of the sputtering lanterns before it settled once more into worried lines.

"Don't worry," he said, "I'll make sure to leave you a leg to stand on. You can trust me—I'm a doctor."

The last was added with a wink so quick she wasn't sure she'd actually seen it. Then his focus was back on the hole, his flashlight directed inside.

"Eniel," he called, "someone's coming in to get you. She'll be with you in just a minute. Don't be afraid!"

He glanced at Oksana and she was caught yet again by the intensity behind his stormy eyes. Tearing herself away, she crouched down and eased onto her stomach, wincing a bit as rocks and pieces of debris poked at her through her thin black t-shirt.

She took a deep breath, purposely not focusing on exactly what she was about to do, and army-crawled through the tiny gap under the roof. The cries of fear from within had subsided to muffled sobs, as if Eniel was trying desperately not to let the sound of his weeping be heard.

Oksana took a couple of steadying breaths and used her knees and elbows to propel herself forward. The dirt beneath her collected against her shirt as she scooted further into the gap, some of it getting inside the low scoop of the shirt's neckline, where it made her skin itch.

She coughed, eyes watering as dust swirled in her face. "I'm almost there," she croaked, hearing the boy's racing pulse only a few feet ahead. "Talk to me so I can find you more easily."

Of course, to her enhanced senses his heartbeat, thrumming blood, and warm body were like a beacon in the low light, but he didn't need to know that. Talking would—hopefully—keep him calmer and listening to him would—hopefully—keep her attention on the here-and-now rather than on a part of the distant past better left buried.

Buried. *Ha.*

"Please," a small voice begged in Creole. "Please, hurry…"

Of course, that was the moment when the spring-loaded epoxy arch of her prosthesis managed to get hooked around something, halting her forward progress. As soon as she felt the constriction of her left leg, coupled with the darkness and sensation of walls all around her, her thoughts crashed down around her like falling icicles.

She was trapped… trapped underground… her foot… what had they done to her foot?

Oksana! Her name was a sharp bark inside her mind, piercing through the momentary confusion.

It was Xander. She blinked rapidly, trying to reorient herself in the present. She was in Haiti, yes, but this small, dark space was a collapsed building, not a—

She cut the thought off harshly.

Focus, mon chou, Duchess said in her mind.

I'm all right, she sent back to them. *My Cheetah just got hooked on something.* She backed up a couple of inches and twisted her leg until she felt the prosthesis come free from whatever it had been stuck on. *I'm free now.*

"Where are you?" called Eniel. "I can hear you but I can't see you!"

There was a movement in the darkness ahead of her. She reached out with all her senses, and the darker shadow coalesced into a child. Male. Young. She could smell his blood in the air and knew that he was injured.

"It's all right. I can see you now," she told him. To the others, she called, "I see him! He's hurt—I'm not sure how badly."

"Can you get him out?" The Australian doctor's voice came back immediately.

Of course, there was no way to know until she got a better idea of the boy's circumstances, but she hadn't crawled in here just to fail. "I'll get him," she replied with certainty.

She crawled forward the last couple of feet, the space ahead of her opening into something a little less confining. She reached out, feeling around the debris and broken glass until her fingers grazed warm skin. The boy caught his breath in surprise at her touch.

"There you are," she said, keeping her voice calm and friendly. "Your name is Eniel, right? I'm Oksana."

Hesitation followed her question, the silence stretching between them. Finally, a small voice answered, "Call me San."

Her brow furrowed in surprise. San, as in the Creole word for blood? She shook off the moment of confusion. It was hardly relevant in their current circumstances.

"Sure thing, San," she said. "Now, what do you say we get out of here? I don't know about you, but I wouldn't mind seeing the sky right about now."

"I can't see anything," the boy said. "I don't know how to get out."

Oksana silently cursed herself for not having brought a flashlight. She might not need it, but it would have been reassuring for Eniel—or San, as he apparently preferred.

"That's okay," she said, "I can see a bit. I know the way out. Can you crawl toward me while I crawl backwards toward the gap?"

Another pause, and Oksana worried that perhaps the boy was pinned by a fallen beam or something. When he answered, his words took her by surprise.

"You... won't hurt me?"

Oksana caught her breath, half from her own reaction to the unexpected question, and half at Duchess', who had obviously been eavesdropping through their link.

Why would he think you would hurt him? Duchess's words were low and dangerous.

Rescue now. Questions later. That was Xander, and when *Xander* was acting as the voice of reason, it was definitely time to regroup.

I heard that, came his mental growl.

She ignored him in favor of reassuring the frightened boy. "No, I won't hurt you, San," she said, putting a bit of will behind the words to calm him into compliance. "Let's you and I get out of here. Can you crawl?"

The pause this time was shorter. "Yes."

"Follow me, then," she instructed, and started to shimmy backward, his small hand grasped in hers. To her relief, he followed.

She continued to push herself the way she came with an awkward hitching motion, feeling claustrophobia threaten once more in the suffocating stillness of the tight space. She focused on the boy whose hand she clasped; the last thing he needed was for the stranger helping him to lose her shit and start gibbering about being trapped.

Hang in there. Xander again. *We can almost reach you – just a little further and I'll help pull you out.*

"We're getting close," she told the boy. Light from outside filtered through the hole behind her, illuminating his frightened face. He had a gash on his forehead that was bleeding freely, but he seemed otherwise unhurt. He did not meet her eyes even though there was enough light now for him to see, his gaze darting around the tunnel instead.

Hands grabbed her right ankle and she gasped, even though she'd had ample warning.

Easy, ma petite, Duchess reassured her.

"Okay," Oksana said, "They're going to pull me out, and I'll pull you. Just hold on, San."

He nodded, wide-eyed, just as Xander tugged her backward. She gripped his hand harder and pulled him after her as they passed through the gap and into the gloriously fresh air.

Well... maybe not *fresh*. The air actually still smelled like garbage and fish, but compared to the stifling, dusty atmosphere inside the collapsed building, it was heavenly.

Once the child was free of the building, Oksana rolled into a sitting position and coughed, rubbing at the dirt on her face.

"Hmm, that's actually not a half bad look for you," Xander said, gaining his moment of revenge for her quip earlier. He, of course, looked enviably unruffled even after having dragged her out of the rubble.

"Thanks for that," she grouched, still trying to brush herself off. And—yes—there was, in fact, gravel inside her sports bra now. *Brilliant*.

Duchess knelt on the ground next to her and reached out a hand to help Eniel sit up. He recoiled from her and looked around with wide eyes.

"Let me take a look at the cut on your head," Duchess said in a gentle voice. "I won't touch it, just let me see."

His red-rimmed eyes glared out from a tear-streaked face, but he turned his head toward her grudgingly. Xander fished his phone out of his pocket and shined the light on the boy's forehead. The blue-eyed doctor leaned in and examined the injury under the light. The tension in his broad athlete's shoulders eased slightly.

"I think you're in luck, my young friend," he said in a light voice, "this just needs cleaned and a couple of butterfly stitches."

"Not lucky," Eniel said in a low voice.

The man sighed and nodded. "Yeah, okay, maybe *lucky* isn't the word. But the reality is, it could have been a lot worse." He gestured for the woman who had been carrying the towels earlier to come over. "Natacha? Would you get Eniel here an antiseptic wipe and some butterfly strips for his head?"

The nurse nodded and hustled Eniel away, the boy casting glances over his shoulder as they left. Duchess rose smoothly to her feet, waving off the hand the doctor offered her. He lifted an eyebrow and met Oksana's eyes, reaching for her hand instead. She smiled and took it, only to practically leap to her feet when a jolt of electricity sizzled from the point of contact straight to the base of her spine, lifting the hair at the back of her neck as it passed. She slammed her mental shields down so quickly that both Duchess and Xander gave her a questioning look.

The man—*oh, god, the man*—jerked his hand back in surprise, his blue eyes wide. He blinked in confusion, and then seemed to shake off the odd moment. "Best move away from the rubble," he said. "There, uh, must be some exposed electrical wires here…"

Of course, that was complete rubbish, since a glance showed that the power was out in the entire area. And both Xander and Duchess were still staring at her, damn it.

"Oksana?" Duchess prompted.

Not. Now. Her mental reply was unnecessarily harsh, but she could feel cold sweat popping out on her forehead, and the same claustrophobic feeling that had swept over her inside the collapsed building was returning. She tightened her shields further, trying not to succumb to sudden, irrational panic.

Xander's green gaze pinned her for a moment longer before he turned his attention to the doctor. He held out his hand. "Sorry—I didn't catch your name, sir."

For the briefest of instants, the Australian hesitated, but then he grasped Xander's hand in a firm grip.

"Dr. Mason Walker, of Doctors Without Borders," he said as they shook.

"A pleasure to meet you, the unfortunate circumstances notwithstanding. My name is Xander. This is Duchess, and our pint-sized search and rescue expert here is Oksana," Xander said gesturing to his companions in turn.

"I'm more than pleased to make your acquaintance," Mason replied, making no comment about their unusual names. "Not many people would have offered to help strangers in such a way."

He shook Duchess' hand next and lowered his proffered arm awkwardly when Oksana gave him a small, painfully self-conscious wave of her fingers instead of offering to shake.

"Hi," she said, relieved when the word didn't emerge as a ridiculous, high-pitched squeak.

"Hi to you, too," he replied, looking at her curiously. Her skin tingled where his eyes moved over it.

Spirits have mercy on her.

It took Mason a moment to tear his attention away, and she almost sagged in relief when he did.

"The clinic building isn't safe," he said as he turned towards a group of nurses nearby. They were all tending to children that had been pulled from the rubble. "We need to come up with some sort of alternative place to shelter."

"What sort of clinic is this?" Duchess asked, clearly thinking about Eniel's obvious fear of them.

"My colleagues and I help with the rehabilitation of child soldiers," Mason said. "It's a serious problem in Haiti these days."

Duchess made a noise of pain. "Child soldiers? *Mon Dieu.* There is truly no end to the depths to which humanity will sink."

"We all do what we can, where we can," Mason said, sounding like a man who had lately spent too much time plumbing those dark depths.

Oksana could sympathize. With a flush, she realized she was still staring at Mason like a slack-jawed crazy woman. She snapped her mouth shut and looked away before he could notice.

From the corner of her eye, she saw him gesture them to follow in the same direction the nurse had taken Eniel. A group of children was sitting on the ground in an area that was relatively free of rubble. Some were crying quietly; others seemed to be in a complete daze.

Right now, she felt a certain kinship with the latter group, to be perfectly honest.

Nurses were moving from child to child, reassuring them and tending to their injuries. Mason joined them, leaning down to speak with each child as he inquired about their wellbeing. Again, Oksana'a gaze was drawn to him without her conscious volition, following his every movement. She was so engrossed that she jumped a bit when Duchess appeared at her shoulder.

"Talk to me," her friend said in a voice so low that none of the people around them except Xander would be able to hear. "Are you all right?"

Was she all right? Oksana had to swallow back a laugh that would have emerged sounding more than a little hysterical.

"No," she managed. "*All right* is not the description that comes immediately to mind."

FOUR

Duchess nodded, as if that much had been obvious. "Is there anything I can do?" she asked instead.

Oksana thought about it for a second and sighed. "No, I just need to think. I don't want to talk about it right now. It's not the time."

Indeed, as if to underline the words, a small aftershock rocked them. Cries from the terrified children rose into the night sky. Oksana looked up for a moment—after crawling through the wrecked building, the view above was stunning, unimpeded by clouds or haze. Stars winked peacefully down on the scene of fear, pain, and chaos below.

After a last unhappy look at Oksana, Duchess turned her attention to practicalities. "What are the options for temporary shelter?" she asked Mason.

He looked up from the boy he was examining. "There are a couple of possibilities. I've got Joni working on it now. First things first, though. We need to get a head count and make sure everyone is accounted for, then search if anyone is still missing."

Xander spoke up. "We aren't very far from the beach here. It's not safe. My friends and I were just going to try and find out if there's risk of a tsunami when your nurse found us."

Mason nodded. "I sent Evens to watch the tide as soon as the trembling stopped. Our radio got flattened under that section of collapsed roof, so we'll have to keep tabs the old-fashioned way. If the water recedes, he'll report back and tell us, so we can make a run for it before it washes back in. As soon as these injuries are treated I'll send the children to higher ground as a precaution, but I'm not leaving anyone behind unless it's life or death."

Of course, Oksana thought. *Of course he had to be competent and handsome and compassionate… and oh dear god, what am I supposed to do now?*

Her traitorous undead heart stuttered as Mason rose and turned to her. She tried to tear her gaze away from his, but it felt like her eyes were glued to the man now pulling out a notepad and pen from a pocket in his scrubs.

"Here," he said, holding them out to her. "Would you mind taking down every child's and staff member's name? I've got a couple of people I still need to treat here. It shouldn't take more than a few minutes, though."

"Of course," Oksana managed, taking the offered items. She was careful not to let their skin touch as their fingers came close to one another.

She worked her way through the group of people, putting a mark on everyone's left hand as soon as she recorded their names. After several minutes of walking around, she had a full count of every child and adult.

As she worked, she could intermittently feel Mason's intrigued gaze resting on her. Doing her best to ignore him, Oksana checked in with one of the nurses.

"How many of the children are injured?" she asked, poised to take notes.

"Just over half," the young Haitian man said, "but all except a few are minor injuries. Mostly cuts, a few sprained wrists or ankles, and a couple of possible fractures. Nothing more than that, thankfully. We were lucky."

She jotted down the final notes, tallied the number of children and staff, and managed to paste on an encouraging smile for the young man.

"I'm glad to hear it wasn't worse," she said.

Dreading it, she crossed the impromptu triage area and approached Mason. He was watching her, a thoughtful expression clouding his attractive features. Before he could speak, Oksana held out the notepad.

"I think this is everyone. They pulled another child out of the rubble a few minutes ago. Mostly minor injuries, thankfully."

A crease formed between his eyebrows in response to her clipped tone. Oksana couldn't help it; there was no room left in her mind for friendliness or an upbeat demeanor in the face of the darkness surrounding her. It pressed in on her as surely as the confining tunnel under the rubble had pressed in on her earlier.

Basic politeness was about all she'd be able to muster until she'd had a chance to get away for a bit and think. She had to keep her distance from this dangerously alluring doctor until she could sort things out in her mind and deal with the emotions that were threatening to swallow her whole.

As if on cue, Xander swooped in on the conversation. "So, everyone's accounted for, then?"

"Yes, thank heavens," Mason said in clear relief, glancing over the notepad.

"Good news," said Xander. "What's the plan now, Oz? Where can we take this lot to keep them safe tonight?"

Mason's eyes lingered on Oksana for a moment before he turned towards Xander and spoke. "Joni managed to get a mobile signal out, and we've arranged for them to be temporarily housed with the American Red Cross. They're setting up tents near the city center."

"Americans?" Xander asked without enthusiasm. "Well, I suppose needs must. Is it far from here?"

"It's a little over two kilometers away. Most of the roads are closed, so we'll have to walk, but the distance isn't what I'm worried about."

Duchess had joined them in time to hear that last exchange. "And what *are* you worried about?" she asked.

"Port-au-Prince is dangerous after dark," Mason said grimly. "The city has been experiencing an upswing in violence recently. No one really knows what's going on, but we suspect that some soldiers from the rebel movement have penetrated the center of the city and are causing havoc to de-stabilize the area."

Xander's knowing green eyes flicked to Duchess, and then Oksana.

"Yes. Well," he said, his tone mild, "we do seem to live in interesting times these days, and I mean that very much in the *Chinese curse* sense. I imagine that the addition of looters and opportunists after the quake won't improve the situation, but we can't exactly stay here."

"And we'll be traveling in a large group," Duchess added. "That should help."

Mason's eyes took the three of them in. "You're willing to assist us in getting the children relocated, then? You've already been an immense help tonight. I can't reasonably ask you for more of your time, but—"

Duchess waved him off. "Some of these young ones have sprained ankles and other injuries that will prevent them from walking. You need all the help you can get."

Mason's reply was heartfelt and utterly without artifice. "That I most certainly do, Madame. I'm in your debt—all of you."

Oksana swallowed around a hard lump that either wanted to be a laugh or a sob—she wasn't sure which. *In our debt, indeed. Would you still feel that way if you knew the truth, I wonder?*

"Right," Mason said, oblivious. "Let's get this parade underway." He put his fingers to his lips and let out a loud whistle. Silence fell as all faces turned towards him.

"Here's what we're going to do," he called in a commanding tone. The sound of his voice sent a shiver down Oksana's spine, and she cursed herself for it. Mason continued, "We have a shelter available in the center of the city. Unfortunately, we don't have access to any vehicles right now. We'll have to walk."

A few of the boys nearby made disparaging noises as they clutched injuries to their feet and ankles.

Hearing them, Mason turned and gave them a reassuring smile. "Don't worry, mates, we'll make sure you get there in one piece. We have some wonderful volunteers who helped us get people out of the wreckage of the clinic. They have agreed to stay and help us tonight. Anyone who needs a lift, raise your hand. Don't be shy!"

The group started clambering to their feet, nurses helping those who could hobble on one leg. Xander walked over to a small boy who was crying silently on the ground with his hand raised, clutching a swollen and bandaged ankle with the other hand.

"Looks like you could use a ride, huh?" Oksana heard Xander ask. The boy nodded as he continued to cry.

Xander gently scooped him into his arms and turned to Mason.

"This lad barely weighs anything, Oz," Xander observed.

"Maybe right now he doesn't. He had some health challenges to overcome when he arrived, but we're going to build him up," Mason said. "Isn't that right, Cristofer?"

"Yes, Dr. Walker," the boy answered in a tremulous voice.

Mason picked up another boy, and the male nurse Oksana had spoken with earlier took a third.

After a brief mental exchange, Oksana pulled a dagger from the hidden sheath at the small of her back, while Duchess pulled one from her boot. The two of them took point, while Xander dropped back to take rear guard. He still carried Cristofer and did not draw a weapon, but with his keener senses and vampire reflexes, he would be able to alert them to anyone approaching from behind long before any of the humans noticed.

Mason came to an abrupt halt upon seeing the lethal dagger held in Oksana's hand. Had she been human, she would have flushed under his disbelieving regard — and once again, she was immediately angry with herself for her subconscious reaction.

"Is there a problem, *Docteur*?" Duchess asked coolly. "I believe you were the one concerned about the children's safety, given the increase in violence in the city, *non*?"

Mason blinked, his eyes flicking from Oksana to Duchess, and back again. She got the feeling that he was assessing them, trying to determine if they actually knew how to use the weapons in their hands. After a moment, he purposely relaxed his shoulders.

"No bloodshed, please, unless it's absolutely necessary to defend the group," he said, speaking English — presumably to avoid frightening the children.

Duchess smiled dangerously, not *quite* wide enough to expose her fangs. Oksana sent her a quelling look, but she only raised a perfectly plucked brow in response. "Really, *Docteur*. Whatever do you take us for?" she asked, all innocence.

Mason stared at her for a moment longer before breaking his gaze away. He addressed the group, giving them the directions to the Red Cross camp where they were heading. *Smart*, noted an objective part of Oksana's mind. *That way, if anyone gets separated, they'll know where to head for safety.*

The group got underway, and after speaking quietly to several of the nurses near the front, Mason dropped back to walk near the rear of the group. *Keeping an eye out to make sure no one wandered off?* It would make sense, given what she'd seen of his protective nature.

Oksana forcibly refocused on their surroundings, watching the eight o'clock to twelve o'clock sweep of their flank, while Duchess took twelve o'clock to four o'clock, and Xander, four to eight.

With one small part of her attention, Oksana listened to the conversation behind her. Much to her chagrin—if not her surprise—Xander seemed to have taken a great interest in Mason and was asking him for more information about the Doctors without Borders mission.

"We were called here after receiving reports of rebel child soldiers being captured by the government," Mason explained.

"A repulsive practice," Xander observed, "but not a terribly surprising one under the circumstances, I suppose."

The doctor nodded. "Sadly not. Things like this have been going on elsewhere in the world for decades. The rebel commanders go into these small, rural villages, murdering the adults and capturing the children. The boys, they make into soldiers, and the girls… well, I'm sure you can imagine," Mason said, sounding tired and bitter.

Oksana's stomach clenched.

"We've had some success bartering the release of the boys who are in poor health, or seem close to a mental breakdown," Mason continued. "We've had little to no success freeing any of the girls, but we won't stop trying. Anyway, once we have them, it's our job to medically stabilize them and start the rehabilitative process."

"That sounds like quite a challenging undertaking," Xander observed. "How much success have you seen in rehabilitating them?"

Oksana glanced back in time to see Mason run a gentle hand over the back of the boy in his arms, who appeared to have drifted into exhausted sleep. He turned a sad, kind smile on the youngster cradled in Xander's sure grip.

"Oh, quite a bit. Wouldn't you say so, Cristofer?"

Dear lord, he has a beautiful smile, Oksana realized, as if it were some sort of divine revelation. She couldn't help but watch the way the young doctor interacted so smoothly and effortlessly with both the children and adults around him.

Cristofer smiled back and nodded. "You help."

"Cristofer was one of the first children ever treated at the clinic. He's been with us for almost a year now and does an excellent job every day," Mason explained.

The boy ducked his head under the praise, but couldn't hide the grin on his face. "I want to be a doctor, too."

"Oh, yes?" Xander asked, glancing down at the boy. "That's quite a good thing to be."

Cristofer nodded with clear enthusiasm. "Dr. Walker shows me all his instruments and lets me listen to his heart sometimes."

Mason chuckled as he gestured the group to turn down a side street. "So far, I've been diagnosed with scurvy, the sniffles, and a broken heart."

Oksana's own traitorous heart lurched, as if in sympathy.

"Well, you don't have a girlfriend," Cristofer said accusingly. "That's why you're sad sometimes."

Mason gave a genial huff and raised an eyebrow at Xander. "We're still working on refining our medical diagnoses, as you may have gathered."

Anything Xander might have said was interrupted when the sound of nearby gunfire rent the night air.

"Get under cover!" Oksana shouted.

The children and clinic workers flattened themselves against the wall of the nearest building. A few of the children cowered and covered their ears with their hands.

A yell of rage and terror caused Oksana and the others to turn toward the middle of the group. Two of the nurses were wrestling with Eniel, the child Oksana had pulled from the rubble. The one who had told her to call him San—the Creole word for blood. She hurried forward and dropped to her knees in front of the boy, who was being forcibly restrained by both arms.

"Let go! Let go!" he raged, tears streaming down his face. He kicked out wildly, temporarily suspended in mid-air by the adults' firm grasp. "Free me, *now*!"

"Eniel," Oksana said in a low voice, trying to catch his eye. "*Hey*. Eniel, look at me."

Eniel closed his eyes firmly and continued to fight, thrashing his head back and forth.

"*Eniel*," Oksana said, more softly. The boy did not respond, but continued to struggle. With a sigh, Oksana reached out very gently with her mental power and touched his mind. She caught a small glimpse of the boy's pain and rage, the out-of-control emotions coursing through his body like acid.

Oksana could sense that he was completely disengaged from their surroundings. Attempting to reason with him would be useless. He was lost in the memories conjured by the gunfire still erupting sporadically from a couple of streets over.

Taking a deep, calming breath, Oksana layered a soft mental blanket of peace over Eniel's awareness. She did not force it upon him — simply offered it to him. For a moment, nothing seemed to change. Eniel continued to exert all his energy on escape, while the nurses restrained his flailing limbs.

Eventually, though, his movements grew less frantic, and eventually stilled. Oksana breathed in and out, allowing her life force to flow around the two of them. She could sense Xander and Duchess' life forces swirling and combining with hers, bolstering her, adding to the tranquility hanging gently in the air.

"There, now," she said. "That's better. That noise certainly was a bit unexpected, wasn't it?"

Eniel breathed in time with her, his thin chest rising and falling like a bellows. He nodded slowly, as if dazed. She could feel that he was clinging to her projection of calm as his anger and anxiety drained away. She made brief eye contact with the nurses, who released his arms and stepped back a bit, giving him space. The boy didn't move, but stood there breathing heavily and staring around, his eyes glittering.

"Are you ready to keep going?" Oksana asked.

"Yes," Eniel answered.

"Okay, good. The shooters are some distance away, but there may be more gunfire as we're walking. We're going to keep moving towards safety unless it gets closer to us, though. Can you do that?"

"Yes." The word was soft, but steady.

Oksana nodded that they were ready. The group continued on, but this time Eniel stayed close to Oksana. He did not speak and flinched anytime the *pop-pop-pop* of automatic gunfire sounded nearby.

Mason appeared beside Oksana and murmured, "Thank you."

"It was nothing," she replied, trying hard not to let her gaze linger on him.

"Bollocks. That was frankly amazing to watch," Mason said conversationally. "Have you worked with kids for long?"

He's trying to start a conversation, Oksana. Don't shut him down, Xander sent, obviously eavesdropping even though he was several meters behind them.

Could you maybe mind your own business? Oksana grumbled silently. *This is bad enough with only me in my head.*

Xander sent the mental equivalent of a shrug. *Hey, if you're so worried about privacy, you should be shielding better.*

She gritted her teeth. *We're trying to herd more than two-dozen adults and children through streets riddled with gunfire and rattled by aftershocks! I appear to be just a tiny bit distracted, for some strange reason.*

So… get un-distracted? She could picture his raised eyebrow as clearly as if she'd seen it.

Oksana groaned aloud in irritation and slammed her mental shields down on him.

"Er… did I say something wrong?" Mason asked.

She swallowed a sigh. "No, of course not. Sorry. I was just thinking. To answer your question, I don't work with kids, but I do enjoy interacting with them."

"Oh?" Mason responded, looking surprised. "What do you do, then?"

Oksana paused, caught out. Wait—hadn't her plan been to avoid him until she could figure out what to do?

"Um, it's a little complicated to explain."

If anything, that seemed to make him *more* curious. "Try me," he said.

Brilliant. How could she possibly explain anything to him when she was still reeling from discovering he existed? This entire situation was a nightmare. What a fool she'd been, to assume this wouldn't happen to her—that she'd have time. Time to come to terms with the reality of what finding her lost love Augustin would *mean*.

She was rescued from her predicament when they turned a corner, getting a view of a large plaza a block or so away.

"Doctor," the nurse named Joni called. "That's it, right?"

Mason smiled in relief. "So it is. Looks like we made it, everyone."

The open area was near the city center, and they were far enough from the ocean now to be safe from any waves that might come their way after the moderately powerful quake. There were several tents set up, where people in civilian clothing were talking to aides with the American Red Cross symbol emblazoned on their shirts.

As Oksana watched, workers scurried about, intent upon their business. Large floodlights illuminated the area, casting dark shadows around bushes and tents.

"Well," Xander said, looking around. "They certainly mobilize quickly. The earthquake was only a couple of hours ago."

"Oh—they were already here," Mason explained. "They've been trying to help with relief efforts following the violence and civil war. We just negotiated an informal agreement where they're temporarily going to house us as well, now."

"Dr. Walker?" a voice called through the crowd.

Oksana looked up and saw an older white man moving towards them, a weary look on his face.

"Yes?" Mason replied.

The man held out a hand, and Mason shook it. "I'm Jeff Sentry, I spoke on the phone to one of your people earlier."

"Of course," Mason said. "How are you?"

Jeff rubbed tired eyes. "Making it. Are these all of the children?"

Xander moved closer to Oksana, still holding Cristofer in his arms.

Mason nodded and gestured to the group. "Yes, this is everyone."

Jeff nodded and motioned for the cluster of people to follow him. He led them through the crowd, which was finally beginning to thin, heading towards a cluster of tents that were positioned off to the side of the operation, as if they had been erected as an afterthought.

"When were you able to get these set up?" Oksana asked.

"About thirty minutes ago. We didn't manage to get the bedding sorted out, but there are stacks of cots, pillows, and blankets inside. It's the best we could do on such short notice. We're running low on supplies at the moment, but we should still be able to feed everyone, at least for a few days."

Oksana used the cover of the children being directed towards tents to move away from Mason.

She could tell that he was still watching her as if fascinated, but she tried her best to keep all her focus onto the task at hand.

"Eniel, which tent would you like to sleep in tonight?" she asked him.

The young boy had trailed behind her for the entire walk through the city. He glanced back and forth, and then looked at her with a lost expression.

"Hey," she said, squeezing his shoulder. His gaze flickered first to her hand, and then back to her face, as if he was surprised she'd touched him. "Listen," she continued, "I know this is really hard, okay? It's perfectly understandable for you to be a little freaked out, but I think these are good people that are going to take care of you, now."

Eniel's lips tightened, and he looked slightly angry. "I'm not a child."

She raised an eyebrow. "Eniel—child or adult, *everyone* needs help sometimes. Let these people do their job, all right?"

He sighed at her words and looked around again. His eyes settled on Mason for a moment, as if considering his options. "Yeah. All right."

"Very good," Oksana answered. She helped Eniel and several of the other less injured boys get their cots set up. They spoke very little, but instead yawned widely. After getting everyone into bed, Oksana ducked out of the tent and found several of the clinic staff huddled in a group a short distance away.

"Everyone settled in?" one of the nurses asked as Oksana approached.

She nodded. "Yes, finally. They were all so tired they could barely pull the blankets over themselves."

A conversation from a short distance away floated to her ears.

"… and I know this operation has been going on for quite a while now, but I think we need more help," Mason said.

Oksana peered around the nurse and saw that Duchess and Xander were deep in conversation with the Aussie doctor. She hesitated for a moment before moving in their direction. Still caught between an unmistakable draw and the desire to be far, far away, Oksana shuffled her steps until she was standing close to Duchess.

"Why is that? Too many children?" Duchess was asking.

Mason's face grew dark and drawn. "No, not exactly."

"So what's the problem, then?" Xander asked.

Mason rubbed a hand against his forehead and looked over at Oksana. Their eyes met for a moment before she blinked and looked down.

"I…" Mason began, but then his voice trailed away for a moment. "Look… I know this will sound crazy, but I've been hearing strange reports from some of the outlying villages. Anytime I try to bring it up with people in my agency, though, I get brushed off."

"Go on," Xander pressed.

Mason took a deep breath and let it out. "There are mutterings from the front lines of the fighting. Villagers have seen what they call *the lifeless*. Child soldiers who blindly obey orders, seem to have no emotion, and are incredibly destructive. Some people are saying that the vodou are preying on the people of Haiti, and have started claiming the island's children, turning them into something like… zombies, I guess, as ridiculous as that sounds."

Duchess made a soft, strangled noise in her throat, matching the feeling of stifling dread that settled in Oksana's chest at the words. She looked over at her friend in time to see all the color draining from Duchess' face. Duchess turned wild eyes on Oksana and Xander.

No. Her mental voice was harsh with denial. *Mère de Dieu – no. Does this evil know no bounds?*

"It's a frightening prospect—I agree," Mason said, clearly misinterpreting her emotion. "I'm sure there's an explanation, though. My guess is that it's a drug cocktail we've never seen before. A lot of these kids come to us high on cocaine—Eniel, for one. But this? I don't know… I can't imagine what it could be, to produce such effects."

The three vampires' eyes met and locked, a single word resonating through the mental link joining them.

Bael.

FIVE

A fierce, red flame of rage encompassed Duchess' aura. In the other's minds, she grew bright, and the light she bathed them in was hot, like fire. *This will not stand,* she swore. *By my life, this demon will pay for his crimes!*

Oksana needed to be away from this place, *now*—the urge to flee growing more difficult to ignore with each passing moment. *Not here, Duchess*, she sent, some of that desperation leaking through. *Not now.*

"*Fuck*, I need a drink," Xander muttered, almost too low to hear. In a more normal tone, he said. "All right, Oz. Here's the deal. It's almost dawn, and we have some business today that can't really be rescheduled. But—" He lifted a finger when Mason drew breath to speak, cutting him off. "—we want to talk with you more about this. Will you still be here tonight, say half an hour after dusk?"

Mason appeared surprised that they were taking him seriously. He nodded. "Yes, I'll be around. I'll try to meet you where we are now, but if I'm not here, just ask for me—I'll be inside one of the tents."

Xander clapped him on the shoulder. "There's a good chap. We'll see you then. Not to worry—

we'll figure out a way to get to the bottom of your strange reports."

Still taken aback, the doctor nodded. "That's... *thank you*. That's just about the first good news I've had all day. I'll see the three of you tonight."

"Until then," Xander said, and Oksana thanked him silently for taking the lead. Duchess was still fuming, her anger no less incandescent than it had been earlier, and she herself was moments away from losing her shit completely and making a thoroughly undignified run for it.

She didn't *actually* run as Xander gave a final wave and headed for the shadows behind the row of tents, but it was a close thing. It was a huge relief to transform into mist with the other two and swirl away into the night air — a far safer option than traveling as owls in a city wracked by random gunfire.

If only she could leave the crushing weight of her past behind as easily as the weight of her corporeal form.

-o-o-o-

Thankfully, the Royal Oasis hotel in the nearby Pétionville suburb did not appear to have sustained any serious damage. Power was out in the area, but the building's generator was running, and lights glowed from the windows of the occupied rooms.

Oksana was no less of a hot mess now than she had been earlier, and it was a relief when Xander waved them into his suite and closed the door, pointing imperiously at the white leather sofa.

"Sit," he said.

Oksana flopped down on the comfortable cushions and pinched the bridge of her nose; Duchess ignored his command and paced.

Xander turned to rummage in his luggage for a moment and came up with a flask. Duchess waved him off in irritation. He shot her a side-eyed look, but conceded that particular battle in favor of standing before Oksana and thrusting the shiny metal container under her nose, instead.

"You," he said, with uncharacteristic firmness. "Drink. Now."

Oksana swiped the flask out of his grip and tipped it up, nearly choking on the liquid it contained. The stuff was lightly aged B-negative—her favorite type, usually—but it had a blood alcohol content so high it was a wonder the donor hadn't succumbed to ethanol poisoning and expired on the spot. How the *hell* did Xander manage to get things like this through customs?

"By hypnotizing the customs officials, obviously," he said, as if she'd spoken aloud. "Don't be a lightweight, Oksana. Bottoms up."

She glared at him as she drained the spiked blood, which had approximately the same delicate bouquet as paint stripper. When she was done, she capped the flask and tossed it in his general direction. He snatched it neatly out of the air.

Within moments, warmth spread from her stomach outward—not an entirely pleasant sensation given that it was paired with an uncomfortable twist of queasiness. Nonetheless, some of the tension bled out of her shoulders, and she leaned forward, resting her elbows on her knees and her head in her hands.

She heard Xander put the flask back into his luggage and settle against the corner of the heavy dresser on the other side of the room. Duchess fetched up near the east-facing window, where the first gray light of dawn would just be starting to peek in through gaps in the heavy curtains.

A small aftershock rattled the building, but everything in the room that was in danger of falling over had already done so before they got here, so Oksana ignored it.

"Right, then," Xander said, matter-of-factly. "It appears we have two competing crises. Somebody pick one to start with."

Oksana made an ugly grating noise in her throat and pressed the heels of her hands more tightly against her eye sockets.

"Dr. Oz it is," he said, and she flipped him a rude hand gesture, not bothering to lift her head. He ignored it. "So. Talk, Oksana. I'd've thought this was an occasion for congratulations, not a reason for me to have to give away my entire stash of liquid courage in one go."

She raised her head to stare at him through narrowed eyes. A glance in Duchess' direction showed that her friend was also watching her with interest, some of her earlier anger having finally drained away.

Oksana didn't much like being the center of attention like this. "And if it had been one of your soulmates we'd stumbled on, you'd have skipped merrily into the sunrise humming *It's a Small World After All*?" she asked pointedly.

"No," Xander said without hesitation. "But that's because I'm a dirty rat bastard who deserves a second chance about as much as Bobby Brown deserved Whitney Houston, and Duchess is a dangerous man-eater. Whereas *you're* a nice person who just happens to have fangs and a bad case of photosensitivity. It's a completely different situation."

Spirits above. She stared down at her hands as if they belonged to someone else. They were shaking. When they didn't stop, she clenched them into fists and stuffed them between her knees.

"You have no idea what you're talking about," she said.

"If he doesn't, *ma petite*, it's only because you never talk about what happened to you when Bael turned you," Duchess said.

"None of us ever talks about what happened when Bael turned us," she muttered.

"No," Duchess said. "We don't. Because it was horrific, and each one of us killed the very people we should have died to protect — or else we wouldn't be here. But that didn't stop Tré from finding Della. It didn't stop Eris from finding Trynn. And now you have found the one *you* lost."

"The one I murdered, you mean," she whispered.

"The one who willingly sacrificed himself to save you," Duchess corrected, "and whose death lies squarely at Bael's feet — no one else's. So, why is it that you look as though you'd rather lose another limb than even trade a handful of words with this man? A man who seems kind and brave, and who risks himself to save lost children?"

The feeling of being trapped—of being hemmed in on all sides with no light, no air, and no hope of escape—returned.

"I don't want to talk about this," she said.

"Oh, well," said Xander, laying the sarcasm on with a trowel. "Problem solved, then. Because I'm *certain* that if you ignore this situation, it will simply go away."

And why not? she thought, a bit desperately. If she could just steer clear of Mason until they left Haiti...

The sofa dipped as Duchess sat next to her. "*Petite soeur*," she began, and Oksana *hated* the careful quality in her friend's normally haughty voice. "We can see that something about this is hurting you terribly, even if you will not tell us what it is. But you cannot ignore the prophecy. Not after what we have all seen over the past months."

"Watch me," she said, knowing as soon as the words passed her lips that they were a lie.

The Council of Thirteen. It was like a taunt echoing in her mind.

An assemblage of thirteen of Bael's greatest failures, and the only force that could hope to stand against him. With the addition of Della and Trynn to their ranks, Eris was more convinced than ever that prophecy referred to vampires.

So... not only was Oksana supposed to relive the night that had turned her into this sad and broken thing every single time she looked in Mason's eyes; she was also supposed to condemn the soul of the man she loved to that same sentence of almost-death. The invisible walls closed in a fraction tighter around her.

"I'm not having this discussion right now," she said again. "End of debate. Move on to crisis number two."

Silence stretched, broken only by Duchess' unhappy huff of breath.

"Fair enough," Xander said eventually. "So. Undead children. We're stopping this—how, exactly?"

If Oksana allowed herself to examine the fact that she was relieved to be discussing this new subject, she would probably break down weeping on the spot.

Duchess had no such compunctions. "It seems likely that Bael has a human or undead agent here on the island. Find that agent and reduce him to his constituent molecules. Problem solved."

"Direct and to the point," Xander stated. "Next problem—how do we find him?"

"Talk to the same villagers *le docteur* spoke with," Duchess said immediately. "The ones who originally tipped him off to the presence of the undead."

Xander nodded, thoughtful. "And, of course, the quickest way to find those villagers is—"

"—to have *le docteur* take us to them and perform introductions," Duchess finished.

Oksana's stomach dropped. "Mason?" she asked incredulously. "You're joking, right? This is just a really bad joke?"

"Of course we're not joking," Xander said, rubbing the back of his neck in thought. "It's not a terrible idea, you know."

"Uh… yeah, it kind of *is*," Oksana insisted, anger flooding in to fill the hollow left by shock. "You're trying to force us together—both of you are! I already told you, *I can't do this*."

Duchess stood rather abruptly and Oksana rose to match her, standing toe to toe. Well… toe to prosthesis, at any rate.

Duchess' blue eyes flashed. "*I'm* trying to rescue innocents from Bael," she said in a cold tone. "It's not immediately obvious what *you're* trying to do, beyond having an existential crisis while elsewhere, children are being condemned to a fate worse than death!"

Taken by surprise, Oksana reeled back a step, the words more painful than a slap across the face would have been. Hands closed on her shoulders from behind, steadying her. She hadn't even seen Xander move from his spot across the room.

"A little more tact, perhaps, Duchess?" he suggested, sounding tired.

Duchess' eyes still snapped fire. "Tact will not save lives. The truth will."

Shame flooded Oksana, tears stinging ridiculously against the backs of her eyes.

"Shit," she said, her voice thick. She pulled away from Xander's support and practically threw herself at Duchess, who caught her and held her tight. "Shit, I'm sorry, *cheri mwen*. I'm so sorry—I can't think, everything's just this big, dark blur and

I don't know what to do. But we have to save these children. Of course we do."

Duchess spoke into her hair. "We can't help you if you won't talk to us, *mon amie*," she murmured.

Oksana pulled back and wiped surreptitiously at her eyes, turning her face away from both of them. "No, I'm… I'm all right. I've got it under control," she said, pushing everything down and back, into the dark space behind her ribcage.

"You won't thank me for this, Oksana," Xander said, "but it's fairly clear that it hasn't occurred to you yet. Whether you're ready to deal with Mason or not, you coming into contact with him means that a vortex of evil and chaos will be closing in around him over the coming days. Like it or not, the safest place for good old Dr. Oz will be with us."

Ice crept down her spine at Xander's words. She barely made it back to the couch before her knees gave out, as visions of everything that could happen to an unsuspecting human in a war-torn country with undead on the loose played like a movie reel behind her unfocused eyes.

The panic that gripped her as she pictured it drove out any delusions she might have harbored about being able to walk away from him and never look back.

"If he is with all three of us, we can protect him," Duchess said.

"All right." The words emerged as a hoarse whisper. The thought of having to stare into the face of the past she had hidden away was terrifying. But the thought of something happening to the fiercely protective doctor who housed the soul of the man she'd once loved more than life itself? That was worse.

"Well, thank goodness for that," Xander said with false lightness. "Now, I'm calling you room service. You need to eat, and I don't trust you to go out and do it on your own."

She sighed and scrubbed a hand over her face. "Fine. Have them send up whatever looks like it has the most sugar in it from the dessert menu, along with a bottle of merlot."

Duchess muttered something under her breath. Xander gave her that vaguely nauseated look that the others always flashed her when she said something like that. He shook it off abruptly and turned toward the room's phone.

"Whatever you say," he agreed. "But—as you're no doubt well aware—I was referring to the *hotel staff* when I said you need to eat."

She nodded, already resigned to the fact that she would need blood if they were about to plunge headlong into god-knew-what in the outlying villages. "Yes, fine. I'll be a *good girl* and eat my Brussels sprouts before I have dessert. Are you two going out for a bite later?"

Duchess waved a hand. "I fed before we left for the peristil last night."

"I'll hit the bar downstairs in a few hours," Xander said.

"When the serious alcoholics start drinking, you mean?" Oksana asked, unable to resist the jab.

Xander's smile was tight, as were his words. "Too fucking right, pet."

Oksana breathed out slowly through her nose and curled against the arm of the couch. Her gaze focused on a threadbare patch in her dark jeans, where rubble from the clinic had weakened the worn denim. In the background, she was vaguely aware of Xander phoning for room service, while Duchess started pacing restlessly once more.

Coping mechanisms, indeed.

-o-o-o-

Mason glanced at the late afternoon sky — a lovely cornflower blue vista that seemed at odds with the dingy surroundings of the overcrowded Red Cross camp. Still, it would have been churlish in the extreme not to appreciate his American colleagues' generosity in allowing the children's presence here after the loss of their clinic building.

The youngsters were safe — at least, as much as anyone was in Haiti these days. Their injuries had been tended, and none of them was life threatening. They'd been fed and had blankets to sleep under. So far, there hadn't even been any serious outbursts from the former child soldiers, whose behavior could be unpredictable, to put it mildly.

Things could have been worse. So much worse.

"Mason?" A familiar, gravelly female voice had him turning on the spot, craning to look over the heads of the people wandering around the camp.

"Gita!" he called, catching a glimpse of rapidly approaching silver hair piled up in a messy bun. "You're back safe! Thank heavens for that."

Dr. Gita Belawan, Mason's partner at the clinic, pushed through the refugees waiting in line for handouts of rice. She was a tiny woman—a stereotypical grandmotherly type whose head barely came up to his collarbone.

"Yes, we made it," she said by way of greeting. "Some of the roads were blocked by fallen trees, but we managed to get back around noon. Seeing the clinic roof collapsed gave me quite a shock, I have to say. Injuries?"

"Several," Mason replied grimly, "but nothing more serious than a simple fracture. Now that you're back with us, everyone's officially safe and accounted for."

Gita had been out in the field when the quake hit, trying to broker more meetings with the rebel military forces in hope of securing the release of more children. They had been taking turns with that duty since they'd arrived in Haiti, so that one of them was always available at the clinic to oversee their young patients.

"Any luck with the rebels?" Mason asked, already thinking ahead about how they might house any potential new arrivals after yesterday's disaster.

But Gita shook her head, her wrinkled face pulling into a frown. "None. They're spooked, and that was *before* the earthquake hit. Things seem worse in the rural areas than they were last time I went out, which is saying something. There's—I don't know—an *atmosphere* around the villages. Like something big is about to happen."

A chill settled in Mason's stomach.

"Anyway," Gita finished, "thanks for leaving that note about where to find you scrawled on the wall. I might've had a right panic otherwise."

"No worries, Gita," Mason said. "Now, why don't you grab something to eat? It's just rice, I'm afraid—they ran out of beans last night and it'll probably be another couple of days until the emergency shipments start getting through again."

Gita snorted. "*Please*. As if I didn't practically live on rice for the first sixteen years of my life, you spoiled Australian."

She gave his arm a quick squeeze, belying her teasing, and let him show her to the mess tent. By the time they made it through the line and emerged again, the sun had fallen below the horizon and the generators were kicking on. Floodlights glared into life, illuminating the camp as the natural light continued to fade.

Gita ate quickly before excusing herself to check on the children and let the staff know she was back safely. Mason lingered outside, curious to see if the three good Samaritans from last night would show up as they'd promised.

He was leaning toward *no*, but a part of him hoped he'd be wrong about that. He tried to put it down to excitement over the idea of someone—*anyone*—giving credence to his worries over the reports from the outlying areas about children being... *changed*. And that was true, as far as it went.

But it wasn't the *whole* truth. The strangers had been oddly magnetic, with an undeniable charisma that intrigued him. In particular, his contrary streak drew him to find out more about a woman who would fearlessly dive into the rubble of a collapsed building despite suffering from claustrophobia. A woman who wielded a dagger as if she'd been born with it in her hand one moment, and calmed a young boy's PTSD episode the next.

And — good lord — she had been *stunning*. Though, of course, she had also acted as though being within ten feet of him made her want to cringe.

Yep. Contrary, that was him.

The other two strangers had landed somewhere on the spectrum between businesslike and congenial. Which made him wonder why the petite, dark-eyed beauty with the Cheetah foot prosthesis had seemed like she wanted to sink down into the ground and disappear whenever she interacted with him.

He was ninety-five percent certain he hadn't said or done anything too terribly offensive. Well, unless you counted giving her an accidental shock when one of them had brushed against an exposed electrical wire in the rubble, or whatever it was that had caused that odd jolt when their skin touched.

So, yeah. He was curious. And possibly harboring a slight crush, because, well, *damn*. There was *attractive*, and then there was *saving a kid's life by risking your own* levels of attractive.

He wanted to hear her story, spoken in that honeyed Caribbean voice. How did she know the others? Her male companion was obviously a Pommy—that posh English accent wouldn't sound out of place reading the BBC news. The blonde woman had sounded French. But *she* hailed from right here in Haiti, he was sure of it. She'd spoken Creole like a native, and the accent clung to her impeccable English as well.

As if his thoughts had somehow conjured them, the trio appeared from the shadows, emerging into the central space adjacent to the tents that had been set up last night. *Bloody hell.* He certainly hadn't been mistaken about her. She was goddamned *gorgeous*.

She also still looked like she'd rather be pretty much anywhere but here. Which raised the question—if that was the case, why *was* she here? Even if her companions were curious enough to want to talk to Mason again, why would she accompany them if she didn't want to be here? Again, he wondered what their connection was with each other.

They came straight to him, as if they'd known just where to find him amongst the slowly dispersing crowd in the camp.

"You came back," he greeted. "I wasn't sure you would."

The blonde woman—Duchess, as he recalled—wasted no time on pleasantries. "You described some very alarming reports from the outlying villages," she said. "We wanted to follow up with you."

Mason nodded, falling into the same businesslike demeanor. "I appreciate that, believe me. You're the first people who've shown an interest.

But, much as it pains me to say it, I've already told you pretty much everything I know—which isn't much."

The green-eyed Pom tilted his head. "So, you've not run across any of these children yourself, then? Just heard rumors?"

"No, I haven't. None of the boys who've come to the clinic have shown the kind of behavior the villagers describe," he said. "They've been brainwashed and hyped up on stimulants, true—but at the end of the day, they're just normal children who've undergone a terrible trauma."

A half-formed memory slipped into the front of his mind, and he went still, frowning.

"What is it?" Oksana, the dark beauty asked—the first words she'd spoken since she arrived.

He took a breath and held it for a moment before answering, new puzzle pieces coming together in his mind.

"Sorry—I was just remembering something Eniel said, shortly after he arrived at the clinic. He talked about some of his friends being spirited away from the rebel camp in the middle of the night—just... *disappearing*, never to be seen again."

"I'd imagine desertions and raids would be a normal occurrence under the circumstances," the man called Xander pointed out.

Mason shook his head, still putting things together. "I thought that at first, too. But Eniel said that they would find the boys' shoes left behind. If they were deserters, they would have put their shoes on before sneaking away. And if it were a case of night raids by government forces, why sneak away quietly with only a few children, when they could capture or massacre the entire group?"

"So, you're saying you believe these disappearances are tied to the appearance of the undead children?" the Frenchwoman asked sharply.

Mason raised an eyebrow, taken aback. "Undead? Let's be clear right up front—*The Serpent and the Rainbow* might've been an entertaining book, but zombies don't exist."

The blonde and the Pommy shared a flicker of a glance that Mason couldn't decipher. He put it aside and chewed his lower lip for a minute, trying to follow this new thread to its logical conclusion.

"Honestly, I don't know that Eniel's report makes any more sense than anything else," he concluded. "I mean, if the rebels are using some crazy new protocol on their child soldiers, why go to the trouble of sneaking them away under cover of darkness? Why not just march them off under orders in broad daylight?"

"Well," said the Englishman, "there's only one way to find out."

Mason's frown deepened. "And that is—?"

Xander smiled, showing very white, very even teeth. "Why, we go see for ourselves, obviously."

"Uh, go… where?" Mason asked, feeling like he was missing something obvious.

The French woman answered. "Go to whatever village you visited when you first heard the reports, of course. And, from there, to the source of the sightings."

Mason blinked, not having expected the strangers' vague interest to escalate into a proposed field trip to the front lines in the space of less than ten minutes.

"You're serious?" he asked cautiously.

"Very," said the blonde woman, sounding it.

"And we want you to come with us, to act as a guide," added the man, as if it was an afterthought.

Wait. They wanted *him* to go along with them? His knee-jerk reaction was to protest that he couldn't; that he was needed *here* with the boys under his care, especially now that they no longer had a clinic.

But Gita was back now. And while it was true that there were a lot of things that needed doing, it was also true that she and the rest of the clinic staff were eminently capable. In an operation like theirs, no single person was indispensable. They'd made certain of that. Stability was too important for these children to risk upheaval if something happened to one of them.

"We completely understand if you're too busy—" his mocha-skinned muse began.

So, she was still trying to get rid of him, then. At this point, burning curiosity about what he'd done to offend her was nearly killing him. Maybe she had something against Aussies? His stubborn streak spurred him to find out, but it was his worry over the alarming reports from the front lines that finally swayed him.

"I am busy, it's true," he said. "However, my partner at the clinic returned today, and I was scheduled to go out and meet with the rebels in a few days anyway. Given what's at stake, it only makes sense for me to head out early and see if anything can be done for these lost children."

"Perfect!" the man called Xander enthused. "You can help me balance out all the estrogen floating around."

Both women scowled at him, and Mason couldn't help wondering how wise it was to antagonize two people who apparently carried concealed knives on their persons at all times.

"Which I say with all the respect and admiration in the world for my two comrades, of course," Xander added, possibly coming to the same — if slightly belated — conclusion.

Their flat stares made Mason think that vengeance would likely be extracted at some unknown future date, but for now, they let it slide. Oksana's gaze met his for the barest instant before darting away. Without a word, she turned and walked back the way they'd come.

The other woman's china blue eyes followed her. She met Xander's eyes, a furrow between her perfectly plucked brows. "I'll talk to her," she muttered. "You get things set up with *le docteur*."

With that, she spun on her heel and followed her friend, disappearing into the darkness beyond the floodlights' pool of illumination. Mason gave Xander a questioning look.

"What was that about?" he asked, hoping for some clue as to Oksana's apparent aversion to him.

Xander flashed a quick smile that did not touch his eyes. "Nothing for you to worry about, mate," he said mildly. "Now, since we're apparently heading out into no-man's land, let's you and I talk logistics."

-o-o-o-

"I don't know how to feel about this," Oksana whispered into the darkness, feeling an unaccustomed need to unburden herself. "If Bael's minions are really taking children from the front lines, this is going to be complicated enough without him there."

"What is it, exactly, that you're worried about?" Duchess asked, moving alongside to walk at Oksana's shoulder.

"I don't know!" she snapped, her frustration spilling over. "Everything. Nothing."

Duchess sighed and tossed her wavy blonde hair over her shoulder. "That's helpful."

"Look," Oksana said, pulling Duchess to a stop in the shadows of the derelict buildings around them. "I can't deal with the fact that this is happening right now. There's too much going on. First Damascus, and now this mess with the children and the rebels—"

Duchess met her gaze squarely, blue eyes glowing. "You can't escape it, though. This is happening, whether you want it to or not."

Oksana frowned at her friend, who looked back with an uncompromising expression.

"I can see this is hard for you, *petite soeur*," Duchess continued, "but you're strong. You always have been. You can get through this like you've gotten through everything else. For, truly, what other choice is there in the end?"

With a heavy sigh, Oksana looked up into Duchess' face. "How on earth do I tell him the truth?"

"The truth? That you were the one who killed him?" Duchess asked.

"All of it." The words were a hoarse whisper. Their truth — the truth of Bael, and the evil that was nearly upon them — was knowledge she wouldn't wish on her worst enemy, much less a soul she'd once loved more than her own life.

"I don't know," Duchess admitted, "but perhaps that conversation can wait for another time. He doesn't need to know any of the specifics right now. Things will make more sense to him after he's been turned."

"What?" Oksana yelped, stepping back in shock.

"You haven't thought that far ahead?" Duchess said wryly. "Come, now, *ma petite*. You need to get your mind back in the game. Think about Tré and Eris. Both of their mates have been turned. With what we know about the prophecy, you need to expect that *le docteur* will be, too."

Oksana made a disgusted noise and pressed a hand to her forehead. "I can't think about that. Let's just see if we can find these missing children, and then go from there, all right?"

Duchess stared at her, but gave in. "You can't avoid this forever," she said pointedly.

Oksana spun on her heel and started walking again. "Watch me try."

SIX

A few hours before dawn, Mason finally sank onto a spare cot in the corner of one of the tents they borrowed from the American Red Cross. His eyes itched and burned with exhaustion, but he couldn't quiet his mind enough to fall asleep. Thoughts and plans chased themselves around his brain, keeping him alert when all he wanted to do was rest.

Knock it off, he told himself sternly. Forcing his eyes to close and his breathing to deepen, he tried to resurrect the talent for napping that had served him well in medical school and, later, as an overworked resident doctor. After lying completely still for what felt like over an hour, he finally gave up.

Bugger. Guess I'm pulling another all-nighter.

He rolled upright and pulled his laptop out of the rucksack full of stuff he'd been able to salvage from the wreckage of the clinic.

Luckily, the battery still had some life, and he was able to connect to the Red Cross Wi-Fi. Good on the Americans. He logged onto Skype and saw that his brother was online.

At least that was a lucky break. He quickly tapped out a greeting on the Instant Messaging app and hit send, hoping that he would catch Jack before he went to get dinner.

Mason: *You busy?*

Jack: *Just trying to finish up some work. Nothing important. How ya doing there, brah? Heard on the news you got shook up a couple of days ago.*

Mason paused, his fingers poised over the keyboard. There was so much that he wanted to tell his brother, but it felt like the words were stuck inside him, like there was a block between his brain and his fingers.

Before he could decide what to say, another message popped up.

Jack: *Isn't it like 4am there? Or am I off in my reckoning?*

Mason: *No, you're right.*

Jack: *What the bloody blazes are you doing up so early? Everything OK?*

Mason: *…I never went to sleep.*

As if to punctuate the statement, Mason yawned widely. He felt as if his jaw might crack open, and his eyes watered.

Jack: *What happened, eh? That's not like you.*

The gentle question seemed to unblock Mason's brain, and he knew where to start the story.

Mason: *It's been one hell of a couple of days. First, we were getting ready to do nighttime meds for the kids, and so everyone was up at the office. The earthquake struck just as we started passing out meds and the roof collapsed on top of us.*

Jack: *Oh my god, are you all right?! They said it wasn't a bad one!*

Mason: *Yeah, that makes it sound worse than it was, honestly. The office was made of some really shoddy materials, or it wouldn't have come down. Thankfully, there were no serious injuries. A few of the kids needed* *help getting out and we have some minor stuff, but nothing too bad.*

Jack: *Jesus, that's awful! I'm glad you're okay but damn, that's bad luck. Especially after the craziness with that kid who got hold of the gun.*

Mason: *Yeah, I hear you on that. I need some sanity, too. Because then? Things got REALLY crazy.*

Jack: *Something worse than an earthquake and a roof collapsing on top of you?*

Mason tapped his fingers over the keyboard, composing his thoughts.

Mason: *Three strangers ran up to the clinic to help us get the kids out. And one of them was this woman…*

Jack: *OMG that is so totally you.*

Mason: *What the hell is that supposed to mean?*

Jack: **snort* What do you think? Only you would pick up a woman in a disaster zone.*

Mason: *I DIDN'T PICK HER UP. I just… I don't know. She's gorgeous. Gorgeous, and brave, and great with the kids.*

Jack: *You totally picked her up.*

Mason: *Not hardly, mate.*

Jack: *…*

Mason: *… but I can't stop thinking about her now. It's like she's just hanging out in my head. She helped get the kids out and they worked with the staff to get everyone to safety. They spent all evening with us.*

Jack: *You've got it bad, brah. This sounds like a serious crush if you're that smitten after only a few hours. That's not like you, Mister Love-'Em-and-Leave-'Em.*

Mason: *Don't be an arse. Besides, she acts like she doesn't want to be within a hundred feet of me. It's* *probably all in my head, and it'll be gone after I've gotten some sleep.*

Jack: *Yeah, maybe. And since you brought it up, when WAS the last time you slept?*

Mason: *Uhhh, I got up at 5am yesterday. I think?*

Jack: *Jesus. Get some damn rest already!*

Mason: *I've been trying. I can't get my brain to turn off.*

Jack: *Uh-huh. Thinking about this woman?*

Mason: *Yeah, I guess. And some other things, too. So you know those weird stories that I've been telling you about? Where the kids go missing and then turn up on some sort of drug making them really screwed up and ultra-violent?*

Jack: *Yeah*

Mason: *Well, I finally have a plan to get to the bottom of those reports. These people – the ones who helped at the clinic – they want me to go with them to some of the remote villages and get a first-hand account.*

Jack: *Going in there to kick ass and take names, little brother?*

Mason: *Haha, yeah right LOL. No, we just want to get some information to see what we can find out.*

Jack: *And you're going with this mystery woman? What's her name?*

Mason: *Oksana, and yeah she's going.*

Jack: *OK, so here's what you have to do. 1) Don't fuck it up. 2) Send me a picture of her ASAP.*

Mason: *LOL all right, fine. I'll get with you once we come back.*

Jack: *You do that, brah. Be safe and let me know how things are.*

Mason: *You got it, J. ttyl.*

Mason turned the power off to conserve the battery and set the laptop on the floor next to the cot. He leaned back, finally feeling like he had siphoned off enough of his swirling restlessness to sleep. As soon as he got settled and pulled a blanket up over his shoulder, though, he heard some of the boys around him starting to stir.

Argh, no, please just go back to sleep, Mason thought, a bit desperately.

Unfortunately, his wishful thinking was not enough to quiet the boys, who were now clambering around and talking to one another.

"Dr. Walker," one of them whispered.

When Mason did not immediately respond, he felt a couple of jabs on his shoulder.

He let out a sigh and cracked open one eyelid. "This had better be an emergency."

"We're hungry," the boy said earnestly.

By the time he had scrounged up a meal for the boys and the other children who had started to wake up, he had long given up on the thought of sleep.

Maybe I can catch an hour or two this afternoon, he thought, stifling a yawn.

-o-o-o-

Oksana, Xander, and Duchess showed up as Mason was helping Gita settle the boys after the evening meal of rice. Mason had to wonder what business they had that kept them occupied during the day—he realized that he'd only ever seen them after the sun set.

Xander tossed him a sturdy rucksack.

"Here," he said. "We packed one for you."

Mason caught it and hefted it, testing the weight. He rifled through the contents and found a medical kit, satellite phone, several bottles of water, and some snacks.

"It should be enough for a day or so traveling light," Xander commented as he hefted his own rucksack over his shoulder.

"What are we doing for transportation?" Mason asked.

"I have some contacts," Oksana said, not looking at him. He watched her curiously as she stuffed several packages of pretzels into her bag.

"Closet pretzel aficionado, then?" Mason asked conversationally. He wanted to learn everything he could about the woman standing before him, and right now, he knew almost nothing. He felt inexplicably drawn to her, more so than he could ever remember feeling toward a woman. The instinct to reach out and touch her was nearly overwhelming—

Jesus, mate, get a grip, Mason thought, mentally shaking his head at himself. A pleasant buzz had seemed to creep over his entire body as he looked at her, but this was no time for fantasizing. There were kids' lives in the balance, for god's sake.

"Among other things," Oksana said, still not meeting his eyes.

Mason blinked in confusion, having completely lost the thread of their conversation. It took an awkward moment for his brain to catch up with her words.

"Oh," he finally said, remembering the snacks. "So you're a non-denominational snack food lover, then?"

"Oksana considers herself a connoisseur of all things that come in crinkly plastic packages," Duchess said.

Mason thought he saw Oksana elbow the other woman in the ribs, but it was so quick he couldn't be entirely certain. "Hmm. It's a trap, you see," he joked. "They get you hooked on one snack, and then it leads to another, and another, and another…"

Almost despite herself, she bestowed a quick smile on him that made his heart soar, before she abruptly turned back towards the others.

"Are we ready?" she asked. "I think I hear our ride approaching."

"Yes, I believe we're good to go," Xander said, after a quick glance around.

"Yeah, we're ready," Mason reiterated, eyeing the battered Land Cruiser that pulled up with some trepidation.

It was well founded, as it turned out. Any thought he had of sleeping on the ride was quickly dashed. Oksana's contact took them along back roads and rutted tracks. The potholes and damaged parts of the road pitched and tossed them like dinghies on a stormy sea.

The experience was not helped by the darkness, broken only by the crazily bouncing yellow beam of the single working headlight. By the time they finally arrived at their destination, many hours later, Mason felt mildly queasy. He rubbed his neck, which ached from being jerked around so much.

"Well. That was certainly unpleasant," he said as he stood and tried to stretch the kinks out of his spine.

Oksana looked sheepish, but surprisingly unruffled by the jouncing. "Sorry about that," she said. "I should've warned you that this gentleman has an aversion to driving the more well-traveled roads."

"What's the problem with at least using a gravel road?" Mason couldn't help asking. While this village was remote enough that there would have been at least some rough travel regardless, they could certainly have used the better roads to start with.

"He tries to avoid drawing too much attention," she answered, her tone evasive.

Mason raised a curious eyebrow at her retreating back before his attention settled on the sway of her hips. He blinked himself back into awareness of his surroundings and followed behind her, only to have his gaze caught by Xander's knowing eye.

"What are you staring at?" Mason asked, a bit defensively, feeling his face heat up despite his best efforts. *Good god above — what had gotten into him?*

"Nothing at all, Ozzie," Xander replied blandly. "Nothing at all."

Right, Mason thought. *So much for subtlety.*

"Look—" Mason began, but Xander interrupted him with a wave of his hand.

"Say no more. You've got nothing to explain to me, old chap," he said.

Mason scowled, trying to get a read on him, but he was distracted when he realized that Oksana and Duchess had led them past the center of the village and were heading towards a run-down building, barely visible in the starlight.

Mason increased his stride to catch up to Oksana. "Have you been here before?" he asked.

She didn't turn to look at him. "Yes. This is Mama Lovelie's place."

"Mama Lovelie? Who's that?"

She did meet his eyes, then—but only for an instant. "You'll see."

With that, she knocked twice. There was a short stretch of silence, but then a sharp command to enter issued from the back of the structure, despite the ungodliness of the hour. Oksana pushed the door open and stepped inside, not waiting for anyone to appear and let them in.

Still feeling confused and out of his depth, Mason followed Oksana inside, with Xander and Duchess right behind them.

"What are we doing here?" Mason asked, lack of sleep erasing the filter between his brain and his mouth. "When I was here before, I spoke to a man on the village council. Will this woman know anything about the missing children?"

Oksana was a black silhouette against the dark gray of the unlit room.

"Mama Lovelie is a mambo—a vodou priestess," she said. "If we're going to embark on such a mission as this, we should have the blessings of the vodou spirits—the loa—first. As a mambo, Mama

Lovelie has a direct connection with them, and can appeal to them on our behalf."

Mason regarded her, willing his eyes to adjust to the darkness. "Do you really believe in spirits?" he asked, genuinely curious.

Oksana hesitated, throwing a look at her companions, who were still standing near the door.

"Yes," she said. "I do believe in spirits. I don't know if they are exactly as we Haitians believe them to be, but it certainly can't hurt to ask for some good fortune with our quest."

Could it hurt? No. But superstition wouldn't help them, either. Still, there was no reason for him to trample on anyone's beliefs, even if he *was* sleep deprived and impatient to get started with what they'd come for.

"I suppose that's true," he said neutrally.

A derisive snort came from across the room. They turned as one to see a small woman with dark skin leaning against a doorframe, holding a lit candle. She had short, iron gray braids covering her head, and there was an odd expression on her face.

"Mama Lovelie, I don't know if you remember me—" Oksana began, only to be abruptly cut off.

"I know who you are," Mama Lovelie said. "Or, rather, I know *what* you are."

Oksana blanched, her *cafe-au-lait* complexion going pale in the flickering candlelight.

Mason glanced towards the others in confusion, only to find that their features had gone cold and wary.

"I know what you are," Mama Lovelie repeated in a quieter tone. "Why have you come here? You see, at my age I don't have a lot of time for small talk. Not when there's work to be done!" She tipped her chin up, looking down her nose at them despite the fact that all of them, except Oksana, were several centimeters taller than she was. She lifted an imperious eyebrow. "I'm a very busy woman, you know."

"Uh..." Oksana began, clearly at a loss.

"Forgive our intrusion, but we need your help with a very important matter, Madame," Duchess interjected smoothly, coming to Oksana's aid.

A slow smile spread across Mama Lovelie's face, revealing white, square teeth. "That much," she said, "is painfully obvious."

Mason wasn't sure if he should feel amused or offended on the others' behalf. The expression on Oksana's face was so gobsmacked that it made him want to chuckle. He stifled it, not wanting to give her any more reason to feel uncomfortable around him. He definitely got the impression that she was second-guessing her decision to bring them here, though.

Oksana appeared to recover herself. "Mama Lovelie, we are here to investigate reports of children disappearing from this region, only to reappear later, but changed."

She indicated Mason with one hand. "This is Dr. Walker—a physician who specializes in helping traumatized children. He tells us that he's heard reports of these disappearances from families in the villages around here. I felt that it would be... *prudent*... to request blessings from the spirits before we venture further into this matter."

"Can't, luv. I'm far too busy," Mama Lovelie said dismissively, and bustled out of the room, taking the candle with her.

Mason couldn't see a damned thing, but the silence spoke volumes.

"Is she really too busy?" Mason asked, when it seemed no one else would break the stunned hush.

Another pause, before Oksana said, "No, I think she's just testing our resolve. Follow me."

Mason heard the rustle of clothing as the others moved to go with her. He could barely make out shapes in the dark, but followed cautiously after the sounds, feeling his way to avoid bumping into anything.

Oksana led them into a modest room at the back, lit with a kerosene lamp. Five small, circular mats were laid out on the floor, as if awaiting their arrival. Candles and incense burned on a low table in the corner.

One might almost think that Mama Lovelie had been expecting four visitors, though of course that was ridiculous. This village was in the middle of nowhere, and it was either ridiculously late or ridiculously early, depending on one's point of view.

Their eccentric hostess stood off to one side, preparing a tray with three cups on it. She looked up as they entered.

"Oh, you're still here?" she asked. "Well, I suppose you'd better sit down and have some *akasan*, in that case."

She finished stirring and handed one cup to Mason and one to Oksana before lifting the third to her own lips. Mason looked down at the milky, anise-scented drink, and back up at Mama Lovelie.

"Aren't you going to offer some to the others?" he asked, more than a little bewildered by the woman's actions.

She waved off his question with her free hand. "They don't want any."

His confused gaze moved to Xander and Duchess. Xander only shrugged. "As bodily fluids go, I can't say milk holds much appeal, no."

Oksana sank gracefully onto the nearest mat and looked up at the others with an expectant flicker of one dark eyebrow. Mason lowered himself down onto the mat next to her, careful not to spill the warm drink he was still holding.

The room seemed very still, as if he had just stepped, completely unprepared, into a church or holy site of some kind. He had never been a particularly religious man, and here he was, apparently right in the middle of a vodou ceremony designed to ask for the blessings of spirits he didn't remotely believe in.

Still, the only polite things to do were to sit down, shut up, and respect the beliefs of others. He only wished it wasn't costing them precious time.

Mama Lovelie finished her drink and set it aside. She knelt on the mat facing Oksana, her head tilting in curiosity like a bird's.

"Why do you come here seeking the blessings of the spirits, child?" she asked. "Surely you have the favor of the goddess?"

"That's… a little up in the air, I guess you could say," Oksana replied, looking more than a bit discomfited.

Mason knew he was missing the subtext, here, but there was nothing to be gleaned from either the mambo's cryptic remark or Oksana's vague answer.

"Why would you say that, child?" Mama Lovelie pressed. "Her light shines inside three of you, and the human has potential."

Mason blinked. The *human*? What on earth was this woman talking about? This conversation was veering straight past *odd* and into *surreal*.

If possible, Oksana looked even warier than before. "Perhaps, but… that's really not why we're here. We just need blessings from—" she began, only to be interrupted again.

"You," Mama Lovelie said in a sharp voice, jabbing a small stirring stick towards Oksana, "do not get to come into my house, asking for blessings from the loa, while you are so desperately trying to hide what you are. What you have become. The cosmos is moving around you and the prophecy will be fulfilled. You cannot flee from this. You cannot stop what has already been set in motion. Your cowardice will anger the spirits and drive them away."

Mason, unable to stay quiet any longer, cleared his throat. "Look, I'm sorry—but do you all know each other somehow? What is this about, exactly?"

Both women ignored him, still locked in a stare-down.

"It's not cowardice," Oksana said, her voice burning with intensity. "*I'm trying to protect him.*"

"How is this protection? You *cannot* protect him," Mama Lovelie replied. "You know that."

Oksana *flinched*, a small, wordless noise torn from her throat. A flicker of sympathy crossed Mama Lovelie's face, replaced a moment later with determination.

"I'm sorry, child," she whispered, reaching out and patting Oksana's knee. "This, you cannot avoid."

"She's right, Oksana," Xander murmured, breaking the tense standoff. "It's time. It's *past* time, in fact."

"It's not!" Oksana insisted, her eyes going wide. "We don't even have confirmation that Bael is behind this—"

"*Petite soeur*," Duchess said gently, "of course he is."

"Right," Mason said. "Would someone *please* tell me what the hell you four are talking about?"

Xander closed his eyes, and when he opened them, they were blazing green with a bright, unnatural light. Mason's heart stuttered once and began to pound.

"What—" he choked out, his eyes caught fast by that otherworldly glow.

Xander smiled, his lips pulling back to reveal lethally pointed canines. "If you'll forgive the misquote—there are more things in heaven and earth, Ozzie, than are dreamt of in your philosophy."

SEVEN

Mason sat completely still, barely even breathing as he stared at the…*man? Creature?* At the *individual* in front of him. He thought he understood now what a rodent must feel like when staring into the face of a cobra poised to strike.

Hypnotic eyes, and the teeth of a dangerous predator.

Both set in the face of a charming Pom who'd chatted with Mason pleasantly and teased him for being from Australia. The implication of the fangs was obvious, but Mason… just… couldn't make his mind go there. He was a *doctor*, for fuck's sake. A man of science. Bad enough that he was wandering around in a war zone searching for zombie children—not that he believed in zombies, either.

The Englishman—who apparently wasn't a real Englishman—continued to gaze at Mason until the silence became stifling. Then, he blinked, and when he opened his eyes, they were once again a striking—but totally normal—shade of moss green. He frowned at Mason, as if perplexed.

"Okay… I'll admit I was expecting a bit more of a reaction that that," he said. Mason opened his gob, but no words came out when Xander leaned over and spoke out of the side of his mouth to Duchess. "Er… I didn't accidentally break him, did I?"

Mason closed his jaw with a snap and looked at Oksana, who seemed to be silently willing herself to sink straight through the dirt floor beneath her and disappear. Then, he looked down at the cup of *akasan* he'd set aside after taking a few sips.

"There was something in the drink, wasn't there?" he demanded, his eyes narrowing as he pinned Mama Lovelie with a suspicious glare. "What did you dose me with? Was it in all three cups, or just mine?"

The mambo snorted. "There were several things in the drink, *blan*. Milk. Corn flour. Sugar. Cinnamon and star anise. A pinch of salt. I'm sorry to say, I ran out of vanilla beans last week, however."

"You're not hallucinating," Oksana said hoarsely. Her eyes flashed angrily at Xander, and Mason was certain he saw a flare of violet light within their dark brown depths. "Xander, how *could* you?"

The look Xander gave her was almost pitying, but there was steel beneath it. "You'll thank me for it later."

Duchess snorted. "She'll *thump* you for it later, more likely," she muttered, before lifting a perfectly plucked eyebrow at Oksana. "But it still needed to be done, *chérie*."

Mason had surreptitiously taken his own pulse during the exchange and run himself through a short cognitive test. Everything seemed... *normal*. And now, he wasn't sure which idea was more upsetting—the idea that he was hallucinating the results of his quick and dirty self-diagnosis, or the idea that he *wasn't*, and the last couple of minutes had truly happened.

"You and I need to talk," he told Oksana, since this madness seemed to center around her, somehow, if their hostess was to be believed.

She still looked like she wanted nothing more than to vanish into thin air, but Mama Lovelie said, "Yes. You two talk. There is to be a ceremony tonight in the village center. I will use it to appeal to the loa for deliverance from the evil that has gripped our country. You may attend and ask for their blessings on your journey at the same time. If the spirits favor you, we will speak in more depth afterward."

Mason's attention was mostly for Oksana, but he was peripherally aware when Duchess rose gracefully from her mat and crossed to the small window in the far wall.

"It will be dawn soon," the blonde woman said. "Will you offer us sanctuary, Madame, or should we leave you in peace and find shelter elsewhere?"

"You may stay," Mama Lovelie said. "I require payment, though."

Xander reached into a trouser pocket. "That's not a problem. Do you prefer American dollars or Haitian gourdes?" he asked.

The mambo laughed—a clear, rich sound.

Xander quirked an eyebrow. "So... Euros, then?"

"Oh, nightwalker," said Mama Lovelie. "You are a sly one, aren't you? I have no use for your paper notes. What I require is far simpler—a few drops of blood from each of the three of you."

Oksana stiffened, her earlier reticence forgotten. "Why do you want it?" she demanded.

Duchess turned her gaze from the window, suddenly watchful. Xander deliberately lowered his eyebrow and pulled his hand from his pocket. "I'd be curious about the answer to that question, as well," he said in a deceptively mild voice.

Mason clambered upright, fighting an unexpected moment of vertigo as his body chose that moment to remind him that he'd barely slept in the last two days. He was so far out of his depth right now that the surface was merely a distant glimmer. Part of his exhaustion-fogged brain insisted that he was the butt of some kind of elaborate joke, and the punch line would come any minute now. The other part was babbling, *now the voodoo lady wants to take blood from the sodding vampires, are you fucking well kidding me?*

Mama Lovelie regarded Oksana with an inscrutable expression. "Why do I want it? Why do you think? There is power in blood."

Mason stepped up shoulder to shoulder with Oksana. "Yet you don't ask for mine. Just theirs."

Amusement was clear in the mambo's reply. "Some kinds of blood have more power than others, *blan*. Perhaps I will ask for yours another day."

Duchess pushed away from the window. "We can leave. There is still time to find someplace else to stay."

Oksana lifted a hand, her gaze not leaving Mama Lovelie's. "Give me your word that you don't intend to use our payment in a way that would bring harm to innocents."

"Oksana. Are you sure about this?" Xander asked, looking at her quizzically.

Mason couldn't stay quiet any longer. "This is mad." He rubbed at his eyes until he saw stars, trying to scrub away the fogginess. "Okay, so look. You're a vodou mambo. I get it. There are certain expectations from the villagers you need to meet, right? You have to display the trappings. But it's *just blood*. The only way it could be dangerous is if it contains disease vectors, or if you transfuse it into a person with the wrong blood type!"

There was a beat of silence, before Xander murmured, "Ozzie... oh, mate. You have *no idea*."

The mambo was still staring at Oksana and ignored his words. "If I am able to utilize it to bring harm to someone, child," she said, her tone flinty, "it most certainly won't be an innocent."

Oksana's shoulders tensed visibly. "So, you *do* know something about the children."

Mama Lovelie snorted. "Am I a fool? Of course I know what is happening on my own doorstep. I already told you—make your peace with the truth, and then, if the spirits favor you tonight, we will talk further."

After seeming to struggle with a moment of indecision, Oksana looked at Duchess and Xander. Her eyes moved to Mason next, but they slid over him like water across an orange peel—as if she found it physically painful to look at him.

"All right," she said. "Fine. We'll pay your price."

-o-o-o-

After Oksana, Duchess, and Xander had each sliced their palms with the knife Mama Lovelie provided and squeezed a few drops of blood into the three glass vials she indicated, the mambo carefully sealed the containers before giving the four of them a quick tour of the house where they would apparently be spending the day.

It was larger than most structures one would expect to find in a village such as this, with four modest rooms in total, plus a raised and covered sleeping porch built against the north wall. Xander and Duchess retired a short time later, giving Oksana what seemed to Mason to be rather pointed looks as they left to get some rest.

Oksana looked… *cornered*. Mason pondered the idea of giving her an out — pleading exhaustion and begging off to sleep for a few hours. But for one thing, he didn't think he *would* be able to sleep until he talked to her and got some kind of mental handle on this insanity, and for another, he thought the other two might well intervene if they thought she was in danger of weaseling out of the conversation.

There were more undercurrents swirling around than he could possibly hope to follow in his present befogged state, but it was painfully clear that they needed to talk. He followed her out onto the sleeping porch as the sky began to lighten with the coming dawn. The outdoor space was homey and welcoming, with a hammock hanging from two of the posts holding up the roof, and a mattress taking up one corner of the floor. A couple of rattan chairs with a low table set in between completed the setup.

Mason flopped down in a chair. Oksana moved to one of the posts supporting the hammock, her smooth, almost feline grace belying her missing lower limb. She leaned against the rough wooden pole at an angle that let her look out across the village, while keeping Mason in the corner of her eye.

The first hint of golden light appeared as the sun breached the horizon, and they watched it from the shadowed porch. Mason let the silence stretch until it became clear that she would not speak unprompted.

"You're uncomfortable around me," he observed, breaking the spell of the morning stillness. "Painfully so. Why?"

Her pause was long enough to make him wonder if she would refuse to speak at all. He let his gaze wander, taking in the low bank of slate-colored clouds hugging the western horizon, illuminated now by the morning sun. A flash of electricity crackled within the gray, swirling mass.

Was there a storm coming this morning? Well, now... how terribly apt.

Oksana sighed—a sound of capitulation.

"It's complicated," she said.

He looked away from the distant lightning in favor of examining her beautiful, melancholy features. "Try me."

Her eyes met his, that spark of glowing violet visible once more within their soulful depths. "You saw what we are, yet you don't believe the evidence of your own senses," she accused.

Mason regarded her steadily. "I'm sleep-deprived well past the point where hallucinations are common, and I still have no guarantee that I wasn't drugged with something in that drink," he said. "I wouldn't be much of a doctor if I immediately jumped to the *least* likely explanation for what I thought I saw, now would I? Occam's Razor cuts both ways."

She gave a frustrated shake of her head. "Then what is the point of us talking, if you won't believe anything I say?"

He frowned. "As you'll recall, I didn't ask you about Xander's teeth, or about that violet glow I've seen in the depths of your eyes. I asked you why you were uncomfortable around me, when I'm not aware of having done anything to make you react that way."

Her eyes flicked back from the view beyond the porch, settling on him properly for perhaps the first time since they'd arrived here.

"Because my presence here has drawn you into danger," she said. "The worst danger you've ever faced."

He snorted. "The worst danger I've ever faced? And you're sure of that, are you? I hate to disillusion you, Oksana, but three days ago I spent a good twenty minutes staring down the barrel of an AK-47 held by a frightened teenager who was hopped up on so much cocaine he could hardly see straight." He gestured at the sleepy village around them. "I assure you that I was in far more danger *then* than I am now—and I hadn't even met you at that point."

His intention might have been to reassure her, but his words appeared to have the opposite effect. Her expression grew devastated.

"The vortex," she whispered. "It's already forming around you."

Mason shook his head, trying to stay on top of the conversation.

"Look," he said. "Maybe you're right, and this isn't the best time to try and have this talk. Like I told you, I'm knackered. I'm guessing you can't be much better off. Why don't you let me bandage your hand, and then we can both get some rest and tackle this subject later today."

Her brows drew together in confusion. "Bandage my hand?"

He gestured at her left palm, which hung loosely by her side. "Yes, that's what I said. I'm a doctor, after all, and that looked like a wicked slice on your palm earlier when you offered up your little unplanned blood donation to Mama Lovelie." A noise of irritation escaped him. "I think our hostess must be the real vampire here."

After the barest hesitation, she pushed away from the post and crossed to stand in front of him, moving like she was caught between the desire to come closer and the desire to flee. She stretched out her hand, palm up, to reveal smooth, unbroken skin.

He stared at her unblemished palm stupidly, forcing his groggy brain to confirm that it had definitely been the left one she cut with Mama Lovelie's sharp little blade.

It was; he was certain of it.

"But... that's..." The words emerged slowly, and with no plan as to how the sentence would end.

He reached out and grasped her hand in his, intending to turn it more fully toward the light. Instead, he sucked in a sharp breath as the same shock he'd felt when he helped her up from the rubble of the clinic ricocheted up his arm and down the length of his spine like lightning.

His jaw hung open. The sane thing would have been to let go. To jerk back, breaking contact. Instead, his fingers tightened on hers. His eyes lifted to her face. She looked as though she wanted to weep—her expression one of the most exquisite pain.

The initial jolt would have been enough to put him straight on his arse if he hadn't already been sitting down. Now, though, the buzz of inexplicable power seemed to settle along his nerves like a comforting cloak, banishing his exhaustion... energizing him.

"What... *is that*?" he asked breathlessly, still not releasing her. There were no exposed wires here. Hell, he'd seen no indication that the village had electricity at all—no lines, no generators.

Oksana was still staring at him as though she were grieving for him, even though he was sitting right in front of her.

"It's the outward manifestation of a bond that draws the two of us together," she said. "A bond that has drawn you into danger—the likes of which you can't even begin to imagine."

After a few more moments, she drew her hand back. He fought a brief, confusing impulse not to let her go before rationality returned and he allowed her fingers to slip from his. As soon as the contact broke, a feeling of emptiness washed over him, exhaustion close on its heels. He blinked rapidly, trying to marshal his fragmented thoughts into some semblance of coherence.

"Your hand. The cut. It's completely healed," he said blankly. "Or am I hallucinating again?"

She shook her head. "It was only a small injury. It healed almost instantly."

"But... *how?*" he asked.

"Because I am a vampire," she said simply.

"No. Vampires *don't exist.*" Even in his sleep-deprived state, he could hear the undertone of desperation behind his words.

Rather than answer directly, Oksana turned away. She walked across the porch and down the rickety steps. Pausing at the edge of the shadow cast by the porch roof, she stretched one hand out in front of her, the movement slow and cautious. Seconds later, she pulled it back and retraced her steps, tension coiling in her shoulders.

A teasing whiff of something unpleasant reached Mason's nose—the acrid scent of burned flesh. When she held her hand out for inspection—the same hand he had held only moments ago—his stomach churned. Skin that had been smooth and uninjured was now mottled red, with ugly blisters rising as he watched.

"Good god," he breathed, and rose from the chair to grasp her forearm. "Oksana, those are second- and third-degree burns! Come inside, I brought a medical kit—"

"Wait," she said, cutting him off. "Watch."

Her voice was tight with pain, but no less commanding for it. The words snapped him back from instinct to logic. She'd never left his line of sight. He'd *seen* her stretch her uninjured hand into the sunlight, and pull it back mere moments later, burned and blistered. This wasn't some easily explained medical condition, like porphyria.

Human skin simply did not react to the sun like that.

As he watched, the blisters gradually subsided. The mottled red burns turned shiny, pale new skin covering them like accelerated time-lapse photography. The skin smoothed and changed shade to her natural mocha tone. He blinked, and when his eyes opened, her hand was once again completely normal and unblemished.

His knees gave out, and he fell back into the chair.

"Tell me what you wanted to tell me," he said. "I'm listening."

The lines of tension in her shoulders eased. She pulled the second chair around to face him and sat in it, leaning forward intently.

"There's a war, Mason," she said. "A terrible, unimaginable war... and you're part of it now. You're part of it, *because of me*."

She sounded so sad—so full of regret.

"There have always been wars, Oksana," he argued. "And I came here because I wanted to help pick up the pieces, not because I was somehow drawn here against my will."

She shook her head. "I don't mean *this* war. Though I suppose this war is part of it, given what we've learned. But it's not just Haiti. Not just Damascus."

"Damascus? The suitcase bomb? That was a terrorist attack," Mason pointed out. "A terrible one, certainly. Perhaps the worst in history, but—"

"No," she interrupted. "It was an opening salvo in the war that will make or break humanity. Only luck and a desperate last-minute ploy kept six nukes from going off in cities around the Mediterranean and Middle East, rather than just one. Can you imagine what would have happened if that had occurred?"

There had been no mention on the news of other nukes, or a broader plot. "That's the first I've heard of other bombs," he said cautiously. "What source did you hear that story from?"

She snorted. "I don't need a source. I was there, along with Duchess and Xander. Our other friends are still in the region, trying to track the movements of the man who orchestrated the attack—and the movements of the forces he unleashed in its aftermath."

He blinked stupidly at her. "You… were in… Damascus? When the bomb went off?"

Her eyes grew far away. "Yes. We were—close enough for the shockwave to drop part of a ceiling on our heads. Close enough to see the mushroom cloud rise... and to sense the screams of the dying victims."

Thinking of how close the sad-eyed woman before him had come to annihilation made something cold and heavy settle in Mason's chest.

"You told me to say what I needed to say to you," she continued. "There are forces in the universe, Mason. Powerful forces arrayed in opposition to each other. Good and evil. Light and dark. When they are balanced, they drive the patterns of nature. Of life and death. But the balance has shifted. My friends and I are victims of that power shift. So are the kidnapped children whose souls are being destroyed. And so, now, are you."

He wasn't ready to tackle all of that, with his thoughts muddled by exhaustion. Instead, he took a different tack.

"You called yourself a vampire," he said. "Help me understand that. The idea of vampires is a human construct, with roots in societal and religious history. It's a reflection of human insecurities and fears about life and death, not a description of a real condition. So... when you say *vampire*, tell me exactly what you mean."

"You've seen some of it," she pointed out.

He thought of glowing eyes, gleaming white fangs, and fresh skin growing over burns as he watched. "Tell me the rest."

Oksana regarded him for a long moment. "I don't know that you're ready to hear what I have to say quite yet," she said eventually. "I could tell you that I was born only a few kilometers from here, in the year 1769. I could tell you that I can change form—even prove it by vanishing into mist and reappearing behind you an instant later.

"I could even tell you that you just tipped over that little side table next to you because I planted the suggestion in your mind, and then told you to forget that I'd given you the command. But you won't believe a word of it."

Mason's eyebrows drew together in confusion. She looked pointedly to his left, and he followed her gaze to see the little table that had stood between the two chairs lying on its side. His hand rested on the edge. He stared down at the upended piece of furniture stupidly.

"I... don't—" he began.

"Yeah," she sighed, sounding suddenly tired. "I know you don't. It's all right. You should get some sleep. We can talk again later."

He was still eyeing the table. As she spoke, he righted it. He wanted to dispute her claims, but his brain felt like a saturated sponge that couldn't take on another drop of water.

"Maybe you're right," he said in a blank tone. He looked up at her. "Tell me one more thing, though. You keep talking about a bond—saying that you and I are being drawn together somehow. What makes you say that? How do you know?"

The slender hand that he had seen healing from second-degree burns lifted to smooth over his cheekbone and cup his jaw. He gasped, a jolt of raw power zapping from the point of contact straight down to the base of his spine where it coiled restlessly, sending heat pulsing through him.

He couldn't look away from the violet glow behind her burning eyes. The look of veiled torment was back on her face, and in that instant, he would have done *anything* to make it disappear.

"This is how I know," she whispered. Her hand slid away, leaving him shaking with reaction. Before he could recover himself enough to speak, she was gone, disappearing into the house.

EIGHT

It was a testament to the depths of his exhaustion that Mason was eventually able to fall asleep, fully clothed, on the mattress in the corner of the covered porch. The arrival of the rain pattering on the metal roof above him was oddly soothing—a natural lullaby.

He dreamed... shadowy, half-formed visions of Haiti as a lush paradise rather than a desolate wasteland of war, deforestation and over-farming. A faceless woman with mocha skin stood by his side, and even though he could not seem to glimpse her features, he knew that she was beautiful.

Beautiful, and *his*.

No one disturbed his rest, and he awoke many hours later to find that he'd nearly slept the day away.

As was often the case after recovering from an all-nighter, Mason almost felt worse after waking than he had before he'd gone to sleep. Still, he knew intellectually that he was better off now than he had been earlier. His thoughts were sharper, lending his conversation with Oksana that morning an almost fantastical, dreamlike quality by comparison.

He needed food, something with caffeine, and—with luck—a basin of water to wash up in. As it turned out, the former and latter items were readily available. Coffee, on the other hand, was apparently in short supply in the village, with the fighting so close around them. He settled for more of the goat milk *akasan*, a pitcher of which had been laid out next to a crock of pumpkin soup and a bowl of rice with black mushrooms.

Xander wandered in as Mason was sitting down with his simple meal. The collar of his spotless white button-down was open, the sleeves rolled up to his elbows. His hands were thrust casually into the pockets of his khakis. Tousle-haired and with a day's worth of stubble shadowing his chin, he looked for all the world like a stereotypical well-to-do British tourist abroad.

"Evening, Ozzie," he greeted. "I see you found the nosh. Our charming hostess had to leave to get ready for the ceremony. We're to follow her once the sun is all the way down."

Mason swallowed his mouthful of soup, and gestured Xander over.

"Let me see your hand," he said. When Xander raised a bemused eyebrow, he clarified, "The one you sliced open last night. I want to see the cut."

Xander sighed. "Ugh, *scientists*. Tiresome sods, the lot of you. But... where would the world be without you, I suppose?" He extended his right hand, palm up, to reveal skin marred only by old calluses. No wound.

Right. Mason lifted his eyes, meeting the other man's quizzical green gaze. "Tell me where you were before coming here to Haiti."

"Damascus," Xander said without hesitation. "Pulling survivors out of radioactive rubble." He raised a pointed index finger. "And, for the record, there are two things about your question that piss me right off. First, it implies that you believe Oksana to be a liar, since you're checking up on her story behind her back. Second, it implies that you think we're too stupid to coordinate our stories amongst ourselves, if we *were* going to lie to you about something."

Mason shrugged, not backing down. "Well, if you get too brassed off at me, I suppose you can always grow fangs and drink me to death. Assuming that's a real thing? I'm afraid Oksana and I didn't quite get that far into the subject."

"You didn't? Funny," Xander said. "That's usually one of the first questions."

"The answer to which, is…?" Mason pressed.

"Short answer? Yes. I most certainly could grow fangs and drink you to death. Longer answer? Doing so would upset a very good friend of mine, so you're probably safe."

Mason nodded. "You do drink blood, then? From humans?"

"Cheerfully, and at frequent intervals." Xander tilted his head. "And to answer the question you're pointedly not asking—no, we don't kill humans to feed. A hint of mental suggestion, a modest blood donation, and off they pop afterwards, none the wiser."

"They're not alerted to something being wrong by the presence of fang marks the next morning?" Mason asked dryly, still caught up in a strange mental give and take—half of his mind sliding into this bizarre new reality, while the other half screamed at him to get a fucking grip and stop encouraging the delusional lunatics around him.

"Vampire blood and saliva have healing properties," Xander said.

Healing properties. Of course they did. Buggering fuck. Mason glanced around until he saw the knife Mama Lovelie had thrust on them that morning, to exact her payment for the lodgings. He reached over and picked it up, using it to open a shallow cut across the meat of his forearm—where it wouldn't be too much of a hindrance if he had to wait for it to heal naturally.

"Show me," he challenged, placing the injured arm flat on the table in front of him.

"We're not your lab rats," Xander observed mildly, making no move toward him. "And besides—what do you expect me to do? Come over there and drool on you?"

An irritable sigh sounded from the room's entrance. Duchess came in, brushing past Xander.

"Don't be more of a prick than usual, *mon chou*," she chided. Her blue eyes glowed in the room's dim light, and she curled her full lips back to reveal razor-sharp canines curving down. She scored her thumb on one fang and squeezed a couple of drops of crimson onto Mason's sluggishly bleeding cut.

The same part of him silently screaming for rationality knew exactly how stupid it was to let a virtual stranger's blood near an open wound like this. The rest of him was oddly unsurprised at the intense itching sensation which ensued almost immediately, his flesh knitting back together before his eyes. He licked his thumb and used it to swipe their mingled blood away, revealing a pink line that faded to nothing as he watched.

"Impressive," he said, meaning it.

"*Impressive*, he says," Xander muttered, tossing a sour look in his companion's direction. "When he has us stuffed into glass tubes with needles stuck in our veins, pumping the blood out of us for research purposes, I'll know exactly who to blame, Duchess."

"Why so worried?" Mason said blandly. "You could always hypnotize me and make me forget what I just saw, right?"

Xander only made a disgruntled noise and turned to leave the room. When he was gone, Duchess's china blue eyes pinned Mason with a speculative look.

"I wasn't sure about you, *Docteur*," she said, "but I believe you're starting to grow on me."

"Er… thanks?" Mason hazarded in response to the backhanded compliment. "Where's Oksana, anyway?"

"In one of the other rooms, pretending to sleep," Duchess said. "Your presence has her… decidedly rattled. I've never really seen her like this before—and I've known her for almost two hundred years."

Mason was getting better at letting the parts of a conversation that were *batshit insane* slide across the surface of his consciousness to be dealt with later. Practice made perfect, he supposed—even when it came to insanity.

"It was never my intention to upset her," he said truthfully. "In fact, I still haven't managed to pry the reason for her discomfort around me out of her. I mean, I get that she thinks we're linked together somehow—and to be fair, I've got no explanation to offer for that crazy electric jolt when our skin touches. But unless she's just really narked about being mysteriously bonded to some Aussie transplant she doesn't know from Adam—"

"I can't tell you that part of the story, *Docteur*," Duchess cut in. "It's not mine to tell."

He subsided with a sigh. "No. I suppose that's fair." His eyes wandered to the small window in the wall across from him. "Looks like it's almost dark out. I gather we need to leave for this ceremony we're supposed to attend?"

"Yes," Duchess agreed. "It's almost time."

"So, what are your thoughts on vodou rites?" he asked curiously. "Are you a believer in the power of spirits?"

"Indeed I am, *Docteur*," she said. "I only remain unconvinced about the desire of those spirits to assist the damned in a foolhardy quest."

Mason forced a smile. "Surely no one is more in need of help than the damned. If they're benevolent spirits, what better deed could there be?"

Duchess' answering smile was cold. "Benevolent? Whoever told you that these spirits were benevolent?"

With that, she pivoted on her heel and swept out. Mason stared after her for a moment before turning his attention back to his soup, mulling the conversation over as he ate.

-o-o-o-

Oksana reappeared just in time for them to leave. If Mason was any judge—which, as a doctor, he was—she'd barely slept. Admittedly, there were several assumptions involved in that statement. Did she even need to sleep? If so, how often and for how long?

Whatever the case, Oksana looked like hell. When her eyes met his before glancing away an instant later, Duchess' words floated through his mind.

I've known her for almost two hundred years.

For the first time, he could almost believe it. It took more than the twenty-odd years of age she appeared to be for someone to amass that much pain behind their eyes.

That pain… it ate at him. It made him want to cut his bleeding heart out of his chest and present it to her as an offering. It also terrified him, because he had never before in his life been prone to that sort of overwrought, romantic rot. *What the hell was she doing to him?*

Ever since that first jolting touch at the clinic, she had fascinated him. The second lingering touch this morning had drawn him completely into her thrall. He needed to get her to tell him more about this strange, otherworldly bond that they apparently shared.

He also wanted to feel it again. Preferably soon.

He followed the others out and shut Mama Lovelie's door behind them, before lengthening his strides to catch up to her. The others hung back, and he wondered if it was deliberate. When he reached her side, he slowed to match her pace. She didn't look at him, but when his hand brushed hers, she didn't pull away. Instead, somewhat to his surprise, she tangled their fingers together and held tightly. The small gesture made his heart lift all out of proportion with what it represented.

Holy hell, you've got it bad, mate, he thought.

Rather than risk breaking the fragile spell by pressing her for more personal information, he asked, "What will be expected of us at this ceremony tonight? I'm embarrassed to say that even after months here in Haiti, I don't know much about vodou beyond the clichéd crap from books and bad movies. Which, I assume, is mostly wrong."

She seemed to relax a bit. "Wes Craven has a lot to answer for, it's true," she allowed, the faintest hint of humor tingeing her voice. "To answer your question, though, nothing will be expected of you tonight. At least, nothing beyond being respectful and not interfering."

"Respectful, I can do," he promised. "I'm brilliant at respectful."

She snorted softly, the noise both unladylike and utterly, inescapably charming.

"See, it's like this," she continued. "Vodou is an African religion. At the risk of being politically incorrect, the loa will only visit those with African blood in their veins. Mine is only half, but when I was young, the spirits seemed to favor me. Right up until the night they didn't."

Mason digested this for a moment, weighing his next words. "Okay… on a scale of one to ten, how disrespectful would it be to point out that every single human being on the planet has African blood in their veins? We all originally came from there, after all."

She blinked up at him, surprise chasing the sadness from her eyes in the moonlight. He caught his breath, unable to look away.

"Not disrespectful at all," she decided. "Merely a bit vexing." She chewed her lower lip thoughtfully, drawing his trapped gaze down to her full, lush mouth. "I'm not sure it's so much a matter of DNA, as of the shared race memory of slavery and conquest."

He nodded, trying to rein in his wandering gaze and his wandering thoughts. "Far be it from me to discount that," he said. "Australia has its own history of ugliness. It still stains the land and its people to this day."

She squeezed his hand briefly in acknowledgment.

"Yes," she agreed. "At any rate, tonight Mama Lovelie will invite the loa to visit the living and possess them. In the Christian tradition, possession is portrayed as something evil. Something to be feared. In vodou, it is our people's means of touching the divine. Many people will be possessed by spirits tonight, and that is considered neither frightening nor unusual."

Mason thought back to what their hostess had told them. "Mama Lovelie said that she would talk with us further *if the spirits favored you*. Does that mean you will seek to be possessed?"

"That may or may not be what she meant," Oksana said. "But, yes, I will invite the loa to enter me." She paused, the tension returning to her spine. "Unfortunately, the spirits haven't chosen me once during the two hundred twenty years since I was turned."

Mason frowned. "Turned. Meaning, into a… vampire?" It was still difficult to get the word out, his rational mind trying to throttle it, unspoken, despite what he'd seen in the last twenty-four hours.

"Yes."

Silence settled around them. He mulled over her words. If such possession—be it real or imagined—was an important aspect of her religion, he could see how its loss might affect her so strongly.

"Why do you think that is?" he asked, wanting to draw her out.

She was silent for another long moment.

"My soul was irreparably damaged," she said eventually, the words emerging so softly that he had to strain to hear them. "The human spirit contains both light and darkness. It's the balance between those forces that makes us who we are."

Mason looked down at her tiny frame. "I can understand that analogy," he said slowly. "But, having watched you risk your life to save a boy you'd never met, I can tell you with certainty that your soul is *not* irreparably damaged."

She waved off his words far too quickly to have properly taken them on board. "My life was never in danger the other night. I'm a vampire, Mason. A roof collapsing on me would hardly have slowed me down."

He continued to look down at her, unimpressed. "But you *are* claustrophobic?"

Oksana shrugged, and he could feel her closing off.

He tried a different tack. "Okay, so I'm apparently not going to win that argument. Why don't you help me understand what you think is wrong with you? With your… soul."

She flickered an eyebrow at him, in irritation… or perhaps in challenge. "A demon ripped it free of its moorings and tore it into two pieces," she said evenly. "But you don't believe in any of that."

No. That was true. He didn't.

"I believe that each of us chooses, every day, whether we act for good or evil," he said, picking the words carefully. "I believe that in the end, our actions are the only metric by which we can be judged. If we leave the world a better place than we found it, who would dare condemn us for the condition of some unseen vital force that supposedly resides inside of us?"

They were approaching the center of the village, and Oksana was spared from answering by the sound of drumming and chanting coming from the grassy open space ahead of them.

"We're here," she said, and slid her fingers free of his. Mason swallowed a sigh of frustration, knowing that further discussion would have to wait.

The scene was both primal and exotic. A large bonfire dominated the open space, throwing golden light over the figures of the village folk. Most were dressed in loose, white clothing. Many were dancing in a slow rhythm around the fire, while others sat on stools or on the ground, singing or beating small drums.

His eyes scanned the chaotic space until they settled on Mama Lovelie, wearing a beaded tunic and skirt decorated with a pattern in the African style. She was bent over a makeshift altar, holding a gourd rattle with a small silver bell attached to the bottom. Smoke from burning incense rose above the low table, curling into the night air.

When Mason dragged his attention back, Oksana had already slipped away. Xander stood in her place, and Mason suppressed a faint, instinctive shudder at the unnaturally silent way they both must have moved when he wasn't looking.

"The ladies went to join the dancing," Xander said. "Can't say I'm in too much of a hurry to join them. I'm guessing you're not, either. Do you have a grasp of what's happening here, out of curiosity?"

"Only in the broadest sense," Mason said cautiously.

Xander only nodded. "I'm afraid I'm barely qualified to offer commentary, but what the hell. Right now, the mambo is running through a very particular set of rituals to summon the loa. First, the one who's a sort of gatekeeper for all the rest, and then all the ones who they're hoping will show up to possess some poor, random sods and *ride them like horses*, as the natives put it."

He eyed Mason sideways before adding, "You might want to settle in. We're going to be here a while."

Mason lifted an eyebrow. "Not a true believer, then?"

Xander made a sharp noise that might conceivably be interpreted as laughter. "Me? Blimey. I'm not a *true believer* in anything, Ozzie."

Mason let his attention drift back to the dancers. Duchess' pale complexion was an anomaly among the swirling mass of dark skin. Oksana also stood out in her t-shirt and denim cut-offs. Mason's eyes followed her movements, graceful despite her high-tech prosthesis. Both of the women were welcomed into the crowd of revelers—*worshipers?*—despite their obvious differences. The sight made a smile tug at one corner of his lips.

"You two looked a bit cozy on the walk over here," Xander observed, his green eyes on Mason rather than the spectacle. "Did you chat about anything interesting?"

Mason bristled. "What's that supposed to mean?"

"Exactly what is sounded like," Xander said. "It's a fairly straightforward question, I'd've thought."

"I'm not sure our private conversation is any of your business, mate."

A spark of brighter green kindled behind Xander's gaze. "You'll probably want to rethink what you consider a private conversation, when you're within range of vampire ears, *mate*," he said. "But, as it happens, you're sniping at a potential ally. I had a talk with Oksana earlier today. Tried to convince her to relax a little and be more herself around you."

"Oh," Mason said, floundering a bit. "Er… thanks?"

Xander smiled, briefly flashing teeth that—while not pointy or elongated—were still disconcertingly straight and white.

"You're welcome, Ozzie. You see, both Duchess and I want Oksana to be happy. That's very important to us. Do you know why?"

Mason felt a frown furrow the skin of his forehead. "She's your friend."

"She is," Xander agreed. "But there are things you should probably know about us, before you spend more time with her. You see, Duchess and I are not good or nice people. We never have been. Oksana, by contrast… *is*."

The frown cleared as Mason's eyebrows tried to climb into his hairline instead. "Wait. Are you… am I seriously getting a shovel talk from a vampire during a vodou ritual?"

"Of course not," Xander said. "That would be ridiculous."

Mason relaxed his tense stance and drew in breath to apologize for jumping to conclusions, but Xander cut him off.

"This could hardly be construed as a *shovel talk*. Because if you hurt our girl, Ozzie, I promise you—*there won't be enough of you left to bury.*"

There was a pause as the drums and chanting swelled behind them.

"O-*kay*, then," Mason said.

Xander patted him on the shoulder. "Good. I'm glad we could have this little chat." He seemed to lose interest an instant later, his attention turning back to the scene unfolding in the grassy lot. "Oh, look. The loa are possessing people already. Capital. Maybe we'll actually be able to get out of here before dawn comes and fries us all."

Mason did that thing again where he let the crazy roll off his back and moved on to whatever came next. Which, in this case, was apparently spiritual possession. And to think, a few days ago, he'd thought his life couldn't get any stranger than staring down the barrel of an assault rifle held by a child who only came up to the level of his chest.

He returned his gaze to the people around the bonfire. Oksana was still dancing, her head thrown back now; her eyes closed.

She was breathtaking. He didn't want to look away, but several other people were acting strangely, now. Some were shuddering in the supportive grip of other worshipers. Others lay on the ground, their backs arching like seizure victims. Mason's instinct was to go to them and check on their vitals—make sure they were all right—but a hand closed around his upper arm, holding him in place with a grip that hinted at inhuman strength.

"Best not," Xander said. "I'm told it's all perfectly normal."

Mason clenched his jaw, but stayed where he was. As he watched, some of the people on the ground rose and began to wander around. They wove their way among the crowd, some strutting, some using an odd, hitching gait, like actors playing some over-the-top role in a pantomime play.

As more people began to exhibit the strange behavior, which Mason presumed was associated with being possessed, the circle of dancers broke up. Those allegedly possessed by loa spoke with the other villagers, or embraced them, or made gestures of blessing over them.

Mason did a double take as he noticed Duchess. No... his first impression hadn't been mistaken. She really was tongue-kissing the hell out of a rather plain looking middle-aged Haitian woman.

Xander followed his gaze. A moment later, he let out a vaguely long-suffering sigh. "Stick your eyeballs back in their sockets, mate. Apparently that villager has been taken over by a male loa. Duchess said something about wanting to find out what the blood of someone possessed by a god tastes like. We find it's best to just let her have her way when she gets like this."

"And... when did she tell you this, exactly?" Mason asked, trying valiantly to get a handle on his *what-the-hell* expression.

"Just now," Xander said. "We can read each other's thoughts. Did Oksana not cover that part, either?"

Just let the crazy roll off like water, Mason reminded himself. *Deal with it later.*

"Oh, dear," Xander said. "Look over there—I do believe that Mama Lovelie has left the building. The lights are on, but somebody else is home."

The mambo's eyelids were fluttering, her head lolling back as she straightened away from the altar and lifted her arms over her head, spreading them wide.

Xander winced. "Ouch. That's a formidable one. Crikey, she's leaking power like a sieve. Can you feel that?"

Mason slanted a look at him. "Run-of-the-mill human over here, mate. I have literally no idea what you're asking me."

Xander's distracted grunt was his only reply.

A moment later, an inhuman shriek shook Mason so completely from his focus that he stumbled back a step. The unearthly wail was followed closely by more recognizably human cries of fear, and he cast around, looking for the source. Next to him, Xander had gone very still.

The hair on the back of Mason's neck stood on end as he saw a disturbance at the edge of the crowd. People were backing away, nearly falling over one another as they fled the terrifying sight in their midst.

It was a girl. A single, raggedly dressed girl, perhaps seven or eight years of age, shuffled into the circle of firelight. A putrid stench tickled Mason's nose as the girl turned dead, milky eyes towards the figure by the altar. In her right hand, she clasped a dagger—dark stains coating the blade.

"Oh, *hell* no," Xander murmured, barely audible over the confusion.

The child opened her mouth again, and the same hair-raising scream filled the night air. Several people shouted commands for her to leave, none of which were obeyed.

The people around the fire stood frozen, as if transfixed by her keening cry. No one moved except for Mama Lovelie, who took several slow deliberate steps forward.

The girl's blind gaze turned towards the approaching mambo. Lank, wet braids swung around her shoulders as the firelight flickered over her unnaturally gray skin. Everything about her seemed to have a cast of decay, including the rotten teeth visible through the rictus of her lips.

"Begone. I command you!" The mambo said, her voice sounding louder and more resonant than humanly possible for such a small woman. Mason struggled with the instinct to cover his ears as he watched with wide eyes, still paralyzed by the sight.

Faster than his eyes could follow, the girl moved. As she lunged toward Mama Lovelie, Mason felt Xander tense beside him and leap forward. In the space of time it took him to blink, all three of the vampires were hurtling towards the girl with inhuman swiftness. The child had the dagger raised, ready to plunge it into the mambo's heart.

Mason tried to rush after them, but his limbs were hopelessly sluggish in comparison to the lightning speed of the events unfolding around him.

The dagger slashed downward in a shining arc.

NINE

Oksana sprang forward, aware of the other vampires doing the same. Knowing even as she flung her body toward the pair by the altar that they would be too late. A small part of her — quickly subdued — felt dismay at the idea of attacking a child, but she knew in her heart that the spirit of the young girl was long gone. Only her body remained, a puppet of Bael's will. For all intents and purposes, she was dead already.

An animalistic snarl ripped from the child's throat, and Oksana's fangs elongated in instinctive reaction. The need to protect Mama Lovelie rushed through her veins like ice water.

Oksana had good reason for being protective of any priestess that she happened to meet. As a youngster, a local mambo had guided her in her journey to open her soul to communication with the loa — a kindness she had never forgotten.

On rainy days, which came often during the stormy season, Oksana would sneak away from the plantation where she and her mother were slaves. She would sit with the mambo, an old woman who lived in a hut not far from their owner's property.

Oksana was a mere girl, and far below the old woman in station. Yet the mambo had schooled her, always treating her with respect and kindness.

"You will be very powerful, Oksana. I can already sense it. Far more powerful than I am." The old woman spoke quietly, brushing Oksana's braids back from her forehead.

"But that's not possible," Oksana answered in her clear, girlish voice. "No one is as powerful as you!" Even so, she preened a bit under the praise of the woman whom she had begun to see as both grandmother and guide.

"We all have our time, child, and yours is just beginning. If you continue with your studying and your prayers, you will become a favorite of the loa."

Oksana stood and hugged the woman around the middle.

"My goodness! You are getting big," the woman observed, patting Oksana's shoulder. "How old are you now?"

"I've seen nine summers," Oksana answered looking up at the woman with adoration.

"Nine, eh? Well, now! May you see many more, little one."

The memory flashed through Oksana's consciousness in the space of a single heartbeat. She and Duchess had been about the same distance from Mama Lovelie when the undead child attacked; Xander was a bit further away. Had the girl been human, they might have had a chance of stopping her in time.

But she wasn't.

An instant before the tip of the knife would have sunk into her chest, the mambo raised a hand, palm out. A wave of power exploded from her, and

Oksana felt as though she had flung herself head first into a pile of pillows. The very air around her absorbed her momentum and she fell to the ground, unable to move any closer.

"What the—" Xander hissed. She could sense that he and Duchess had both met the same impenetrable force.

Oksana stared at the tableau in front of her, wide-eyed. The girl stood frozen, the knife halted mid-arc.

"Oh, child. You have been gone for some time now, haven't you?" There was compassion in the voice emerging from Mama Lovelie's mouth—but it was not the voice of the mambo. It was the voice of the powerful loa who now possessed her. "It is time for your soul to rest."

Oksana heard her start to mutter in tongues. The undead child who had been standing before her, still as a statue, crumpled to the ground. Her unseeing eyes rolled up, and she lay unmoving. In the distance, a plaintive wail of despair rose and fell on the wind before trailing off to nothing.

Some of the people who had been standing near the fire moved forward to examine the body, wearing expressions of the deepest disgust.

"Sprinkle the corpse with bitter herbs and wrap it up, but be careful not to touch it," the possessed mambo instructed. "Also, the knife is coated with poison. Throw it in the fire."

With that, Mama Lovelie's body sagged. The power holding Oksana and the others back disappeared at the same instant, and Oksana scrambled upright. Only the mambo remained, now. The loa who had possessed her and saved her life was gone.

Mason jogged up to Oksana. Electricity crackled between them as he took her upper arm. He gave her a quick once-over before turning his attention to the girl. Two men were already rolling the small body up in a blanket.

"Wait, I'm a doctor," he said. "I should check on her first—"

Oksana shook her head, lifting a hand to catch his and hold him back. "There's nothing to check, Mason. Believe me. Let them deal with her."

He resisted for a moment, but a glance at the girl's milky eyes and decomposing flesh before the blanket covered her face seemed to stop him. She felt a faint shudder travel through his body.

Xander had recovered himself enough to approach Mama Lovelie, who still appeared disoriented.

"Are you well, Madame?" he asked, a hand hovering near her elbow. "The knife didn't break your skin?"

She waved his offer of support away, shaking off her moment of weakness. "Of course not. Erzulie Fréda Dahomey would never allow her servant to be harmed in such a way. As the spirit of love, she is far stronger than a single child tainted by darkness."

"Why was the girl sent?" Oksana asked. "This was hardly a random attack."

Mama Lovelie raised an eyebrow. "I expect she was meant as a message."

Mason was still watching, with sick fascination, as the child was taken away, but now his attention turned back to the mambo. "A message? From whom?"

Bael? Oksana thought to the others. *But... that doesn't really make sense, does it?*

No, I agree, Duchess replied silently. *Bael prefers grand gestures. If this had been his doing, that poor* enfant *would have been strapped into a bomb vest, or something equally horrendous.*

Mama Lovelie's dark eyes played over them, as though she were somehow aware of their silent exchange. "There is a powerful bokor in the village west of here. He is a twisted thing of pure evil, who has committed heinous crimes in the name of money and power. This was his doing, I am certain."

"And he is the one you planned to speak with us about tonight... if the spirits favored us?" Xander asked, his voice level.

"Just so," Mama Lovelie confirmed. "Come. I must complete the ceremony to close the door between our world and the spirit world. When that is done, we will talk."

-o-o-o-

It was not yet midnight when the five of them returned to Mama Lovelie's home. Their hostess waved them into the main room before collapsing rather abruptly into a rickety chair by the table.

Is she all right? Both concern and curiosity colored Xander's silent question.

Oksana gave the mambo a quick once-over before sitting across from her. *I think she's just drained from the ceremony*, she replied. *I've seen similar things before.*

That was a lot of power she was hosting, Duchess put in.

Mason, meanwhile, had been poking around until he found a pitcher of water and a cup. He set the drink before the mambo, who shot him a glance of thanks.

"You're certain you weren't injured at all?" he asked her.

Oksana felt the now-familiar ache take up residence in her heart again. Why did Mason have to be so kind? So earnest? So intelligent?

So damned handsome?

Mama Lovelie waved him off, though not as brusquely as she might have done the previous day. "Of course I wasn't, *blan*. Don't fuss."

"You said there was a… what was it? A bokor?" Xander asked, getting them back on track. "Forgive my ignorance, but what exactly is that?"

"A sorcerer for hire," Oksana said. "Someone with both power and a lack of scruples, who is willing to perform dark magic for money."

"Don't tar all bokor with the same brush, child," Mama Lovelie said severely. "Nothin' wrong with taking handouts in exchange for a bit of spirit work. Lots of bokor out here, you know, and not all of them are Dark."

Oksana had definite opinions about anyone who charged money for what the loa would willingly give for free, but airing them would only derail the conversation.

"This one is Dark, though?" Duchess prompted.

Mama Lovelie's lip curled. "This one is twisted. He has committed heinous crimes without fear of reprisal."

"Crimes like what we saw tonight?" Xander asked, looking vaguely ill.

"Just so. Rumors are circulating that he is hunting at night, plucking children out of war-torn areas and destroying their souls."

"Destroying their souls? How is that even possible?" Mason asked, and Oksana could sense him struggling to reconcile what he'd seen with what he believed about science and medicine. "How could that girl have been walking and holding a knife, when her body was obviously undergoing the decay of death?"

The mambo looked at him with an expression of pity.

"The soul, while in some ways a discrete entity, is also two-fold, *blan*. The two parts are known as *gros-bon-ange*, which controls the body, and *ti-bon-ange*, which is the personality. While they are united, the person exists in balance, with the body's base needs held in check by the conscience."

"Two parts? That sounds familiar," Mason said, turning his eyes towards Oksana, who nodded.

"Yes," she said. "The Light and the Dark."

Mama Lovelie shook her head. "It's not that simple, child. *Ti-bon-ange* and *gros-bon-ange* are not good and evil. They just *are*."

Mason frowned. "So, again, what exactly happened to this child?"

Mama Lovelie sat back in her chair, regarding him. "Through dark sorcery, a powerful bokor can divide the soul, literally ripping out the ti-bon-ange and leaving simply a body that moves and functions without a will. There is no moral compass to moderate behavior. The victim becomes extremely impressionable. This is what is happening to the children of our villages."

"Their souls are being ripped in two and the ti- … ti—" Mason stopped, as if trying to remember the word.

"Ti-bon-ange," Xander offered helpfully.

"Yes, that. The ti-bon-ange is just… gone? Forever?"

A troubled expression filled the mambo's face. "Gone forever? I believe so, yes. There are still some practitioners who believe a person can be reunited with their missing ti-bon-ange, but I have never seen this. I do not know how it is done."

Mason sighed and rubbed the heel of his hand over his forehead. "Okay. Let's say that I believe this. You're basically talking about turning children into… *zombies*."

He looked like he wanted to choke the word back as soon as it passed his lips, but Mama Lovelie only nodded.

"Yes. It is slavery in its worst form. Our people knew slavery for many centuries, but nothing the whites did to us was any more horrific than this."

"And these children are being bought and sold?" Oksana asked, aware that if the man they were after was a bokor, there must be money involved. Already, this seemed like a much more organized venture than simply creating child zombies and turning them loose on a war-torn country.

"Oh, yes," said the mambo. "Some of the children, he sells to the military commanders and militia men. They do their superiors' bidding better than regular child soldiers because they have no emotional needs."

Mason's face had gone pale, Oksana noticed, and she knew he must have been thinking of the battered and damaged children in his care back in Port-Au-Prince.

"You can't help these children, Mason," she said quietly "The best we can do for them is stop this bokor before he adds to their ranks any further."

"That's true," Mama Lovelie agreed. "There is nothing a foreign doctor like you can do to save the *gros-bon-ange* from their fate. All they need is burying."

The words were innocent, but Oksana couldn't help the faint shudder that snaked along her spine. She was aware of Duchess shooting her a concerned look, but she ignored it.

Xander cocked his head. "I notice you said that only *some* of the children were being sold to the military. What about the others? What happens to them?"

The mambo sighed. "Therein lies a strange tale, nightwalker. Some, he sells to the soldiers. But others are packed onto boats and shipped away. People say he is sending them across the ocean; selling them in faraway lands."

A chill went through Oksana—one that had nothing to do with the temperature. This sounded frighteningly familiar.

"Selling? To whom?" Duchess asked, her usually mellifluous voice sounding strangled. She was staring hard at the mambo, blue eyes unblinking.

"There is talk of some rich European man who seems to be a—" the mambo paused as if considering her words. "—collector."

"*Bastian Kovac.*" Xander's words emerged as a hate-filled growl. "It has to be."

The noose closed a little tighter around Oksana's neck, as the full weight of the danger she'd put Mason in became apparent.

"Who's Bastian Kovac?" Mason asked, frowning.

"A rat bastard in serious need of burning, staking, beheading, and anything else I can come up with before the next time we meet," Xander grated.

"The man behind the attack in Damascus," Oksana said simply.

Mason's eyes widened. "Wait. You're saying that the three of you had a run-in with this bloke in Damascus, and then you randomly came to Haiti only to find that he's somehow involved here as well?"

Xander cocked an eyebrow. "We didn't randomly come to Haiti."

Mason's gaze moved to him. "Okay. So why did you come here?"

"Because you're here, Ozzie," Xander said. "We followed Oksana's bond with you."

Oksana leveled a glare at him. *Shut up, Xander,* she sent, her eyes burning holes in him. *Seriously. Not. Another. Word.*

In her peripheral vision, she saw a faintly glazed look come into Mason's gaze for a moment before he appeared to shake it off.

"Let the crazy roll right off your back, mate," he murmured, low enough that a human wouldn't have been able to hear it. He cleared his throat. "Okay, then. So we've got this bokor arsehole trafficking children, both locally and internationally. But... how is he getting away with it? I mean... that girl was..."

"A walking corpse?" Xander supplied helpfully. "Not all of them are like that. Not... the newer ones."

Mama Lovelie nodded. "That little girl had been gone for ages. A fresh gros-bon-ange might look pale or sickly, but not dead."

Mason ground the heel of his hand against his left eye socket. "This whole thing is..." He trailed off and shook his head.

"Horrific," Duchess agreed quietly. "And we're stopping it."

There was silence for a moment before Mama Lovelie levered herself out of her chair and nodded.

"Let me think on things for a while," said the mambo. "This bokor. This *man*—if he even can be called that anymore—he is a very formidable practitioner. I am drained now. I must rest and figure out what to do. We will talk again later."

Without another word, she turned and walked slowly toward the back room.

Silence settled over the group once more, after her footsteps had faded. Oksana tapped her fingers against the worn surface of the table—a thoughtful rhythm.

"Should we call the others here?" she asked eventually.

Xander and Duchess shared a look, but it was Mason who spoke first.

"The others, meaning your friends who stayed behind in Damascus?"

She nodded. "Yes. I'm sure they would come to our aid without hesitation, but with the state of things in the Middle East, it might still take some considerable time for them to book travel and get here."

"Not to mention the fact that what they're doing is important," Xander said. "Bastian Kovac is obviously a big part of this puzzle, and they're already trying to track him down."

Duchess's blue eyes flashed. "We can't wait. How many more children will be defiled and subjugated while Tré and Eris are trying to arrange connecting flights?"

"Agreed," Oksana said, fighting another shiver of unease. "We can't just rush in blindly, though. You saw tonight what kind of power a talented bokor might wield. We'll need an edge of some sort."

Xander leaned back in his chair and crossed his arms, looking unhappy.

"Yes, I for one am well aware of the capabilities of vodou practitioners," he said, and Oksana knew he was once more thinking of Madame Francine, his eccentric acquaintance in New Orleans. "We'll just have to wait for our mambo friend to recharge her batteries and come up with something for us. Best if we get some rest, too, I suppose."

Oksana's mouth tilted down. *And how many more children will be defiled while we nap here, safe and comfortable?* she wondered, echoing Duchess's sentiment.

Of course, neither of the others could offer an answer.

Mason looked around the table, taking in their expressions. "Xander's right. It won't do these children or anyone else any good for us to go blundering in and get ourselves captured or killed by this bloody wanker, whoever he is. We'll come up with better plans when we're rested."

Duchess pushed back from the table abruptly and stalked off toward the back of the house. Xander rose as well, but spared Oksana a tight smile first.

She's just upset about the children, he sent.
I know, she replied. *We all are.*

A moment later, Oksana found herself alone with the man who was the reincarnation of her dead soulmate. The bond between them, which she had been trying all evening to ignore, tugged painfully at her heart.

Over the decades and centuries, she had grown used to being alone, even when surrounded by her friends. She carried the guilt over what had happened all those years ago walled up inside her damaged soul, jealously guarding it as though it were some kind of sick treasure. By pushing that pain down deep inside, she was able to continue.

In some ways, she prided herself on being a happy person—at least, to all outward appearances. Cheerful Oksana. Eccentric Oksana. The vampire who dined on Crackerjacks, Twinkies, and pinot noir, with only an occasional blood chaser as required. Yet, after a scant couple of days spent in Mason's presence, she had already turned into a sharp-tempered emotional wreck.

No wonder Duchess and Xander were worried.

And now, here was her soulmate, sitting only a few feet away from her. Hale, hearty, and whole... and still with that old, unconquerable drive to help those less fortunate than himself. No doubt about it—Oksana was completely doomed.

Mason sat back, regarding her with interest. "So. Rescuing people from collapsed buildings. Stopping evil witch doctors and battling knife-wielding zombie children. Is this just a typical day for you lot, or what?"

There was a hint of despair behind the choked-off bark of laughter that slipped past her control. "It's starting to feel like it, I'm afraid. Though... it wasn't always like this. For many years, it was just the six of us—wandering around, pursuing our various interests, and occasionally trying to make a little excitement for ourselves to relieve the boredom."

"That sounds all right," Mason said. "Did you work, or—?"

"Xander's the entrepreneur among us," she replied. "Though the rest of us do have money, of course. Honestly, it's hard *not* to amass wealth when you live for hundreds of years. Invest a few dollars here and a few dollars there, and it just sort of happens while you're not paying attention."

Mason snorted. "I'll admit, I can't really relate to that sentiment. I know doctors are supposed to be loaded, but in my experience it's all scrounging for grants and wondering where the money for the next truckload of medical supplies will come from."

He regarded her, tilting his head. "Though I must say, I have a difficult time picturing any of you clocking in at a nine-to-five gig."

Her laugh this time was a bit more genuine. "Yeah, I suppose I'm more of a night shift girl, myself." She shook her head at herself before sobering. "We don't age. And after a few years of not changing appearance, people start to talk. We tend to move around a lot."

"But always as a group?" Mason asked, clearly fascinated.

"Not always," she said. "Lately, though, it's safer if none of us are alone. We've learned that the hard way."

"Because of this war you've been trying to tell me about."

"Yes," she whispered. "Because of Bael."

A furrow formed between Mason's eyebrows. "All right. I'll bite. Who or what is Bael?"

Oksana took a deep breath and let it out slowly, trying to ignore the thundering of her pulse as the conversation veered in precisely the direction she didn't want to go.

"Bael is the name of the demon who turned me. Who turned all six of us—the six original vampires, I mean. He is the Darkness. The force that seeks the destruction and desecration of the world and those who live in it."

To his credit, Mason did not immediately denigrate her words, but sat mulling them for a long moment.

"I'm not sure what to say to that," he replied eventually. "I've always found that humanity was perfectly capable of manufacturing its own evil, without the need for gods and devils pulling strings in the background."

Right. He wasn't quite there yet. And that wasn't surprising, she supposed.

"I sincerely hope that you don't end up with first-hand proof of Bael's existence," she told him, knowing deep down what a futile hope that was. "Humanity is a microcosm of universal forces, it's true. Humans choose every day whether to act for good or ill. But the true horror of Bael is his ability to take away that choice and steal a person's free will. Do you think that child tonight chose to act in the way she did?"

"No," Mason said, very quietly, "but I also work with brainwashed children every single day. Their agency wasn't taken away by a demon. It was taken away by ruthless men with access to illegal drugs and a basic knowledge of psychology. I don't know exactly what happened to the girl tonight, Oksana. But I do know we need to stop it. For now, we're agreed on that, and it will have to be enough."

She studied him, noting the pall of exhaustion that still seemed to hang over him. A pang of guilt at yet again keeping him from his rest accosted her. It was followed by a traitorous sense of curiosity about what it would feel like to sneak into bed with him while he was sleeping. Would he sense her nearness and roll over, still half asleep, to curl around her? Would his strong arms feel the same as Augustin's had, so many long years ago?

She shut down the unwanted train of thought, appalled at herself.

"You should… get some rest," she said tightly. "You look dead on your feet, and it's going to be a long couple of days."

He nodded and yawned, not protesting the change of subject. "Yeah, I could definitely use some more sleep."

"Go on, then," she said. "One of us will come and wake you up whenever Mama Lovelie decides to talk to us again."

Mason nodded, stifling another yawn. "Okay. Goodnight, Oksana."

"Goodnight," Oksana answered. She turned to go to the back room where the others were resting.

Still, she couldn't help glancing over her shoulder as Mason headed for the sleeping porch, an unaccountable feeling of longing pulling at her divided soul.

TEN

Oksana didn't fall asleep until just after dawn, thoughts and worries chasing themselves around and around inside her head like a dog chasing its own tail. It seemed only moments later when a familiar voice intruded on her thoughts.

Are you awake, ma petite? Duchess asked, the words flowing along the mental connection that wove a gossamer web across the three vampires' awareness.

Oksana startled into awareness, rousing from a restless doze. She glanced at her watch and found that it was just after eleven-thirty in the morning. Sunlight streamed from underneath the worn curtains drawn firmly across the window.

"I am now," she replied dryly, glancing up at the figure hovering in the doorway.

"My apologies," Duchess said with the barest hint of contrition. "But it's growing late, and Xander left a few minutes ago to see if Mama Lovelie was ready to speak with us. I thought I'd take the opportunity to talk to you, while he talks to her. We're worried about you, *mon chou*."

Oksana frowned at her friend. "I'm all right."

"Are you, now? I'm pleased to hear it," Duchess said tartly. She flopped down on the end of Oksana's bed and crossed her arms. "So. You've found your mate. Now what?"

Oksana groaned and pulled the dusty pillow over her head. It smelled vaguely of mildew. "Can we not do this thirty seconds after I've woken up?" she asked, the words muffled.

"Why not? It seems like a perfectly good time to me," Duchess retorted. "We need to have a plan, *n'est-ce pas?*"

Oksana pulled the pillow away in disgust. "Yes, fine. We need a plan. But I think our *plan* should focus on disrupting Bael's hold on Haiti, stopping the flow of undead children to Bastian Kovac, and helping the government re-establish peaceful talks with the rebels. Not on my…" She paused before finishing, "… predicament."

Duchess raised a graceful eyebrow. "I disagree. You said yourself that we needed the mambo's help for those other problems. Your predicament, as you so charmingly put it, is the *only* thing we can deal with at the moment. So. Talk to me, Oksana."

Oksana swallowed a growl and threw the disgusting pillow against the wall. "I can't, though!" she insisted, struggling to keep her voice low enough not to be heard by everyone inside the thin-walled house. "That's not what's most important right now."

Duchess's sky-blue gaze was almost pitying. "You're what's important to me right now, *petite soeur.*"

Her friend's soft words took Oksana by surprise. Duchess might be inclined toward pet names and fleeting caresses, but she was not frequently given to flights of genuine tenderness.

Oksana opened her mouth to say... something, but no words came.

"You can stop putting everyone else's needs before your own just this one time," Duchess continued. "It's all right to think about *yourself* in this situation, because this situation is undeniably overwhelming. It's also terrible timing."

Oksana laughed bleakly, covering her face with her hand. "Yeah, it's definitely terrible timing. Though I'm not sure what would constitute *good* timing."

"You know what will happen, *non*?" Duchess's tone was uncompromising. "It's obvious that you fascinate him. A blind woman could see it. He wants you. After all, you're the other half of his soul."

"That's the part I can't afford to think about," Oksana murmured, still hiding her face in her hand.

"Why ever not?"

Oksana sighed, and felt the ridiculous burn of tears behind her eyes. She was glad that her face was covered, but that, too, was ridiculous. The pain in her heart was beyond shielding; Duchess would have been able to feel it from a mile away—much less an arm's length.

"I can't let myself get my hopes up," Oksana admitted. "Think about it, Duchess. Both Eris and Tré are far older and more powerful than I am, but it was all they could do to keep Della and Trynn from falling into Bael's clutches. What if I'm not strong enough to keep Mason safe?"

"It's not just you, though, is it?" Duchess said. "Don't you know that Xander and I would give our lives to protect you and yours?"

Oksana swallowed hard, the ache in her chest growing sharper. "I don't *want* you to give your lives protecting me and mine," she said, very quietly. "I don't want you to give your lives for anything, period. Please, don't make me talk about this any more."

She felt the mattress shift as Duchess leaned forward to squeeze her knee in sympathy. "Very well, then. We'll leave it for now. I just wanted to make certain you were all right."

The laugh Oksana let out was not a pleasant noise. "Yeah… no. I lied earlier. I'm not remotely all right. But thanks, all the same."

"Well, then. In that case, you'd better get your *derriere* off that mattress, you layabout. We've got things we need to do," Duchess said briskly, reaching down next to the bed and tossing Oksana her prosthetic leg.

"Supportive friend to drill sergeant in the space of two seconds," Oksana muttered. "Why am I not surprised in the least?"

With a sigh, she tried in vain to smooth her hair into something presentable. Maybe she would get it done in braids again one of these days, to make it easier to deal with. She'd been sleeping in nothing but a camisole and her underwear, so she pulled on a fresh shirt and her cutoffs from the previous night. When she was dressed, she stuck her left leg, which ended in an ugly stump below the knee, into the padded plastic sleeve of the Cheetah foot and stood up.

Oksana brushed past Duchess to get to the ewer and basin in the corner.

When did I get so dependent on hot showers? Oksana wondered, as she splashed lukewarm water on her face and neck.

About five minutes after they were invented, if you're anything like me, Duchess replied wryly. *Now, hurry up.*

Oksana snorted and busied herself buttoning the white shirt over her camisole top as she and Duchess exited the room. They found Xander waiting in the hallway.

"Is Mama Lovelie ready to talk to us?" Oksana asked.

"In a few minutes. Do you want to wake Mason?" Xander asked.

Oksana stood irresolute for a moment. She wanted nothing more than to slip silently into Mason's room and find him sleeping quietly. It would be a perfect opportunity to sneak into the bed next to him, curl up, and rest for a few minutes listening to his strong heartbeat and the gentle sound of his breathing. She could wake him up by running her hands over his soft, warm skin and—

A soft whistle like a birdcall dragged her attention once more to Xander, who was waving a hand back and forth in front of her unfocused eyes. "Oksana?" he prompted. "You still with us?"

She blinked "Oh. Yes. Sorry, I was… uh… just worrying about what the bokor is doing to those poor kids."

The lie wouldn't have convinced a total stranger, much less someone who'd known her for more than a century. She was thankful, though, that her dark complexion hid the hint of a blush rising up her neck.

"Right," Xander said, drawing out the word. "Well, if you think you can keep your hands off your pet Aussie for longer than five seconds, you should probably go get him up. I mean... *wake* him up."

She threw him a dirty look over her shoulder as she wheeled and walked to the door leading onto the sleeping porch.

Oksana raised her hand, hesitating, and glanced back again. She could practically feel her companions' interested gazes burning holes in her back.

"A little privacy, maybe?" she suggested, a hint of a growl behind the words.

Neither of them replied, but she could sense Xander's wash of amusement as he allowed Duchess to herd him further into the house.

With a sigh of relief, Oksana knocked on the door and waited. No sound came from the porch beyond. Oksana stretched out her awareness, hesitantly probing the space on the other side of the door for a moment or two before she sensed Mason's presence. He was still sleeping.

She knocked again, louder this time, and felt him jerk into wakefulness. Drawing her senses back inside herself, Oksana took a step back as soft footfalls approached the door.

Mason opened it just a crack, and one sleepy eye appeared. Oksana could see that his hair was tousled and messy from sleep. A small, traitorous part of her wondered how it would feel to run her fingers through it, straightening the tangled strands. It looked so soft…

An unexpected revelation hit her.

Good god. She could… *actually have that*, she realized, as if the thought were truly penetrating for the first time. If she reached out — right here, right now — he wouldn't stop her. She could have him. Have someone again, for the first time in over two hundred years.

Only… she didn't dare. Once she took that step, she'd be lost. And if she were lost, he would be, too. Lost to Bael, if she was too distracted — or too weak — to protect him when the moment came. And it *would* come. Of that, she had no doubt.

She had to stay strong. She couldn't let herself fall into the past. Not the good parts. Not the bad parts. She had to stay grounded in the here and now.

"Hey," she said, pleased when her voice reflected none of these troubling thoughts, all of which had tumbled through her mind in the space of a second or two. "It, uh, sounds like we're about to be granted another audience with our hostess. I assume you'll want to be there?"

Mason opened the door wider, blinking at her owlishly. "Yeah," he said, his voice gruff with sleep. He scrubbed his hands over his face, trying to rouse himself further. "Give me a couple of minutes and I'll be right out."

"Take your time."

Relieved that nothing further was required of her, Oksana escaped back into the depths of the house.

-o-o-o-

Mason wandered into the sitting room a few minutes later, yawning and stretching the kinks out of his back. Xander pinned him with a look, lifting an eyebrow at his less than put-together appearance.

"Thought you humans were supposed to sleep at night and stay awake during the day," the vampire observed.

"And I thought vampires were supposed to be nocturnal," Mason shot back. "You seem pretty chipper for midday."

"He's always like this," Duchess said. "At least, he's like this when he's not hung-over."

"Yes, it's true," Xander agreed readily. "The level of sobriety I've been suffering lately has become truly vexing."

Let it roll off, Mason reminded himself. Rather than risk being drawn further into the exchange, he moved to stand next to Oksana, who tensed at his approach. He was really, really starting to dislike seeing that reaction from her.

"Good morning, again," he said quietly, taking in her rather brittle and red-eyed appearance. "How did you sleep?"

"Oh, you know…" she said vaguely. "Not bad. You?"

Mason would lay money on that being a bald-faced lie. He let it pass, however, and replied, "Better than I expected, actually. Of course, that's probably down to me having been up for almost thirty-nine hours straight before we arrived here."

"Hmm. I guess that'd do it," she said, relaxing a bit.

"Suppose so. I had some crazy dreams, though," he mused. "Wish I could either skip those completely, or at least remember them properly when I wake up. I don't usually dream like that."

Oksana stiffened again at his words, but the exchange was interrupted by Mama Lovelie's arrival. She was dressed in a loose white caftan and looked much better than when they'd returned here last night after the interrupted ceremony. The mambo gestured them to sit on the mismatched chairs scattered around the room before pulling up her own seat and facing them.

"So," she began, "you four intend to confront this bokor, despite the strength of his magical abilities."

"Yes," Duchess said. "We won't allow this destruction of young lives to continue. Not when we have any chance at all of stopping it."

Their hostess leaned back and tapped her chin thoughtfully. "Then I must commend you for both your commitment and your energy in pursuing it." She quirked a dark eyebrow. "Ah, to be young again."

Duchess let out a derisive snort. "I'm far older than you, Madame. As I suspect you are well aware."

"Yet you still fight the battles of the young," the mambo retorted.

The two women locked eyes, sizing each other up. There was a beat before Xander replied, "When necessary, you bet we do. The question is, can you help us?"

"The bokor is very dangerous, as I told you last night," said Mama Lovelie. "He is far more powerful than I am."

"How did he become so powerful?" Oksana asked.

The mambo sighed and shook her head. "It's a sad tale. That any man should feel such greed and lust for power is a sickness within humanity, a cancer that cannot be cured."

Silence reigned for a long moment; nothing could be heard but the sighing of the wind through the open window. The curtains were drawn against the sun to protect the vampires from its direct rays, but the summery smells of light and life still wafted through the sitting area.

"He was born a man, just like any other," Mama Lovelie continued, "and raised in a village west of here. As he grew up, he learned the ways of our people, the traditions that drive us, and the deep spirituality we share. He was sensitive to the loas' presence, and often feasted at their table. Over time, he became immensely powerful by anyone's standards, and acquired considerable wealth through bartering and trading.

"Exactly what happened next is a mystery, but the people around here say that one night, he went into the forest, drawn there by the darkness. He engaged with the most sinister of the loa, some of who were jealous of his successes. They enticed him, promising him greater influence and a position of vast power in exchange for pieces of his soul. He accepted. The more of it he bartered away over the years, the more blackness has been woven into his blighted spirit."

She fell silent and shook her head again. "I dare not challenge him directly."

Mason watched Oksana cross her arms, a stubborn expression stealing across her lovely features. "There must be something you can do. You can't just stand by while this evil perpetuates itself, practically under your nose!"

The mambo gave her a fixed look. "You should learn to listen better, child. I said, I dare not challenge him *directly*."

Mama Lovelie rose abruptly and walked around the room, looking at each of them in turn, as if appraising their possibilities. When she reached Oksana, the mambo stretched out a hand and touched her temple. Mason felt it more than saw it as Oksana shivered, her dark eyes sparking with brilliant violet.

"I might be able to weave a spell around one of you, drawing on the darkness that resides within you," the mambo mused, returning to her seat. The crease between her eyebrows was the only thing that communicated her displeasure with the idea.

"And that would make us strong enough to destroy the bokor?" Xander asked. Mason could make out the glint of battle shining in his eyes, brightening their natural moss-green color. The mambo scowled at him.

"I do not know if it would be enough or not," she replied. "But I do know it would weaken the spell-bearer, perhaps permanently."

"Wait. It wouldn't be reversible?" Mason asked, suddenly not liking the direction the conversation was going, even though he told himself firmly that he didn't believe in any of this fanciful witchcraft rot. But, even still... "I thought vampires healed really fast?"

"Yes, we heal. Much faster and more completely than humans, at least in some respects," Duchess replied immediately.

"You speak of the physical," said Mama Lovelie. "Whereas I speak of the spiritual."

"I'll do it," Oksana said.

"No," Duchess snapped. "I'm the oldest. If something like this is to be done, it should be me."

"Oksana," Xander said, lifting his hand in a suppressing gesture. "Look, it's not that we don't think you're a total badass and everything, but you're really tiny and you've only got one leg—"

"Your point, Xander?" Oksana asked, glaring at him.

"—So I don't think you're the best candidate for a major spiritual warfare knock-down-drag-out, if you know what I mean," he finished.

Oksana bristled. "You really have no idea what you're talking about. This isn't a matter of physical size or strength. A deep connection with the loa and an understanding of the spirit world is going to be of more importance than how vertically challenged I happen to be!"

Before Mason could open his mouth and join Xander's side of the argument, Mama Lovelie interrupted.

"Oksana is correct," she said. "You must remember that she is a daughter of Haiti. None of the rest of you can claim that heritage."

Mason felt a muscle in his jaw twitch. "This is crazy. Not that I necessarily believe in this stuff, but we need a plan that doesn't hinge on someone being permanently injured, physically or... otherwise."

"Mason," Oksana said, laying a hand on his arm. "I appreciate the concern, but this may well be the best way... if not the *only* way."

His skin tingled under her light touch. "Why?" he demanded, turning to meet her eyes. "Why is this the best way?"

For once, she didn't look away. "Because I have a connection to this land. I was born here; this is my birthright. These are *my* spirits, *my* loa, and maybe this is what will convince them to finally welcome me home. If any one of us has a chance of drawing enough power from them to defeat this evil man, it's me."

Their eyes remained locked, Oksana's hand still burning with that strange energy against his skin. Despite himself, Mason felt his heart stutter and beat faster. He opened his mouth to speak, but Oksana forestalled him.

"I'm right, aren't I, Mama Lovelie?" she asked, turning everyone's attention back towards the mambo.

"You are, child," the mambo answered. "I believe you alone will be able to challenge the bokor, but only if the loa choose to bless you and take your side."

"I still don't like it," Duchess said, brushing her blonde hair away from her face with an impatient gesture.

"Seconded," Xander said tightly.

"Thirded," Mason agreed.

"Too bad, since I don't see that we have much of a choice right now," Oksana answered with a sigh. "I do realize this isn't ideal." Ignoring their unhappy looks, she turned back towards the mambo. "We still need an actual *plan,* though. This is too vague."

The mambo nodded her agreement. Xander pressed his thumb and forefinger to the bridge of his nose.

"All right," he said. "Let's suspend rationality for just a moment and say that we all agree to this. You're just going to waltz in there, battle the bokor while we sit twiddling our thumbs, and then we take the kids away to… where, exactly?"

"Bring them back here first, and then try to reunite as many as possible with their families. Take the ones who need additional care on to Mason's clinic," Oksana replied promptly, and Mason forced himself to move beyond the crazy vodou trappings of the plan and focus on logistics instead.

"The clinic that was destroyed in an earthquake, you mean?" Xander asked.

Mason waved the question off. "I'm sure that the Red Cross and Doctors Without Borders are working on finding us an alternative location, even as we speak," he said. "They're very resourceful, and they have a lot of contacts on the ground in Haiti. That part of the plan is sound enough. Though I don't know what, exactly, we're going to be able to do with children whose souls have been partially destroyed once we get them back. There's no research or treatment regimen in place for something like this."

Duchess frowned, her attention turning back to the mambo. "You said there might be a way to reunite the two parts of their souls?"

Mama Lovelie shook her head. "I said some people believe there is, but that I've never seen evidence of any such thing. For one thing, the bokor is the one holding the children's stolen ti-bon-ange. And I can't imagine he'd give them up willingly."

Mason could barely suppress a shudder at the thought of being responsible for the wellbeing of a group of corpselike children without any will or self-awareness. Nausea washed over him as he envisioned them all trapped in the bokor's village, held captive in a pit or something, bumping around blindly in the darkness. And the others expected him to take them away and fix them? If they were like the girl with the knife, how the hell was he going to do that? Even their resident expert seemed to think it was impossible.

"Maybe they'll be turned already, and maybe they won't," Oksana said grimly. "We'll just have to see once we find them."

Please, Mason thought, *let them still be whole.* As a physician, he was equipped to deal with trauma. But not with the living dead.

Duchess looked as ill as he felt. "We need to find them as soon as possible," she said. "He mustn't be allowed to destroy any more innocents than he already has."

"Right, so how about this?" Xander asked, after a moment of thoughtful silence. "We send in Oksana to battle the bokor, armed with Mama Lovelie's spell to make her more powerful. He's so busy dealing with her that he doesn't notice the rest of us getting the kids out. Then, Duchess and I go back once the children are safe, and help Oksana finish him off. That way, if he has guards with him in the village, they won't have time to hide or move the children once they realize they're under attack."

"That's a slightly better sounding plan," Mason said, thinking that at least Oksana would have some backup. He had to admit, he was unable to summon any real remorse about the idea of seeing bloody revenge meted out on this twisted bastard, despite the Hippocratic Oath he'd taken.

"Yes. The sounds reasonable," Duchess said. "We'll leave the children with you, *Docteur*—hidden close by, but out of sight. You're best qualified to care for their medical needs, if they have any."

Again, the sense of being in over his head accosted him. Would he be able to do anything at all for these kids, if the worst-case scenario came to pass and they were all like the girl from the ceremony? Still, if it came to that, he knew he would have to try.

"Some of the children who've ended up at our clinic have been in bad shape," he said grimly. "Many of them are extremely emaciated or hopped up on drugs, so I'm used to seeing that. But whatever is ultimately to be done for these youngsters, I won't be able to do much of anything out here in the bush. I don't have the supplies or the staff."

"Do you think you could reach anyone at your clinic who might be able to get out here and help us?" Oksana asked.

"We can't really spare anyone," Mason replied. "The kids that are there already need all the help they can get, especially after the quake. And even if I could get other people, it would take time to get a message back, and more time for someone to travel here and join us."

"*Docteur*," Duchess said calmly, "we all realize this isn't ideal, but we still have to do our best get these children to safety, given the circumstances. You understand that, I know."

"Of course I do," he snapped. He took a deep breath, knowing that they were short on options, and the clock was ticking. "Look. I'll go along with this plan, but I want you all to know that I strongly protest the parts of it that put Oksana in danger."

"Duly noted," Xander said, not sounding much happier than Mason felt. "So, the tentative plan is for the mambo to put a spell on Oksana, who will hopefully gain enough power from the loa to challenge and distract the bokor in a fight. Duchess and I will rescue the kids and bring them to Mason, who will keep them hidden and care for them as best he can, given the obvious limitations. Then, Duchess and I will join Oksana, in case she hasn't finished the bastard off yet. Afterward, we can share our power with her to counteract any lingering effects of either the spell or the fight."

"Do you believe this can work?" Oksana asked, turning towards the mambo.

The woman gazed at each one of them again, her deep-set eyes troubled as she silently appraised the determined group.

"I think it will be possible for the four of you to save at least some of the children," she said heavily, "but at what cost, I do not know."

No one had anything to say in reply.

ELEVEN

That afternoon, while Mama Lovelie prepared what she would need to complete the spell, Oksana slept under the shade of the covered porch.

-o-o-o-

You deserve a better life than slavery, Oksana," Augustin whispered against her temple, his arm shifting to cradle her more closely against his chest. Oksana blinked up at the waving branches of the tree above them, patches of blue sky shifting and appearing between the ever-moving leaves.

"No one deserves slavery, Augustin," she said quietly. "Unrest is spreading across the island, even now. There will soon come a day when those who have been trodden down will rise up and demand their freedom."

They were propped against the old tree's thick, knobby trunk, hiding away from the prying eyes of the household. For months now, the two of them had been sneaking away to catch private moments with each other — stolen kisses, soft words, fleeting caresses.

"I know," Augustin said, his voice heavy with foreboding. "And you're right, on both counts. Your mother certainly didn't deserve the treatment she received at your father's hands. In fact, I wake every morning asking myself how you can even bear my touch, after what she endured."

"That was different," Oksana said quickly, pushing away from his chest so she could look at him. *"Don't you* ever *compare yourself to… that man!"*

Oksana's father had been a white French slave owner, and her mother had been his property. So had Oksana, until the Frenchman had sold her to Augustin's father at the age of ten. Augustin had been only a year older than she was, in fact. As children, they'd had little direct contact, though Oksana occasionally caught Augustin watching her with interest as she went about her duties.

Shortly after he turned seventeen, Augustin's father had died of a fever, leaving him in charge of the plantation and all its slaves. Three years later, Augustin had kissed Oksana for the first time, setting her heart alight and altering the shape of her world in the space of a heartbeat.

He was her owner, and she was his property. Just as Oksana's mother had been her father's property. But there, the resemblance ended.

Augustin had never forced Oksana, only wooed her. He had never exerted his power over her to gain what he wanted. He had only ever shown her his love, and she loved him in return.

Now, her beloved gazed up at her with soulful blue-gray eyes and an earnest expression. "How can I fail to compare myself to him?" *he asked.* "Until now, I've been no better than he. But that changes, today."

She stared at him in incomprehension. "What are you saying, Augustin?"

"Today, I am asking you to become my wife."

Oksana blinked several times in rapid succession, certain that she had heard him incorrectly. "Wh-what?"

"I want you to be my wife," he repeated. *"A free woman of color. In fact, I intend to free all my father's slaves and offer them honest, paid employment instead."*

Augustin's lips widened into a hopeful smile as Oksana stared at him, completely dumbfounded. "Please say yes, Oksana."

"Yes!" she blurted. "But... what will the other slave owners say?"

"Why should I care?" he countered. "I have never allowed the words of others to influence how I manage my own affairs."

Oksana opened her mouth and closed it again, unable to think of any reply to that.

Augustin lifted her hand and brushed his lips across her knuckles, setting her skin tingling.

"I care nothing for what they say, Oksana," he continued. "I want you. I want you now and forever. You are irresistible, intoxicating, and blazingly intelligent. I would be proud to stand next to you and support you as we flourish together."

Leaning forward, Oksana grabbed the front of his shirt and brought their lips together in a searing kiss.

-o-o-o-

She woke with a start, breathing heavily as she tried to orient herself. Looking around with wild eyes, she found that she was reclining in the shadows of a sleeping porch overlooking a small, flourishing garden. Birds chirped in the distance, and the same sweet-smelling flowers bloomed that had been blooming in Haiti for hundreds of years.

"I thought I heard noises," a concerned voice said. "Nightmare?"

Oksana rolled into a sitting position and whipped her head around. Mason stood in the doorway. Unbidden, tears rose to her eyes and overflowed at the sight of him. His expression morphed into shock, and he was kneeling at her side in an instant, his fingers tilting her chin so he could look at her more closely. Energy rippled between them at his touch.

"Oksana," he breathed. "*Christ.* Your eyes—"

She swiped at her cheeks, unaccountably embarrassed by the watery, rust-colored streaks that she knew would be there.

"Sorry," she said wetly. "Sorry, it's nothing. I'm not sick or hurt—the blood in my tears is just a vampire thing. I'm fine."

Mason's face lost its panicked edge, but he didn't let her go. "You're not bloody fine. You're crying."

Yeah... bloody crying, she thought, a bit hysterically. *Bloody tears…*

God. He needed to stop touching her like that, before she—

"Please don't cry," he murmured. "Whatever it is, we can—"

She surged forward and kissed him.

For a moment, he froze, and so did she—appalled by what she was doing. Then, he made a low noise into the kiss. Before she knew what was happening, gentle, unassuming Mason—physician to Haiti's hurt and frightened children—had his hands tangled in her hair and was taking possession of her mouth as though he would die without the feeling of her breath mingling with his.

Oksana's undead heart slammed against her ribcage, the ragged rhythm echoing the word *home… home… home…* along every fiber of her body. The spark of energy between them flared almost painfully, before settling, warm and intense, along her nerves. She changed the angle of their mouths, lips slanting against his as the kiss deepened.

And just like that, she was no longer kissing a man she'd met only days ago—she was kissing Augustin. The sense of completion—of utter, incontrovertible *rightness*—flooded her until she thought she would overflow with it.

"Oksana…" he murmured into their shared air. "*God…*"

Their foreheads rested together for the space of a handful of heartbeats, and then he was delving into her mouth again, his tongue tangling with hers. She didn't realize that she'd climbed onto his lap until the brush of her breasts against the hard muscles of his chest sent a wash of heat rushing through her to settle low in her belly.

The sudden clench of need in a part of her that had been cold and dead for so long was beyond shocking. Her body was still trying to get closer, closer, *closer* to his, as if she could somehow climb inside of him and disappear. As if merging their bodies might finally knit the torn parts of her soul back together.

Someone was making a high-pitched, needy noise. At first, she didn't even recognize the whimpering sound as having come from her. One of Augustin's hands had abandoned her hair in favor of sliding down to rest low on the small of her back, pressing her hips to his where she straddled him. His hard heat ground against her liquid warmth through two layers of clothing, and with no further warning she was gone—completely lost in the past.

Instead of straddling Mason on a shabby mattress, she straddled Augustin in a huge four-poster bed, curtained by gauzy white material that turned it into a cozy love nest, hidden away from the outside world.

Augustin cradled her face tenderly, pressing his lips gently to her cheeks, her forehead, her eyelids—teasing her until she caught his mouth with hers for a proper kiss. She pulled away after a few moments, meeting his hazel eyes, her expression sobering.

"Augustin, I want to, but we can't right now. I have to leave before dark, so I can perform the ceremony."

Augustin tucked some of her braids behind her ear and regarded her seriously. "You believe one of your spirits will descend tonight, to tell you the best place and time for the slaves to rise up?"

"I hope they will," Oksana said. "Lately, it feels as though the loa are pulling away. It frightens me. I don't know what I've done to offend them."

He stroked his knuckles over the curve of her cheek, and she closed her eyes, savoring the caress.

"Do you think it's because of me?" he asked after a short pause. "Because you married an outsider?"

She drank in his handsome European features, troubled by his words. "You've done as much for our people as anyone, Augustin. Supporting the slaves behind the scenes. Talking to the slave owners and trying to sway them toward emancipation. Why should the loa punish me for loving you?"

Augustin's lips twitched in a brief smile. "Why do supernatural beings do anything?" he asked. "If you think it would help, I'll come along tonight and offer a sacrifice. There's a bottle of fine rum in the cellar, and I daresay we can spare a cockerel or two in pursuit of a good cause."

Oksana smiled brilliantly and kissed him again. "You're a horrible Catholic, my love," she said. "Has anyone ever told you that?"

He snorted. "So many times I've lost count, starting when I was six and asked the local priest why he was wearing a dress instead of trousers. I have a poor track record with deities and their earthly representatives, I fear. Now, shall I come tonight? Even if my offering doesn't sway the spirits, you know how much I adore watching you dance."

Love swelled in Oksana's heart until she thought it might burst. "Yes. Come along with your rum and your cockerel. Who knows? It certainly can't hurt."

The tiny part of her mind that still maintained some awareness of the present quailed. *No, no, no,* it chanted. *Don't come along... please, no, you mustn't!*

But it was too late. She and Augustin were no longer in the cozy, gauze-curtained bed. Instead, they were outside, and it was dark.

No, no, please, no…

The ceremony was a small one. Large gatherings risked too much attention these days, with tensions running as high as they currently were between the slaves and the foreign plantation owners.

About a dozen people gathered around the trunk of an ancient mapou tree, chanting and offering sacrifices to Papa Legba—the gatekeeper of the spirit world. Oksana felt unaccountably off-balance. The energy tonight felt… wrong. She wasn't alone in the feeling, she could tell—several of the older slaves were busy setting out geometric markings of protection on the ground around the group, while others hung trinkets in the branches to appease the angry spirits.

Oksana raised her voice in rhythmic song, calling for the protective spirits to come down and join them. She was aware of Augustin seated on a blanket nearby, watching the proceedings with the same fascination he always did. At first, his presence had made the others nervous, but his respectful demeanor and the offering of one black cockerel and one white cockerel in addition to the bottle of good rum had quickly appeased them.

Now, if only it would appease the loa.

It frightened Oksana on a deep level to feel the way the spirits seemed to be avoiding her lately. Since her childhood, they had been as much a part of her life as any earthly presence. But now, when she needed them most, they floated just out of reach.

She felt vulnerable. Unprotected. When the oldest of the hounci present in the circle cried out, "The loa do not favor us tonight! We must close the portal to the spirits before evil enters," it came as no surprise. Several other voices rose in agreement, breaking the chant.

In the very next moment, freezing black fog descended from the mapou tree's branches. She heard Augustin shout something, fear in his normally steady voice. Before she could call back, though, the fog surrounded her, filling her mouth and nose like foul, oily water.

Oh, my child, crooned a chilling voice, *you thought opening yourself to these foolish folk spirits would make you strong. Instead, they only opened the way for me.*

Oksana flailed, panic overtaking her. She tried to flee, to escape the suffocating mist. But she couldn't even breathe without drawing the darkness deeper inside herself, and jagged flashes of light started to flash behind her tightly closed eyelids as her lungs burned.

Begone, she thought desperately. *Begone, evil spirit, begone!*

The dark voice laughed, a grating sound that scraped against her skin like sandpaper. *Witless girl,* it taunted. *You think yourself more powerful than me? You have much to learn.*

A terrible weight drove Oksana to the ground, crushing her until she felt ribs snapping like sticks. She opened her mouth to scream, but the greasy black fog rushed in, choking her before she could emit so much as a squeak.

You are mine. I will do to you whatever I please. Take from you whatever I please. And what pleases me tonight is to take your soul.

A horrible tearing feeling in her chest brought tears to her eyes. At first, she thought her broken bones must be slicing into her organs, but it was even worse than that. Fire erupted inside her, burning up every bit of moisture in her body. An agony worse than anything she had ever known overtook her. Her last thought, before thought became impossible, was a plea for the spirits to protect her — to protect Augustin and the others from this terrible evil.

There was no reply.

-o-o-o-

Thirst beyond bearing brought her back to something that might have been called awareness. She was empty, so very empty, and if she didn't fill herself up *right now*, the madness swirling at the edges of her mind would consume her.

"Oksana!" The hoarse shout was audible now through the clearing darkness. The fog disappeared, sinking into the ground she was lying on. "Oksana — dear God, no!"

Hands were grasping her, lifting her, cradling her against something warm that thrummed with the nourishment she craved. She *had to have* that warmth, that life, that sweet liquid rushing under the tender barrier of skin. She had to have it *now*.

Nothing else mattered. Her terrible injuries didn't matter. The cries of fear and alarm echoing around them didn't matter. Only the gaping emptiness mattered. Only the succulent, rushing fount of life hovering over her was real.

"*Loup garou!*" other voices were crying. "Hurry, hurry! Get nets and weapons!"

Hands tried to drag the thrumming source of life away from her, but it only held her more tightly, growling, "Get away from us—get your hands off! *I'm not leaving her!*"

She groaned, the sound scraping along her parched throat like broken glass.

Gentle fingers tilted her face upward, until her lips and teeth were only inches from throbbing veins hidden under thin, breakable skin. A blue-gray gaze looked down at her, wide and frightened.

"Oksana, my dearest love," The voice choked. "Mother of God, your eyes! What has happened to you? What can I do?"

Another voice answered. "You can do nothing for her, *blan*. Evil has stolen her soul! You must get away from her, before she kills you and uses your blood to strengthen herself!"

The hands holding her tightened again, and Oksana's lips pressed against the salty flesh—all that stood between her and what she needed to fill up the emptiness. Her canines lengthened and sharpened, scraping at the inside of her cheeks.

"Wait," the voice above her said, oblivious to the threat she posed. "She looks so pale. You say my blood can... help her, somehow? Can strengthen her? I've seen your people give blood offerings to the loa before—"

"No, fool! You mustn't!" The other voice cried, even as her fangs sank into the delectable banquet before her.

Her victim gasped, shuddering in her grip as her fingers dug into him like talons. "Oksana," he croaked, "It's all right, beloved… if this will save you—" An ugly gurgling noise erupted under the choked words. "All I have is… yours… it always has been…"

The sweet lifeblood flowed over her tongue, bringing relief from the agony of thirst and longing. She shook her head back and forth savagely—a mindless attempt to get *more, more, more* until the spurts slowed to a trickle, and then, to nothing.

She wailed in frustration, giving the bloodless corpse a final shake and letting it drop. More warm bodies approached from behind her. She whirled, ready to pounce, but a heavy rope net enveloped her before she could spring at them. The wail rose to a shriek as she tore at the tangled ropes confining her.

"Is he dead?" frantic voices babbled. "Did she kill him?"

Something about the words penetrated the haze of bloodlust in her mind, and a new kind of emptiness replaced the aching thirst. Her thoughts were still mired in animal rage at the net trapping her, though, and she could not concentrate on the slow-growing feeling of dread hiding beneath the panic.

"Is she cursed? What should we do with her?" the onlookers asked, and the commanding voice replied, "Bring a coffin, and someone go find me an iron spike and a mallet."

Oksana roared, her body twisting and rippling. Feathers erupted from her blood-soaked skin, her limbs trying to contort into new shapes and failing.

"Look. Her human soul is gone," the commanding voice intoned. "She is *loup garou* now. She is cursed, and her spirit has merged with an animal's. Give me one of the poisoned darts."

A moment later, something sharp pierced her neck and lodged there. She tried to scrabble at it with her hands, but they were hopelessly tangled in the ropes. She struggled and spat and screamed and snarled, but the dart remained lodged in place.

Numbness stole across her senses by degrees, radiating outward from the stinging point embedded in her neck. Her feverish thrashing grew slower. Less coordinated. Gradually, her body went limp. Her open eyes stared upward. She was aware of what was happening, but unable to move or make a noise.

She was aware of the net being removed.

She was aware of Augustin's broken body lying nearby like a child's discarded rag doll, when the jostling as she was moved made her head loll in that direction.

She was aware of being lowered into a simple wood coffin, and of the fierce agony as they nailed her left foot to the bottom with the iron spike, to keep her from wandering free of her grave.

She was aware of the lid closing, and the coffin being lowered into a hastily dug hole.

She was aware of the dirt raining down on top of her, burying her and muffling the sounds from above until there was nothing but the noise of her sluggish heartbeat reflected back at her.

She was aware of the air growing stale. A board in the coffin lid cracked under the weight of the earth above. When a trickle of fine dirt started raining down onto her face, she couldn't even move enough to close her eyes or roll her head out of the way. Blind panic swallowed her, sending her into the blessed relief of darkness.

When her consciousness returned, the paralysis had lifted. She flailed, trying to get away from the soil covering her eyes, nose, and mouth. Her arms hit the side of the coffin and her forehead impacted the lid, which lay only inches above her face. At the same moment, her left foot exploded in icy agony as it jerked against the iron spike nailing it in place.

Unaccustomed strength flooded her limbs. She went mad, tearing at wood until she could reach her left leg, then tearing at flesh, sinew, and bone with the single-mindedness of a trapped animal set on escaping its prison at *that very instant*, or else dying in the attempt.

There was a horrible cracking noise, followed by a ripping, tearing sensation, and she was free of the icy burn of the iron that had pierced her. The coffin lay in splinters around her, dirt sliding and shifting in to take its place. She turned her attention to the wet weight of it pressing down on her from above, clawing at it with bloody fingers.

-o-o-o-

Escape was the only thought in Oksana's mind as she scrambled backward, away from arms that tried to hold onto her for only an instant before letting go. Someone was saying something—sharp words of worry. Questions. She couldn't understand any of it. Nearby, the sun burned in a sky hazy with low clouds. She fled its terrifying heat, seeking shelter in the darkest place she could find, aware that she was half-stumbling, thumping into walls and using her hands to pull herself along.

When she could go no further, she put her back against an unyielding surface and curled up into a ball, rocking. Her eyes were unfocused; her mind blank as it tried to reject the horror of what had been done to her. Of what she had done to herself.

Of what she had done to the man she loved.

Time passed; she could not have said how much. A silhouette filled the doorway, its shape familiar. Oksana blinked, and the silhouette resolved into Xander, bleary-eyed and disheveled from interrupted sleep. He paused, looked at her intently for a long moment, and then wandered further into the room, giving her a wide berth. A moment later, he fetched up against a bare stretch of wall next to a low altar lit with candles, and slid down to sit across from her, still regarding her with a steady green gaze.

"Did I wake you?" Oksana asked faintly. She looked around at the space Mama Lovelie used for ceremonies, taking it in, along with her position jammed into one corner. "Sorry—I didn't realize I wasn't shielding. I don't... quite know what just happened." She scrubbed at her eyes. They were wet.

Xander drew his knees up and rested his chin on them, searching her face. "No, Oksana. You didn't wake me," he said, with studied casualness. "Your cute doctor did. Said you, and I quote, 'demonstrated several symptoms typical of a PTSD episode,' and I should come check on you. You want me to go get Duchess for you instead? I'm afraid I'm no one's idea of emotional support."

Oksana shook her head. "No, let her sleep. Again, I'm sorry about that. I don't know why Mason woke you rather than just coming after me himself."

A smirk tugged briefly at one corner of Xander's mouth, making the years fall away from his handsome face. "Ah. Well. About that. I might or might not have given him the shovel talk the other day, you see."

Oksana blinked, her eyes going wide, some of her earlier horror draining away to be replaced by shock. "Xander. You didn't."

Xander shrugged, still watching her. "I might've done. So, talk to me. What happened? Do Duchess and I need to start scouting places to dispose of a body?"

Oksana shivered and looked away. "Don't even joke."

But Xander wouldn't let it go so easily. "Oksana. Did he do something to upset you?"

She scowled at him. "No, he didn't. Don't be ridiculous."

"Then, what?"

Another tremor wracked her, and she hugged her knees. "We were... sitting together on the veranda. It was nice, at first. But then, I started remembering the night I killed him. The night Bael tried to take me." She met Xander's eyes again. "Did you know my foot is still buried here on the island somewhere, in an unmarked grave outside the capital?"

His brows drew together. "I'd always wondered why it didn't just grow back. Jesus, Oksana." He took a slow breath and let it out. "You know, the others almost seem to delight in wallowing in the horrific natures of their pasts. But you and me—we're different. We really... don't. And I'm starting to think... maybe... we're not doing ourselves any favors by pretending that horror never happened to us."

"I can't go back there, Xander," Oksana said. "I can't. If being with him means reliving it like this, I don't know what I'm going to do."

Duchess chose that moment to enter the room, silently crossing to curl up at Oksana's side and pull her into a one-armed embrace. "It will work out somehow, *ma chérie*."

To Oksana's surprise, Xander rose and crossed to crouch in front of her, pressing a chaste kiss to the top of her head. He stroked a callused, long-fingered hand over her hair before settling back to sit on his heels.

"It will, you know," he agreed. "If His Royal Broodiness and the Emotionally Constipated Bookworm can make it work for them, I have no doubt you can do it as well. You're probably the most deserving of any of us. Right now, though, I'm honestly more worried about this vodou spell. Are you absolutely sure you won't let me confront the bokor instead?"

"Or better yet, let me do it," Duchess said. "As I said earlier, I'm the oldest, and the most powerful. Xander's a mere babe in arms by comparison— barely past his hundredth birthday."

Oksana shook her head. "No, it won't work right. The loa are African folk spirits. You two don't have the same connection with them that I do. Let's save Xander's youth and your power for putting me back together afterward, in case it all goes wrong, shall we?" She looked down at her prosthesis, and her voice turned wry. "Well, the parts of me you can find, at any rate."

Duchess pulled her in close and pressed a sisterly kiss to the top of her head in the same place Xander's lips had brushed earlier. "Always, *petite soeur*. You know we'll never let you fall apart."

TWELVE

Mason paced up and down the short hallway in front of the door where Oksana had disappeared after fleeing his embrace. His hair was mussed from running his hands through it, and his emotions felt just as messy right now.

She'd kissed him. And what a kiss it had been, until—

The door opened, and Oksana emerged, still looking pale. Her friends flanked her on either side, and she looked up at each of them in turn, as if for support. Duchess squeezed an arm around her shoulders before letting it slide away, while Xander placed a hand on her back in a brief, supportive gesture. Then, they peeled away and left her alone with Mason. Xander's disconcerting green gaze pinned his for a long moment as he walked past, heading toward the sitting room.

When the others were gone, Mason looked at Oksana, trying to quiet the muddle of worry, attraction, and existential dread currently clamoring for supremacy.

"You've been assaulted in the past, haven't you," he said, not even making it a question. "I've seen that kind of reaction before. It was a PTSD flashback. I won't ask you to tell me details unless you want to, but please tell me how I triggered you, and how I can avoid it in the future."

If anything, she paled further. "You already know how I was assaulted," she said, and her voice was steady even if her hands were shaking. "A demon violated me and tore my soul into pieces. He left no part of me untouched." She bit her lip, worrying at it for a long moment. "But... when I told you about that before, I didn't tell you about the worst part."

He frowned. "You don't have to—"

She interrupted him. "In the mindless bloodlust that followed, I ripped out my husband's throat with my teeth and drank his blood until he died."

Mason's stomach lurched, as he tried to reconcile what he knew of the woman before him with the words she'd just spoken. If she hadn't stated it so calmly, so matter-of-factly, he might have been able to convince himself that it was part of some delusion or bizarre coping mechanism her mind had come up with to deal with past trauma. But...

"Several people witnessed it," she continued in the same flat voice, "and men from the village brought a heavy net to trap me. There was a hounci present. He knew the secret of preparing poisons laced with magic. I was still weak, and the villagers managed to subdue me with the poison long enough to seal me in a coffin. They nailed my left foot to the bottom to keep me there. Then, they buried me alive. As soon as the poison wore off, I broke my own leg and ripped it free of my body to get loose. Once that was done, I clawed my way up from the grave. They'd left a teenage boy behind to keep watch over me for the first few nights. I killed him, too. I didn't regain anything approaching sanity until days later, when I found myself crawling aimlessly around a cane field in the dark, dragging the bloody stump of my left leg behind me."

Mason felt blindly for the wall behind him and half-slid, half-fell into a seated position against it. "And... this is what you flashed back to, when we kissed?" he asked, his voice a hoarse whisper.

She nodded slowly, still looking a bit distant. A bit untethered. "It's because of Augustin. My husband. You're hi—" She paused, as if reconsidering her words in mid-sentence. "You... remind me of him."

He looked up at her dark, angelically beautiful features, lost for words.

"We should go after the others," she continued, as if they'd been discussing lunch plans rather than murder, vivisepulture, and violent self-dismemberment. "Mama Lovelie will be wanting to perform the spell on me soon."

She reached a hand down to him and he took it without thought. The contact tingled, and the strength that lifted him to his feet was—

Inhuman. Her strength was inhuman. Her balance as she hefted his larger frame upright didn't waver a millimeter, despite the prosthesis on her left leg. A few more chunks in the foundation of his rational belief system crumbled, leaving him off-balance, even if *she* wasn't.

"I want to talk more about this," he said, hearing his voice as though it were echoing through a tunnel.

She nodded, the movement small and hesitant. "After we rescue the children, though," she said. "We need to stay focused on them right now."

"All right," he replied after a beat, not sure if waiting would make the conversation easier or harder.

They followed the path the others had taken, back to the room with the mismatched chairs. Inside, in addition to Duchess and Xander, Mama Lovelie awaited them with three young women in their late teens or early twenties. The newcomers appeared nervous but determined.

Mason looked at the mambo in confusion, wondering if these three were supposed to be part of this spell ceremony… thing, and if so, in what capacity. Xander pinned Oksana with a stern look, and Mason caught her brief grimace in response.

"Our hostess ordered in for us," Xander said mildly. "No need to go out for takeaway tonight. We might've had a rocky beginning, but I'm starting to warm to her."

It took a moment for Mason to manage a vampire-to-English translation, and when he did, he blanched. Xander couldn't mean—

"Hello," Oksana said quietly in Creole. "Do you understand why Mama Lovelie brought you here?"

One of the girls seemed a bit braver than the other two, and she stepped forward, her chin jutting out.

"Yes," she said in the same tongue. "You're nightwalkers, and you're going after the missing children." She gestured to the young woman next to her. "Our brother was taken." She jerked her chin toward the third girl. "So was her little sister. The mambo says you need blood to bolster your strength before you go off to fight the bokor. You can have ours."

"I'm fairly sure this marks the first time I've ever had someone volunteer," Xander mused. "It's a bit odd, honestly."

"The first time?" Duchess muttered. "Really? I'll introduce you to some Goth clubs I frequent in Los Angeles one of these days."

Mason felt Oksana sigh more than he heard it.

"You're certain?" she asked the girls, and all three of them nodded. "Very well, then. Do you want to forget afterward that it happened?"

"No," said the young woman who had spoken up earlier. "This makes me feel like I'm doing something to help."

Her sister nodded agreement, but the other girl raised her hand in a tentative motion, like a student in a classroom. "I'd... rather not remember. I don't like blood."

"Of course," Oksana said, her demeanor softening. "Come here, *pitit mwen*. Thank you for your gift—you are very brave. I promise you won't feel a thing, or remember it happening."

The girl swallowed and shot a look at Mama Lovelie, who smiled and nodded encouragement. "Go on, child. I'll make sure nothing bad befalls you."

She squared her shoulders and came forward, taking Oksana's hand when she raised it invitingly. Oksana glanced in Mason's direction for a bare instant before her eyes slid away, as though she were embarrassed at the idea of him watching.

For Mason's part, his thoughts were still whirling so badly that he didn't know how to react. Again, the part of him that was a doctor cried a silent warning about the dangers of bite wounds, infection, and blood-borne illness. His inner scientist anticipated the next few minutes with detached fascination. And the man in him ached for the woman he was so quickly growing to care about.

Unsure what to say, and feeling every inch the outsider that he was, he kept quiet.

Duchess flickered an eyebrow at him that seemed almost challenging. "No words to offer, *Docteur*?" she asked blandly.

Mason met her gaze and then Xander's, but his eyes were on Oksana as he spoke. "I trust you wouldn't be doing this if there was any danger to you, or to these young people. Given that, I'm not really in a position to speak on the subject, beyond wondering why none of you approached me if you needed blood."

"It seemed rude to ask, under the circumstances," Xander said, "and, besides, I don't particularly relish the idea of going into a dangerous situation with a human suffering from a temporary iron deficiency."

Oksana's eyes flickered to Mason's and away again, then she seemed to steel herself, her attention solely for the girl in front of her. "Don't mind them, *ti chou*. Look at me for a moment. That's it…"

He watched as the girl met Oksana's glowing violet gaze, her plain features going through a complicated series of expressions before growing slack. Her eyes drifted closed, and a hint of a smile played at her full lips.

"There, now," Oksana said, brushing her knuckles over the girl's cheek. "Nothing to worry about."

The young woman made a noise of sleepy contentment and did not resist when Oksana lifted her left arm, cradling her wrist. Oksana paused, tension visible in her shoulders, her eyes darting to Mason's yet again. Sensing that he was the one causing her distress, Mason took a deep breath and tore his eyes away.

Across the room, Xander, too, held his—*victim's? Donor's?*—arm, lifting her wrist to his mouth. Duchess was not so coy, and had slipped behind the oldest, most outspoken of the girls and tipped her head to one side, baring her neck. The vampire's eyes glowed vibrant blue as her fangs sank into the young woman's dark flesh.

Mason stared, unable to help it—both captivated and repelled. There was something undeniably sensual about the act. Even drinking from a person's wrist, as Xander was, it looked as much like a seduction as an attack. He fought not to let his eyes return to Oksana, to watch her lips caressing the third girl's skin, but his reaction to what he was seeing was wrong on so many fucking levels—

The process was quick. Much quicker than he would have expected. Before he'd decided on the right words to mentally chastise himself for his decidedly unscientific reaction, it was over. Duchess wiped a tiny trickle of blood from her donor's neck and popped the finger in her mouth, sucking it clean.

Xander flipped the other girl's arm over and dropped a courtly kiss to her knuckles. "All right, poppet?" he asked politely.

The girl blinked, seeming to come back to herself. "Y-yes, nightwalker. I barely felt a thing."

Mason finally lost the battle not to look at Oksana. She was steadying the youngest girl, who looked a bit confused.

"What happened?" she asked, no alarm in her voice, only curiosity. "Mama Lovelie, I—"

The mambo waved her off. "Don't worry, child. You came with the others to offer a blood sacrifice, which was very courageous of you. It wasn't needed after all, though. The nightwalkers will leave soon to look for your sister and the others, and we will tell you when there is news."

"Oh." The girl blinked large brown eyes up at Oksana. "Thank you, nightwalker." She stiffened her spine, lifting her chin. "If you need my blood when you return, you only have to ask."

Oksana smiled, though her eyes were sad. "Thank you, Beatrice. Your offer honors us."

Mason was quite sure that the girl had not told Oksana her name.

With difficulty, he dragged his mind back to practicalities. "You're feeling all right?" he asked, directing the question mostly to the other two villagers, though he watched Beatrice from the corner of his eye. "Not dizzy or weak?"

"A little tired," said the older one. "It's fine though."

"Do have a bit of faith, Ozzie," Xander said, mild irritation crossing his features. "We're not going to impose unduly on people who made such a generous offer. What exactly do you take us for?"

Mason ignored him in favor of addressing the young women again. "Eat something, and drink plenty of fluids tonight. Fruit juice if you have it, or *akasan*. Something sweet."

"Something sweet? That sounds brilliant, actually," Oksana muttered, so low Mason barely caught it.

"Please, just get our siblings back," the oldest girl said solemnly. "No matter what it takes."

-o-o-o-

After the young women left, snacking on the honey cakes Mama Lovelie had given them when they went, Xander turned to Duchess and Oksana.

"That was rather strange," he said, crossing his arms and leaning back against a convenient section of wall. "I wasn't joking when I said no one had ever offered me their blood freely before. Well... no *human*, I mean." He scowled. "At least, not since..." The words trailed off, his eyes growing distant for a moment before he shook it off. "Anyway. It felt different. Unless it's just me?"

"Not just you," Oksana said, her eyes fixed on the floor.

Duchess shrugged. "As I said earlier, there are rare places and situations where humans will offer their blood, though not with a true understanding of what they are doing. I suppose it adds a certain piquancy to the meal."

Mason looked from one of them to the other. "Why would that matter? Blood is blood. Nothing about its composition changes based on the donor's mood. Unless there's something about the stress hormones—?"

Xander waved an irritated hand. "Ozzie. *Ozzie*. We're vampires. We don't live on the chemical composition and nutrients in blood. We live on the life force of the people we drink it from."

Mason tried to let the bizarre assertion roll off his back like all the rest, but he'd apparently reached capacity when it came to crazy proofing himself.

"*Life force?*" he echoed. "All right... seriously. What does that even mean? I'm a doctor. I've seen more people die than I care to remember. Life is nothing more than a collection of chemical and electrical processes. When those processes break down—*poof*. No more life. It's not some magical force that you can take from another person like drinking through a bloody straw!"

Mama Lovelie snorted. "Oh, *blan*. How little you understand, for all your fancy book learning. As certain as you sound, you'd better hope you're wrong... since that's exactly what your pretty *kòkòt* will try to do to our enemy tonight."

He shut his mouth, taken aback.

"Is it time, then?" Oksana asked. "Are you ready to cast the spell?"

"Yes," the mambo answered. "Come, let us go to the altar room."

She herded them back to the room where Oksana had fled earlier, after their kiss. Once there, Mama Lovelie turned to her. "Tell me, child. How do you travel?"

"As mist, or as an owl," Oksana said without hesitation.

The mambo nodded. "Hmm. In that case... hair, feather, blood, I should think."

"More blood?" Xander asked dryly. "No wonder you topped us off first."

Oksana ignored him, twining her fingers through a few strands of hair and tugging sharply, then handing the little tuft to Mama Lovelie. She submitted to another bloodletting without complaint, and Mason watched as the cut healed in seconds.

What happened next, though...

Reality twisted, and where Oksana had stood a moment before, there was now a dark owl with white flecks decorating its wing feathers. It perched on one leg, the other curled protectively against its body, terminating in a stump.

"What—?" Mason asked in a faint voice.

"Need to sit down for a minute, mate?" Xander asked. "Owl got your tongue, perhaps?"

Duchess held out an arm, and the bird flapped up to perch on it, fluttering its wings daintily for balance before refolding them. Even Mama Lovelie took a moment to admire the striking transformation.

"The goddess is present in you three, no doubt about it," she said softly, before becoming businesslike once more. She plucked a small flight feather from the owl's wing and made a tisking noise when the creature pecked at her in retaliation. "Cheeky…"

The owl spread its wings, and Duchess gave it a little boost as it flapped away. Oksana dropped lightly to the ground an instant later.

Mason's jaw was open. He snapped it shut. "But… that… that's…"

"Hmm… I do believe the realization train has finally arrived at the station," Xander observed. "About time."

"*That's impossible*," Mason finally got out. "And you just did it anyway, right in front of my eyes."

Oksana shrugged, not looking at him directly.

"Everybody out. You're distracting me," Mama Lovelie commanded in a no-nonsense tone. "Leave me be for a few minutes. I'll call for you when I'm done."

They filed out. Mason turned on Oksana. "You're an owl," he said stupidly.

She met his eyes and scowled at him, which was such an improvement over her earlier looks of discomfort and embarrassment that he nearly smiled.

"Well, not all the time, obviously," he amended. "But… how do you make your clothing disappear and reappear? And your prosthesis?"

"Centuries of practice," Oksana growled.

A snort, quickly stifled, came from Xander's position behind him.

"Just wait until she disappears into mist on you at an unexpected moment," Duchess said.

"Okay... look," Mason said, scrubbing a hand over his face. "Either I have, in fact, gone completely troppo, or else I'm here at a vodou priestess's house with a bunch of vampires who can transform into birds, and absorb humans' life force by drinking their blood. Since we're apparently about to go hunting a sorcerer who's turning children into undead zombies, I'm willing to work on the second assumption until the men with white coats and butterfly nets show up for me. Deal?"

"Deal," Oksana said softly.

"Fine by me," Duchess put in. "As it happens, some of my closest friends are clinically insane."

"You do realize that the men with white coats stopped carrying butterfly nets in the nineteen-fifties?" Xander added helpfully.

"Case in point," Duchess murmured.

They were silent for a bit, Mason mulling over what he'd seen, and the others apparently content to let him stew. After what felt like half an hour or so, Mama Lovelie called them back in. She held out a blackened dagger balanced across her open hand. A small cloth pouch was fastened to the base of the hilt with twine.

Duchess looked at the blade curiously. "Isn't that..."

The mambo nodded. "The knife the child tried to use on me, yes."

Mason looked at the soot-covered weapon more closely. "But the fire will have destroyed the poison on the blade," he said. "That's why you had it thrown into the flames, wasn't it?"

She shrugged. "That wasn't me; it was the Maîtresse Dahomey, possessing me. But the poison is of no use to us, *blan*, though the bokor may well try to employ magic-laced poison against Oksana during the battle," she said. "No, it was the knife itself that I needed. It carries the imprint of both the bokor and one of his gros-bon-ange creations. Now it carries Oksana's imprint as well."

Oksana took the weapon, testing its weight and balance. "This will kill him?"

"It will drain him. If your strength is greater than his strength, it will destroy him," Mama Lovelie explained. "You need only break his skin—even a tiny cut will release the magic."

"And if his strength is greater than Oksana's?" Mason asked.

"Then it will destroy her."

"This is utter and complete madness," Mason stated baldly.

"This is warfare," the mambo retorted. "And warfare always brings madness in its wake."

-o-o-o-

Minutes later, the sound of a sputtering engine outside broke the early evening peace. The vampires had been discussing last minute plans and contingencies, but they looked up at the approaching racket.

"Ah, good," Mama Lovelie said. "He came."

"Who came?" Mason asked, angling a glance out the window, where an ancient Ford truck with a generous flatbed was coming to a halt in front of the house, its brakes squealing in protest.

"Beatrice's grandfather used to be the village healer before his oldest daughter—Beatrice's aunt—took over. Their family is one of only three in the village to still have a working vehicle with fuel in it. I asked the girl to tell her grandfather what was happening and request his assistance. I fear that you may have need of additional help."

Mason took that in for a moment. "He was a healer, you say? A medical man? What kind of training does he have—do you know?"

Mama Lovelie shrugged. "The same as any village healer, though I believe he also went to the city to learn from some American missionary doctors for a few weeks when he was younger."

Mason met the others' eyes. "Better than nothing," he said. "If he's willing to risk the danger, this bloke really could be helpful to us."

A stoop-shouldered man with wiry gray curls exited the truck and walked up to knock on the door.

"Come in, Anel!" the mambo called.

The door creaked on its hinges, admitting the newcomer.

"Evening, Esther," he greeted, his voice hoarse with age and cigarettes. "Heard you've got some folks heading out to do something brave and stupid."

"It's almost like he's known us for years," Xander quipped, reaching out to shake his hand. He cast an admiring glance out the window, taking in the ancient vehicle outside. "Love the truck, by the way. Nineteen-fifty-eight F-500?"

Anel gave Xander the same sort of once-over Xander had given the truck. "Fifty-nine, in fact. When they introduced the four-wheel-drive option."

"Ah, brilliant!" Xander enthused. "Though it does sound like your engine timing is a bit off. I could take a peek under the hood for you when we get back."

The old man shrugged, a hint of wry amusement lurking behind his dark eyes. "If you like, friend. Though there's only so much to be done for an aging inline six-cylinder engine with no access to either parts or machine tools."

"Even so," Xander said, "I could still have a look."

Both Duchess and Oksana were staring rather pointedly at their fellow vampire, Mason noticed. A moment later, Xander cleared his throat and backed off a bit.

Mason came forward to take his place and offered his hand. "Dr. Mason Walker. Pleased to meet you. Mama Lovelie said you were a medical man as well, and might be willing to help us?"

"Well met, Mason," the man said, shaking his hand with a firm grip that belied his obvious age. "Call me Anel—everybody else does. If you're going after these poor children, I'll help you as much as I'm able. Though I'm sure you know there's not much to be done for the ones like that girl they buried today."

"Even the use of your truck would be immensely helpful," Oksana said. "We can't ask you to risk yourself by coming—"

Anel made a scoffing noise. "Nonsense. First off, I'm one of very few people who can sweet-talk that old junk heap into running for more than ten minutes at a stretch. And second, one of the few benefits of being elderly and decrepit is that you can take foolish chances, knowing you don't have all that much left to lose."

"Well then," Xander said cheerfully, "welcome aboard. The evening express to Crazytown is about to embark."

"I don't suppose you have any medical supplies with you?" Mason asked. "I know they're scarce these days, but we're not sure what we're likely to find if we do get these kids out."

"I brought along whatever I could scrounge," Anel told him. "Nothing fancy, but I've at least got some clean bandages and herbs for a sedating tea."

Duchess cocked her head. "And did your *petite-fille* Beatrice tell you about the three of us?"

Anel raised a bushy eyebrow. "She did, nightwalker. But I mostly leave that sort of thing to Esther, here." He indicated Mama Lovelie with a small wave of his hand. "So, are we ready to go?"

With a deep breath, Mason looked around the group. "As we'll ever be, I imagine. Assuming we know *where* we're going, of course. Do we?"

The mambo answered. "The most recent gossip says that the bokor is holed up in the village of Savaneaux, about ten miles from here."

Anel nodded. "Hmm. Makes sense. The war's already been through there. Not too much left of the place, I imagine. The people who weren't killed will have fled to other villages, most likely."

"In that case, let's get underway," Xander said. "Moonlight's burning."

Anel shrugged. "Fine by me. I can fit two of you in the cab, but the other two will have to ride in the back."

"That's not necessary," Oksana said. "Mason can ride with you, but we'll fly."

"Yes, better to get a view from above," Duchess agreed. "We'll have more of an idea of what we're up against."

"Whatever you say," Anel told them. "Like I said, I try to leave those sorts of things to other people."

-o-o-o-

An hour or so later, the truck was creaking and jouncing along a disused road leading into the abandoned village of Savaneaux. Mason had climbed into the cab of the old vehicle, and when he'd turned back, Oksana and the others had disappeared.

Occasionally, the flash of a feathered wing would appear in the illumination of the ancient headlamps, only to disappear an instant later. Anel kept up a steady stream of conversation, asking Mason about what he was doing back in Port-au-Prince with the child soldiers, and telling stories about the odd and amusing things he'd seen over the years as a village healer.

Distances could be deceiving in Haiti with the rough, pothole-riddled roads, but Mason thought they must be getting close. His suspicions were confirmed a few minutes later when a familiar dark-haired figure appeared in the middle of the road in front of them and lifted a hand, palm out.

"*Merde*!" Anel cursed, hitting the brakes and causing the truck to judder to a stop. "Give an old man a heart attack before we even get to the village, why don't you!"

Flapping wings descended on either side of Oksana, and an instant later, Xander and Duchess were flanking her. She came around to Anel's side of the cab.

"There's no cover to speak of ahead," she said. "We should leave the truck here and go the rest of the way on foot. The engine noise and headlights will draw too much attention. Savaneaux is a little less than a kilometer away, just over the next hill. Anel, you should probably stay here with the truck."

Anel snorted. "Don't be ridiculous. I may be old, but I can still walk. And if you need my help with the children, you'll need it in Savaneaux, not here."

"It will be dangerous, Anel," Mason warned.

"Really?" Anel said dryly. "A rogue bokor tearing children's souls apart and you think it might be dangerous? Not only can I still walk, Mason, but I'm also *not an idiot*."

As much as he hated the idea of putting the old man in harm's way any more than they already had, Mason knew that they needed his help.

"Then I guess we'd better get going," he said. "We'll take the most vital of the medical supplies with us and leave the rest in the truck. Hopefully the fact that the fighting has already been here and moved on means the supplies—and the truck, for that matter—will still be here when we get back."

"Give me the dagger," Oksana said. "I'll approach with you on foot, while Duchess and Xander fly in and start searching for the children."

Mason rummaged in his pack and came up with the blackened knife, wrapped securely in sackcloth. Something about it sent a shiver up his spine as he handed it over to Oksana. She took it, being careful not to let their fingers brush as she did.

Another faint shock passed through Mason as Xander and Duchess took to the skies—not as owls, this time, but as pale swirls of mist. He'd been warned, of course, but even so…

"Come on," Oksana said, watching them as they disappeared into the night air above. "Let's go."

The approach to the village was indeed exposed. Deforestation was rampant on the island, most of the trees around populated areas having long ago been harvested for building materials and cooking fires. The overworked soil meant that only low tufts of grass and weeds hugged the ground around Savaneaux, offering no cover.

As they grew close, it became apparent that the village was, in fact, deserted. No lamps or hearths lit the falling-down buildings, and the quiet was absolute. So absolute that Mason had sudden doubts as to whether their objective was even here. They were operating on rumor and hearsay, so there were surely no guarantees.

"What happens if we don't find him? Or the children?" Mason whispered.

"He's here," Oksana replied in the same low voice. "I can feel him, and the others have just located the place where he's keeping the children. At least some of them are still whole."

"How can you know that?" Mason asked.

"Duchess told me," she said. "We can communicate mentally across moderate distances, as long as we aren't shielding our thoughts."

Telepathy. That's right, the vampires had fucking *telepathy*. Xander had alluded to something of the sort, but Mason had mostly discounted it. A hundred new questions jostled to join the thousand he already had, but this was not the time. He'd seen enough by this point that his first reaction wasn't to assume she was delusional, though a few days ago it probably would have been.

"All right," he said, quashing any other words that might have tried to slip free.

"Look," Anel said, pointing at a relatively large structure illuminated by the weak moonlight. "The peristil is still mostly intact."

He was right—one corner of the roof had collapsed, but the rest of the open-air building appeared undamaged.

"That seems like a good place for the others to bring the children once they're free," he said. "Can you convey that to them?"

"Agreed, and yes, I'll tell them," said Oksana. "There's no one nearby. Let's go in."

The shadows under the peristil roof were so deep as to be almost impenetrable, even though the structure only had two walls. Anel flicked the wheel of an old metal cigarette lighter, and the tiny flame lit the area around them sufficiently to show that everything of value had been cleared out during the looting.

"This will do," Oksana confirmed, and set to pulling items from Mason's knapsack.

He'd assumed the bottle of spirits inside had been intended for disinfecting wounds or instruments, and the flour, for preparing food if they were forced to stay in the bush with the children for any extended length of time. So he was surprised when she opened both and began sprinkling them onto the dirt floor.

"What are you doing?" he asked.

Anel answered. "She's laying out protective markings, to keep the bokor's power from gaining entrance to this place."

"And here I thought you didn't deal with the spirit world," Oksana chided. "Though I should warn you, if the loa don't favor me, they may not come, and the protection won't work." She straightened, frowning at the bottle and the bag of flour. "In fact, maybe you should be doing this."

Anel waved the words away. "I wouldn't have the first idea about it, nightwalker. Besides, I've never been able to draw anything more artistic than stick figures. *Bad* stick figures, at that. We'll be safer leaving it to you."

Oksana looked unhappy, but she resumed laying out the complex geometric patterns around the edge of the usable space in the damaged building. Anel's lighter flickered out a few moments later, but Mason could still hear her moving around. By the time she was done, his eyes had adjusted enough to make out the other two as darker shadows against the gray.

When Oksana approached him, he lifted a hand, aiming for her shoulder, but finding the graceful sweep of her neck instead. She shivered at the touch, but it didn't feel like a negative reaction, so he let his fingers slide down to grasp her upper arm.

"I'm going now," she said. "Stay quiet and stay inside the markings I laid down. With luck, this won't take long and the others will get the children to you shortly. They're waiting to make their move until I can distract the bokor."

"Can you tell where he is? Will the others know where to find you afterward?" Mason asked, his misgivings growing as she prepared to leave.

"There's a lone person moving around near the square at the center of the village," Oksana told him. "That's where I'm headed."

She started to pull away, but he tightened his grip on her arm.

"Be careful," he said.

"I'm a vampire. We're hard to kill," she replied. "Don't worry about me; worry about the kids."

He took a deep breath. "We need to talk, afterward—once the children are settled. Promise me, Oksana."

That odd sense of foreboding—of dread, almost—was still swelling in the pit of his stomach.

"I—" she began, only to cut herself off. She seemed to waver for a moment, and then a small hand was cupping his cheek, guiding him down to her level. Soft, full lips pressed against his, and his fingers squeezed her arm convulsively.

"I promise," she whispered, after pulling back with every indication of reluctance. An instant later, she slipped away, leaving him with his hand still poised in midair, grasping nothing.

He stood there for several moments, fighting the sick feeling churning in his gut.

"Well, well, Dr. Mason Walker," Anel said. "That's a hard path you've chosen."

His hand fell. "What do you mean?"

The old healer made a scoffing noise. "Loving a nightwalker? Such creatures aren't of our world."

"It's not really something I chose," Mason said. "It just sort of… happened."

He crossed his arms, tucking his hands under his armpits as a sudden chill swept over him despite the balmy island night. What was causing this awful sense of impending disaster? Everything was going smoothly so far. Going exactly to plan, in fact. He started to pace, feeling as if he had to move or he'd crawl right out of his skin.

"You want to follow her, don't you?" Anel said. "You sense that something is wrong."

Mason swallowed the growl of frustration that tried to rise from his chest, and continued pacing. "I can't follow her. I need to stay here and help the children when they arrive."

Silence stretched, broken only by the sound of feral dogs yipping in the distance.

"You should go," Anel said eventually, his voice quiet in the darkness. "I'll stay. I may not have fancy letters behind my name, but I can bandage cuts and calm frightened children—I've been doing those things longer than you've been alive, son. Your heart knows something your mind doesn't about what is going to happen. Best listen to it."

Mason's instincts pounced on the offer, demanding that he accept it and go now before it was too late. He clenched his jaw.

"Are you sure?"

"I'm not in the habit of saying things I'm not sure of, Mason. The village square is in that direction." Anel took Mason's shoulders and pointed him the right way. "Go. *Hurry*."

Mason took a deep breath and went.

THIRTEEN

Torches burst into flame around the village square, illuminating it as Oksana approached with the dagger held ready in her hand. It was clear that the bokor was making no effort to conceal his presence, for all that he was still hidden from her view.

A laugh echoed around the open space, harsh and chilling.

"Well now, little nightcrawler," a deep voice boomed, "look at you! Neither *loup garou* nor *gros-bon-ange*… whatever am I to make of you?"

She did not respond, knowing the sound of her own voice would make it more difficult to pinpoint the small noises that might alert her to the man's location — the rustle of fabric, the beating of a heart. Oksana looked around carefully. Several of the rough buildings around the edge of the common area were badly damaged, as if by mortars. But a couple on the northwest corner had escaped the fighting relatively unscathed.

She lifted her chin, scanning the shadows with sharp eyes. The darkness under the cover of a front porch was broken by a white slash of teeth bared in a cruel grin.

"Come out. Face me," she called.

The bokor stepped from the shadow of the building, still grinning. His expression reminded her of a shark's.

He was powerfully built, and darkly handsome. The loa had not been miserly in their gifts when they aided him, but the nature of the deal he had struck was visible within his cold, flat eyes. It was apparent from that blank abyss the loa had not been stingy when extracting their payment, either.

I have him, she sent to Xander and Duchess. *Get the children. Hurry.*

"Why would you do this?" she asked the bokor, hoping to draw him out while the others worked. "Why *children*?"

Her enemy titled his head, as if considering her. "The path of least resistance is always the best path," he said. "The spirits require payment in souls—more and more, every year. Children are easy prey. Simple to acquire and to control."

Oksana's stomach churned with disgust, but she forced herself to stay calm and in control. "And when you can no longer make the payments your masters require? What then?"

He laughed, short and harsh. "I will ensure that day never comes. The world's appetite for corrupted innocence is endless. As long as human sheep continue to breed, there will always be children. And there are powerful men in the world who will always pay well for compliant slaves."

Bile rose, hot and sharp. "*Bastian Kovac*," she spit.

The bokor's brows drew together as if she had surprised him, but she was distracted at the same moment by twin flashes of horror flaring through the telepathic link.

Christ! Xander's mental voice was equal parts revulsion and dismay. *Oksana — some of these kids are okay, but a bunch of them have been turned. He's armed them, and — damn it! Look out, Duchess!* There was a moment of confusion across the bond. *— And they're fighting back.*

Oksana nearly clutched at her chest as she felt the sharp stab of Duchess's distress over whatever they were seeing.

Ma petite, her friend said, *this won't be as quick or simple as we'd hoped. Please be careful!*

"Problem?" the bokor asked solicitously, that slow shark's smile spreading across his features again.

Fangs lengthened into lethal points behind Oksana's lips, and she felt her eyes burning with a predatory light. "Oh, yes. You and I have a definite problem. Don't worry, though. If I have anything to say about it, it will only be a temporary one," she said, and sprang at him.

He met her in a clash of bodies, his movements faster than a human's. Shockingly fast, in fact. She dodged and ducked, gauging his strength — also inhuman. She only needed to get in the quickest slash, the tiniest cut, but he was larger, and had a longer reach than she did. Every move she made, he blocked.

She swirled into mist, trying to get behind him, but in the instant it took her to rematerialize, he was always ready and waiting to meet her next feint. The fight became a brutal dance, whirling ever faster as they angled for advantage.

The mental link, which had been quiet as the three vampires focused on their individual fights, flared with agony, the unexpected pain bursting through her shields.

Son of a bitch! Xander cursed, before he tamped down on the unintentional broadcast.

Oksana spun away, staggering back a few steps to gain distance as she recovered from the distraction. In the space of a heartbeat, the bokor pulled a small wooden tube from his belt and raised it to his lips.

A sharp sting embedded itself in the base of Oksana's neck, cold numbness spreading outward from the tip of the poisoned dart. Her eyes went wide, panic clawing at her mind as the past rose up. She stumbled sideways, her muscles growing weak and unresponsive. The view of the village square faded, replaced by the echo of darkness and the memory of wet earth trickling down onto her face through the gap in a coffin lid.

Oksana screamed.

-o-o-o-

Mason made his way cautiously through the silent village, knowing that he'd help no one by running headfirst into the bokor, or anyone he might have here assisting him. The village was small enough that once he was clear of the peristil, he'd been able to see a faint, flickering glow emanating from the direction in which Anel had indicated the central square lay.

He kept to the shadows of the burned and damaged buildings, wincing whenever his feet accidentally kicked against bits of debris. The sounds he made seemed far louder than they probably were, but he couldn't help pausing each time — waiting to see if he'd been detected by anyone, human or inhuman.

With his own hearing strained to the utmost, he could make out indistinct voices coming from the lit space ahead, though not what they were saying. He tried to move faster, but still without drawing attention to himself.

Then, the scream came.

Every nerve in his body jolted into shrieking life, straining toward the sound of *Oksana in danger*. He sprinted forward, all thoughts of stealth forgotten between one heartbeat and the next. Teeth gritted, arms and legs pumping, he rounded the last building blocking his view.

In the center of the open space, Oksana was down, bracing herself on one hand and one knee, the fingers of her other hand scrabbling feebly at something in the side of her neck. The spelled dagger lay forgotten on the ground at her feet. Her eyes were open, wide and unseeing.

A tall, muscular man circled her, grinning down at her with gleaming teeth, his dark face set in lines of cruel glee. Mason didn't stop, didn't think. He just charged — his years as a rugby fullback propelling him toward his target. Dark eyes looked up, flashing with inhuman power, but the bokor had registered his approach an instant too late. Energy crackled around the man's body, but

Mason hunched, slamming into him low, under his opponent's center of balance.

It felt like hitting a goddamned brick wall, but at least it was a brick wall that toppled under the onslaught. Mason's lungs seized, the breath knocked out of him, but he knew he couldn't afford time to recover. He rolled free and lunged toward Oksana, whose eyes had snapped back to the present, blazing violet in the torchlight.

Mason dove for the dagger, his hand closing on the scorched hilt at the same moment Oksana shouted, "*No!*" The word was hoarse and choked with agony, and she scrabbled forward clumsily toward him, her movements slow and uncoordinated.

He'd meant to grab the knife and immediately lunge toward the bokor, who was already rolling smoothly to his feet a couple of meters away. All it needed was a cut, supposedly—he just had to break the man's skin anywhere he could.

But as the knife settled in his hand, a strange, terrifying sensation flooded his body. The blade was pulling at something inside him, drawing the energy from his muscles and the will from his mind. He staggered upright by virtue of sheer stubbornness, but made it only a couple of steps before he crashed back to his knees, the impact jarring his teeth.

"Mason!" Oksana cried, "Let it go; *let it go!*"

She tried to reach him, but fell flat on her belly, her fingers tangling in the fabric of his loose trousers. His mind was reeling from the sudden weakness. Let *what* go? Did she mean the knife?

Was it still in his hand? He couldn't tell... dizziness was clawing at his awareness, trying to drag him down.

"It's draining your life force," Oksana whispered, "trying to add it to mine and fight the poison. But you're human—you're not strong enough! Please let it go!"

Mason toppled onto his side. If he was still clutching the blade, he couldn't feel it... couldn't unclench the muscles of his fingers to release it. Gray fog swirled around the edges of his vision.

A cold laugh came from above them. He rolled his head in the direction of the noise, his heart laboring as it tried to pound faster, while at the same time, all the energy drained out of his body.

"Oh," said the bokor, "this is priceless. Do I have that crusty old bitch Esther Lovelie to thank for this entertainment? It positively reeks of her pathetic powers."

He kicked a booted foot into Mason's side, rolling him onto his back and ignoring Oksana's feral snarl of rage. In his peripheral vision, Mason saw her try to claw at the man's leg, but her movement was slow and he merely stepped out of the way, still laughing.

"Touch him again and I'll torture you until you beg for death," Oksana grated, but Mason could hear the undercurrent of fear behind the threat.

The bokor snorted. "Will you now, nightcrawler? Or will you lie there, helpless, watching while I slit this one's throat before I drive a stake through your rotting heart?"

He strode away, wavering in and out of focus as Mason's vision swam. Drawing breath was becoming a struggle—he had to concentrate very carefully to make his diaphragm pull air into his lungs and push it back out.

Mason saw the bastard walk over to a half-collapsed porch and grasp a thin length of broken board that had once been part of the railing. He jerked at it sharply, and a piece of the wood snapped off in his hand. It was about the length of his forearm and ended in a jagged point where the thin board had cracked and split. He turned and approached again, his other hand pulling a curved blade from a sheath at his waist.

"No," Oksana moaned, her fingers still clenching at Mason's clothing as she tried and failed to rise. "No, no, no..."

Fear had drained away along with everything else inside Mason, but now a single thought crystallized with diamond-edged clarity.

Oksana was a vampire. She was practically helpless—poisoned—and this fucker was coming at her with a sharpened wooden stake in his hand.

The bokor walked casually up to them, his lips twisted in a sadistic smirk. Mason hated that smirk with more passion than he'd ever hated any goddamned thing in his entire life. The fucker used the pointed end of the stake to shove Oksana onto her back and placed the tip casually between her breasts.

"What does it feel like to watch someone with whom you share a soul-bond bleed out onto the dirt, nightcrawler?" he asked, examining the gleaming blade of the hunting knife held in his other hand with casual interest.

Oksana growled and tried to push upright, as though she would impale herself without thought if that was what it took to get to the man standing over them. At the prospect of seeing that stake slide into Oksana's chest and pierce her heart, a massive adrenaline dump flooded through Mason, his body's last-ditch effort to combat the effects of whatever was happening to him.

Was he still holding the dagger? Fuck, he couldn't even tell. This was his only chance, though—*their* only chance. Using the last terror-fueled bit of strength in his body, Mason half-rolled, using the resulting momentum to help swing his heavy, unresponsive arm in an arc toward the outside of the bokor's knee.

His vision clouded over with gray fog, but the bokor cursed and cried out, staggering backward. For an instant, everything went silent… or perhaps Mason's hearing had gone now, as well as his vision. But, no. That theory was shot down a moment later, when the bokor began to howl with agony.

Oh, good, Mason thought, right before the drain on his energy accelerated into a whirling, sucking maelstrom, dragging him toward darkness. The last thing he heard before his senses shut down was Oksana's piercing shriek of rage and denial joining the bokor's.

-o-o-o-

Oksana screamed for help with the desperation of the freshly damned. Her cries echoed through the she bargained. *Just this one thing – this one, tiny thing.*

For long moments, nothing happened. Even Duchess's formidable strength was fading, and Xander had nothing left to give except the unspoken support of his presence. Mason's life force dimmed, then flared brighter, flickering in fits and starts.

"Mason," she whispered, "please come back to me. *Please.* Don't leave me alone in the dark again."

That energy sputtered, but then blazed higher. Mason's jaw moved, his throat working weakly under Oksana's numb fingers. Duchess sucked in a sharp breath, and Mason's shaky hand lifted to grasp her forearm, holding it to his mouth.

"That's it, *Docteur*," Duchess said, relief loosening the tight line of her shoulders. "Have it all. Take everything you can pull from me – I'll get more later."

He drank with single-minded focus until Duchess wavered, and finally slumped against Oksana's side. Mason still seemed dangerously weak as well. He did not open his eyes or move again once Duchess's arm fell away from his lips.

But he was *alive*... albeit, sentenced forever to the same shadowy half-life the rest of them were. Oksana held Duchess with one clumsy, heavily weighted arm, and Mason with the other. Xander's weak grip still clasped loosely around her leg.

"Thank you," she murmured to the dark sky above her, and the vampires at her side. Tears shook free of her body, her chest hitching, but she didn't fight to stop them. "Thank you so much..."

They lay together, exhausted, the first indigo wash of predawn prickling against Oksana's back.

"Dawn's coming soon," she rasped. "We'll have to get under cover."

There was a beat of silence.

"That... may actually be a bit of an issue," Xander said.

She tried to drag her tattered composure together enough to take stock. "You and Duchess could still feed from me. Would poisoned blood be better than no blood?"

"Perhaps," Duchess whispered weakly, "but if we're all poisoned, there's no one to feed Mason when he wakes."

"There's no one to feed him *now*," Oksana pointed out with growing worry. "You're both bone dry."

"Anel's still here, looking after the children," Xander said.

As if on cue, an engine coughed into life in the distance. Moments later, the sound changed, growing further and further away until it faded to nothingness.

"Ah," Xander corrected himself. "Anel is *not* still here with the children. Because that would be too easy, apparently."

"He's probably gone to get help," Duchess murmured.

Oksana forced her mind back into gear, knowing decisions had to be made. "Xander, drink from me. My body is already fighting the poison. Between us, we'll get the others under cover, somehow. With luck, Mason will sleep through the

FOURTEEN

"*Mon Dieu –* " came a new voice from the edge of the square.

That heartfelt curse was quite possibly the sweetest sound Oksana had ever heard. Duchess slid to her knees next to Xander, blood streaking down her upper body from a bullet graze in the side of her neck, and a thicker trail dripping from a hole blown through her hip.

"Oksana's blood is poisoned, and I'm running on empty," Xander grated. "How much do you have?"

Duchess's china blue eyes hardened. "Whatever it takes, that's how much I have," she said grimly. She eased Xander aside, and he flopped onto his back nearby, grunting.

"Bloody, buggering *shite*," he groaned, still clamping a hand over his side. After a moment, he seemed to get a handle on the pain. "Duchess... the children?"

"With Anel," Duchess replied shortly. She spared only an instant to cup Oksana's tear-stained face in one palm before she set to work, opening her wrist and letting the blood drip into Mason's mouth.

"We should have waited," Oksana whispered. "We should have called the others."

"Doctor *Hero* here should've stayed the hell back and followed the damned plan," Xander retorted in a tight voice, not moving from his spot on his back.

"If he had, the bokor would have staked me while I was weakened by the poison, and then gone after the rest of you," Oksana said, new tears threatening.

"Jesus fuck," Xander growled, and Duchess's expression hardened into granite.

"We were shielding our minds," Duchess said. "Trying not to distract you with what was happening on our end. We didn't know, *petite soeur*."

Her friend's complexion had been porcelain and cream to begin with, but it was already paling to chalk as she drained the contents of her veins into Mason's mouth. Even weakened by gunshots and blood loss, though, Oksana could feel Duchess's power bolstering hers, helping her contain Mason's spirit between them. Xander reached out clumsily, a hand grasping Oksana's right ankle. His younger, badly depleted life force twined with theirs, as well.

She held her breath, waiting. Still praying to any power that might listen. Mama Lovelie had said on two occasions that the goddess—the Angel Israfael—was with her, but Oksana had spent hundreds of years blaming the angel for her trials. If Israfael had not weakened, if she had not ceded the cosmic battle of Light and Dark to Bael, how much suffering could have been avoided?

Please, Angel of Light, Goddess of Love... grant me this one thing and I will dedicate my life to your will, the remaining strength she had stolen from him to gather up his fractured spirit, trying to keep it from leaking away into the night like water held in cupped hands.

She cradled him close and prayed for a miracle from the only source left to her. Long moments later, the sound of potential salvation reached her ears.

"*Oksana!*" Xander's voice was hoarse with pain. He staggered into the circle of torchlight, covered in blood and clutching one hand against a horrific slash in his side, as if worried about what might fall out if he didn't hold everything in. He stumbled to his knees beside her. "Dear *Christ*—"

Oksana knew how she must look, crouched over Mason's deathly still form with his blood staining her lips and running down her chin. Wild-eyed and tear-streaked.

"Help me!" she begged, frantic. "Xander, oh, god, please! I have to turn him, but I'm poisoned—my blood will kill him!"

In all the decades she'd known him, Oksana had never seen Xander look as shell-shocked as he did now, like he'd been peering into hell and seen things too awful to live with. Some small and distant part of her quailed at the thought of what could have caused that dull, haunted flatness now hiding behind his normally sharp green eyes.

That paled before her terror for Mason, however. Xander blinked, as if trying to recall himself from whatever abyss threatened to claim him. Without hesitation, he tore his fangs into the wrist that wasn't pressed against the open gash in his side. Blood only dripped from the fresh wound rather than spurting, but he pressed it to Mason's slack mouth.

"Make him swallow," he croaked, swaying a bit as he clenched and released his fist, trying to squeeze more blood through his depleted veins.

Oksana forced numb fingers to work, panic lending her strength as she massaged Mason's throat muscles, willing him to swallow even as she strove to keep his shattered spirit from floating away.

"Mason," she whispered, "please don't leave me... *please*, I'm so sorry... I'm *so sorry.*"

"Duchess is with the unturned children," Xander whispered, sounding frighteningly weak. "The turned ones collapsed into dust as we were trying to subdue them."

"Mason killed the bokor," Oksana said in a faint voice. "The undeads' existence must have been tied to his life force in some way." She felt the soul cradled by hers flutter weakly. "Xander, I can barely feel him. It's not working!"

Xander swayed again and shook his head as if to clear it. He lifted his wrist to his teeth and tore the wound open wider before lowering it back to Mason's lips. "Keep trying. Don't give up on him, Oksana. You mustn't—you're all that's keeping him here."

abandoned village, and also along the mental connection with her fellow vampires.

A few steps away, the bokor's shouts of pain faded into choking noises as his strength failed under the combined essence of her life force and Mason's. His body crumpled to the ground, collapsing into itself until only a pile of dust remained. And still Oksana screamed.

Any satisfaction she might have hoped to gain from the defeat of their enemy was as nothing compared to the sight of Mason's body sagging, the muscles of his chest going soft and lax with a single, slow exhalation. The poison spreading through her bloodstream was the same thrice-damned poison that had paralyzed her on the night she was turned. She could feel it combining with the drain of having Mason's essence siphoned through hers by the knife's spell, the dual forces trying to freeze her limbs into immobility.

But she was no longer a newly turned vampire, weakened from shock and terrible injury. She had been growing in strength for more than two hundred *fucking* years since then, and she would *not* lie here, powerless, while the man she loved breathed his last a mere arm's length away.

Oksana moved, dragging herself forward, forcing her body to comply. Her hands fell on Mason's unresponsive form, her senses questing outward, seeking the spark, the tiny, precious flame that glowed at the heart of every living being.

No, no, no... she chanted, feeling that tiny light flickering like a candle in a hurricane. Feeling the sluggish way Mason's heart stuttered and paused, stuttered and paused.

Desperation lengthened Oksana's fangs and made her eyes glow with inner light. There was only one way Mason could survive the next few minutes. Or rather, there was only one way he could *fail* to survive—but still come back afterward. Even as she plunged razor sharp teeth into his defenseless jugular, the knowledge that her poisoned blood would ultimately be his death sentence burned through her like acid.

She could take from him, rending his soul as hers had been rent, but the willing sacrifice of her poisoned blood afterward would not save him, as Augustin's sacrifice two hundred years ago had saved her.

No. It would only doom him.

And, yet, what else could she do? Turning him was their only chance—even if it was, in reality, no chance at all.

Bloody tears streamed down her face as she pulled his sweetly intoxicating blood into herself, wrapping her decimated strength around the flickering remnants of his life force while praying ceaselessly to spirits who had abandoned her centuries ago.

Please, she beseeched. *Please, help me save him! Somebody... anybody—*

Oksana felt Mason's soul rip free from its moorings, torn by the force of her assault on his blood. But she could not give him back the blood she'd taken—now mingled with hers—without poisoning his weakened body. Instead, she used daylight hours, anyway. And if no one has come by dusk, we'll... I don't know. Look for some animals for Duchess to drink from, I guess. I heard dogs barking in the distance earlier."

"Dog blood? Be still my undead heart," Duchess mumbled. "I can hardly wait."

"I'm open to alternative suggestions," she replied pointedly.

Since there were none, Oksana eased Duchess and Mason to lie flat, then scooted around to offer Xander her wrist. He took it, and a moment later, she felt the puncture of fangs and the deep, drawing sensation as he drank. When he was done, he dragged the back of his hand across his mouth. She could see that the torn flesh of his wrist was already starting to close over.

"*Ugh*. No offense, luv," he said, as he carefully eased into a sitting position, "but that shit in your blood is truly foul." He went quiet for a moment, as if listening to his body. "Although... on the positive side, now I can barely feel my guts trying to fall out. Of course, I can barely feel my hands and feet, either. Or, you know, my face." His brows drew together thoughtfully. "Actually, I withdraw the *foul* comment. This concoction is kind of growing on me. I don't suppose you have the recipe?"

"Talk to Mama Lovelie," Oksana said, her voice tight. "Just keep it the hell away from me, unless you want a very small, very pissed-off amputee going medieval on your Pommy arse."

"Message received and understood," he replied, and cautiously pulled his blood-soaked hand away from his side to check it. "All right, let's move this circus sideshow indoors before someone here ends up with a bad case of sunburn."

Both of them reeled like drunkards from the poison, barely able to grasp anything with their clumsy fingers. Their legs were weak and uncoordinated.

Oh, how the mighty have fallen, Oksana couldn't help thinking as she and Xander dragged first Mason, and then Duchess, across the dusty square, all thoughts of dignity abandoned in favor of practicality as the sun's rays lightened the eastern horizon.

They made it inside with about five minutes to spare, collapsing in a looted hut that had miraculously escaped mortar fire. There was very little of use left inside, but the roof was intact, which was the most important thing as the sun rose. Flies buzzed around them, drawn by all the blood.

"Well, this is certainly cozy," Xander said, faux cheerful. He nudged a discarded bottle out of the way with his foot. It sloshed as it rolled over, still about halfway full, to reveal a Rhum Barbancourt label. "Oh, you have got to be joking. They looted the place, and left *rum* behind? Now that's just cruel and unusual punishment, that is."

Despite decades spent in the pursuit of rampant alcoholism, as a vampire, without a human's blood to filter it through first, the rum was useless to Xander.

"You could always offer it to the loa in exchange for a conveniently timed rescue party," Duchess muttered.

"Give it here," Oksana said, stretching across, careful to avoid jostling Mason's head in her lap. She made a couple of unsuccessful attempts to unscrew the cap with uncooperative fingers before growling in frustration and breaking the glass neck against the edge of the cook stove next to her.

Xander stared at her as she tipped it up, ignoring the sharp edges of the glass against her lips as she downed the contents. The rum burned in her stomach like acid as her body rejected and neutralized it.

"I won't bother to ask how the hell you can stand to do that, because you never answer with anything more than a shrug," he said finally.

She let the bottle fall to the dirt floor with a hollow clank. "I never answer because you're asking the wrong question," she muttered.

He pondered that for a long moment. "You're right. Forget the how. *Why* do you do that?"

She thought of all the human food and drink she'd forced into her aching gut over the decades—the brief moment of pleasure as her taste buds activated, followed by the discomfort or outright pain as her stomach refused it and her body broke it down into useless waste that offered no sustenance.

"Because Bael cursed me to drink only blood, but he won't stop me from swallowing whatever food and drink I damn well please," she said.

"Even if it hurts like the devil afterward," Xander finished, looking at her with new understanding.

"Even so."

They were quiet after that, huddled in a corner of the hut that would not lie in the path of the sunlight streaming through the structure's small windows. Mason was as still as death, but Oksana could feel the faint, reassuring thrum of the life force hidden beneath his pale skin. If no one came, though... if she or Xander weren't recovered enough to fly for help, what would the evening bring? They needed blood—untainted blood—and she wasn't at all sure an animal's blood would suffice.

-o-o-o-

It was midday, and Oksana was trying not to succumb to the lethargy caused by daylight combined with the magic-laced cocktail of poison slowly working its way out of her veins. She'd been keeping watch while the others—who were in far worse shape than she was—dozed.

The rattle of an aging combustion engine split the peace of the deserted village, growing louder as it approached.

"Xander," she hissed, knowing he was the only one who would be able to muster any sort of useful defense with her if the approaching vehicle carried foes rather than friends.

"I hear it," he mumbled. "It's the same truck, isn't it? Anel's Ford?"

"I think so," she agreed.

Which doesn't mean rebels or someone else didn't hijack it, Duchess sent along the mental link, rather than expend the energy needed to speak aloud.

"What've we got for weapons? Just in case?" Oksana asked, drawing her personal dagger—*not* the spelled one Mama Lovelie had given her—from its sheath.

"Four blades, and a pistol I took from one of the chil-" Xander cut himself off, his jaw clenching. "From one of the undead."

Assuming whoever was approaching was human, there wasn't much they'd be able to do to a group of vampires, unless they'd come prepared for an afternoon of staking or decapitation. Which did not, of course, mean that things wouldn't become very unpleasant, very quickly, depending on how heavily they were armed.

Even weakened, she and Xander could *probably* overpower a truckload of humans using mental influence, unless they burst in with automatic weapons already blazing. The bigger worry, though, was Mason. Oksana honestly had no idea how vulnerable he might be right now. He was alive—turned—but he hadn't drunk his fill from Duchess before her blood ran out. Would he awake as a ravenous berserker, or would he be weak and susceptible to injury or death?

Oksana held her breath as the vehicle rattled into the square outside their shelter. Its rusted doors creaked open, and she heard unfamiliar male voices speaking. She tensed and met Xander's eyes, clutching her dagger in fingers that still tingled with numbness.

The truck doors slammed shut, and the voices quieted. After a tense moment, a new voice carried to them.

"The bokor is dead," Mama Lovelie proclaimed. "I can no longer sense his power here. Ah—it appears the loa have claimed their debt—these ashes are all that remain of him."

Oksana nearly sagged in relief, and Xander slumped back against the wall he'd been using for support. "Oh, good," he said. "The mambo-led cavalry is here. And it sounds like she's brought along some carry out for dinner."

FIFTEEN

Mason's nightmares were all the worse because they felt so frighteningly real. He saw Oksana. His beloved. His wife—her eyes glowing from within as she ripped into the flesh of his throat like a wild animal. Pain tore at his awareness. His lifeblood spurted... pulsed... then slowed to a trickle as his heart stopped and his consciousness succumbed to the darkness.

Now, the same bloodlust flooded him, drawing him toward warm bodies with pounding pulses that sounded like beacons. The emptiness inside him was insatiable, as cold and bleak as the vacuum of space, and if he didn't fill it with that tempting warmth, he would go mad.

Each time he tried to rise, hands held him down—how were they so strong? *Nothing* should be able to keep him from reaching what he needed! But, still, they restrained him, and instead of warm flesh, his fangs—good Christ, his *fangs?*—sank into pale, cool skin. The sweet nectar that flowed through the wounds soothed the ache of icy, burning hunger, and sent tendrils of power coiling through his body, but it still wasn't... *right*. It wasn't the nourishment he craved most.

Blessed darkness claimed him, and when he dreamed again, it was of a woman sitting next to his bedside, weeping silently, her face hidden in one hand. The sun was low in the sky, slanting through a small window to paint the wall across from him with a square of light that hurt to look at.

"Oksana?" he rasped, and the scrape of his voice against his aching throat made him realize that he was awake, and this part, at least, was real.

Her head whipped up, and he was struck again by the rusty brown streaks of her tears. This time, though, the jolt of shock hit him low, in his stomach, making it cramp and rumble.

"Mason?" she asked. "You're awake? Do you know where you are?"

He tried to gather his scattered thoughts into something coherent. "Yes, I'm awake, I think. And… sorry, no idea. What's wrong? What's happened?"

Her expression started to crumple, though she fought against it valiantly. Bits of memory began to trickle in.

Telling her and the others about the missing youngsters.

Mama Lovelie. Anel. The scorched dagger. The—

The bokor.

"Oh, god—Mason," Oksana choked. "I'm so sorry."

The bottom fell out of his aching stomach. "Sorry? For what? You don't mean… the children…?" A new memory slotted into place. He'd done something—he'd left Anel alone, ignored the plan—

She shook her head. "Duchess and Xander were able to save about two dozen of them." Her voice was hoarse. "The others had already been turned."

He digested that for a moment. *Some of them had been saved.* That was the part they needed to focus on. "So, there are two dozen children who are safe, and who wouldn't have been without our help."

She nodded and tried to swipe away the bloody tear tracks on her face, but more spilled over even as she was trying to hide them.

"You're not just crying for the lost children," he realized. "Oksana. Tell me what's wrong."

She stared at him with bloodshot eyes, her chest shaking with emotion for several moments before she mastered it. "I killed you," she whispered. "*Again*. Oh, god, Mason…"

He reached out, grasping her wrist when she would have covered her face again. "Oksana, sweetheart—I'm right here. It might feel like someone used me for punt practice, but I'm sure I'll be right as rain in a day or two."

She gazed down at him, and Mason had never seen anyone look so sad in his life.

"No," she said quietly. "No, Mason—you won't be. You've been turned. You're like me now."

Stark denial stiffened his shoulders and drew his expression into tense lines. "Don't be ridiculous," he said reflexively. "I remember… I tackled that arsehole who was trying to kill you, right? I must've gotten clocked in the head, or something. Maybe I've been out for a while, but I'm fine now—"

She only continued to look at him with that awful expression.

"No. Stop looking at me like that. This is crazy," he said, and cautiously swung into a sitting position. He still felt like someone had squeezed him through his great-granny's laundry wringer, but there was strength in his limbs despite his aches and pain. He pushed past Oksana and stood, glancing around the room until his gaze settled on the small rectangle of sunlight against the wall. It made his eyes water, but he strode over to it, intent on putting a stop to this nonsense right the hell now.

"Look, I don't remember exactly what happened last night, it's true," he said, and stuck his hand into the too-bright light. "But you can see I'm not—"

Agony erupted in his hand, smoke and steam rising from the skin as it blistered. "*Sweet bleeding Christ!*" he gasped, staggering backward. He clutched his wrist, wide eyes flying to Oksana.

She was still in the chair, one hand clenched in the bedclothes, her eyes twin pools of agony every bit as intense as the fiery pain in his hand.

"I'm so sorry," she said again, and fled the room.

-o-o-o-

Mason sat on the edge of the bed, staring at his hand. The pain of the second-degree burns was enough to take his breath away, but as he watched, the blisters started to subside. Intense itching spread across the ruined skin. He could not have said how much time passed, but it was surely only minutes as, right before his eyes, delicate pink skin grew across the damaged area.

At the same time, the ache in his stomach that had formed a sort of somatic background noise intensified. It grew harder and harder to dismiss, though a part of him was trying valiantly to do so.

No, the rational part of his mind insisted. *It's just the power of subconscious suggestion. This is all some kind of huge mistake, or maybe it's just another dream. It sure as hell doesn't mean that you're actually a vampi—*

As though merely *thinking* the word somehow gave it physical power, a stomach cramp doubled Mason over, flooding his mind with thoughts of *hunger violence blood*. Everything around him suddenly seemed terribly loud. There were no warm bodies *inside* the building, but *outside*...

The sun had slipped behind the horizon while he was busy staring at his miraculously healing hand. Between one breath and the next, he was lunging toward the window, and the tempting heartbeats that lay beyond it.

A small figure appeared between him and his objective as if by magic, one hand splayed across his chest to halt his progress. Unthinking rage flickered at his awareness like flame, trying to send his rational thought up in a fiery conflagration.

"*Stop.*" The single word echoed in both his ears and his mind, ringing like a French-accented bell and interrupting the spiral of unthinking, furious need.

He doubled over again, clutching his stomach. Panic overtook anger. "Duchess? Oh, god... what's—what's wrong with me?"

"Nothing is wrong." The hand closed on his upper arm and manhandled him back to the bed with far more strength than it should have had. "Well, nothing like what you're thinking, at least. You're hungry, and you need to feed."

Feed. Not *eat*. Mason shuddered, coming back to himself a bit more. He looked up, taking the blonde vampire in properly for the first time since she'd come in. She looked like hell. He got the impression that wasn't a normal state of affairs for her, to put it mildly.

"Where did Oksana go?" he asked, fighting the growing compulsion to launch himself at the nearest vein he could reach.

"To deal with her issues in private," Duchess said.

While Duchess had never been warm with him during their short acquaintance, Mason was struck by her flat tone and her flat eyes, their usual brilliant blue now looking more like the color of ice.

"Something's happened," he forced out through gritted teeth, clutching at the ravenous pit that was his stomach. The desire to *rend tear consume* rose again. Images from his nightmares flashed through his memory, and a horrible, heart-stopping thought assailed him. "Oh, god—I didn't..." He swallowed bile. "Duchess, did I hurt anyone?"

The children? The unspoken words hung in the air.

She tilted her head, as if assessing him. "No, *Docteur*. You didn't hurt anyone except the bokor." There was a faint pause. "Well, to be accurate, you *did* actually get a decent strike in on Xander while he was helping to restrain you this morning. But the rest of us generally work on the assumption that Xander deserves it whenever someone punches him. Even if he hasn't done anything recently, it's a fair bet that someone, somewhere owes him one."

Mason winced, but his combined relief and mortification disappeared under a new onslaught of hunger.

"Drink," Duchess commanded, thrusting her wrist at him. "And now that you're past the worst of the blood frenzy, concentrate on not doing more damage than necessary. Also, you should try stopping before you're completely full."

"I don't want to hurt you—" he managed, between rounds of painful cramping. To his horror, he felt his canines lengthening into points, prodding at the inside of his lips.

Duchess snorted. "I'm a four-hundred-year-old vampire, *Docteur*. While I may not be quite up to full strength yet, I assure you that nothing you can do to me with your little baby fangs will result in any serious damage."

She might have been several inches shorter than him, with dark circles under her hollow blue eyes and a half-healed furrow on the side of her neck that looked like nothing so much as a bullet graze, but something deep in the same part of him that longed for blood recognized the aura of power that surrounded her. Nothing human in him controlled his instinctive grab for that proffered arm, or the way his razor-sharp canines sank into the cool flesh of her wrist. Yet the part of him that sensed her power kept a veneer of control for the first time, drinking without turning it into an attack.

"Better," she approved, when he dragged himself away, feeling deeply discomfited by what he'd just done... yet undeniably sated, at the same time.

He sat back, running a shaking hand over his face.

"I can't... do this," he said, overcome by a sense of *wrongness* that he couldn't escape. "For god's sake, I'm a *doctor*."

"You are doing this," Duchess said, still in a flat tone. "It will be better for you, once one of us can knock some sense into Oksana."

Longing filled him upon hearing Oksana's name, rising with a strength that he didn't understand. He tried to call on logic... to focus on learning more facts about what had happened. About what was happening around him.

"You're injured," he said, examining the furrow in her neck more closely. "Why are you the one feeding me when you've got a half-healed bullet wound and you look like hell?"

"Two half-healed bullet wounds, to be precise," she corrected. "They'll disappear eventually. In the normal course of things, I would feed from one of the others to heal my injuries more quickly. But Oksana was poisoned during the fight. Do you remember that?"

He remembered hearing her scream, finding her on the ground, nearly unable to move. "I saw the symptoms, but I could only guess at the cause. She's all right now, though?" She'd *seemed* all right—if very upset—when he woke up earlier. "And what about Xander?"

"Oksana is largely recovered from the effects, but it still lingers in her bloodstream. Xander was badly injured, and he fed from her even though she was poisoned. It was the only way the two of them could recover enough strength to move us under shelter and defend against possible threats. I did not drink from her, to ensure there would be someone untainted left to feed you."

He remembered Duchess squeezing a few drops of her blood over the cut he'd carved into his arm as a test, mere days ago. "So vampire blood heals other vampires as well as humans?"

"Our blood and saliva do, yes," she said, and then seemed to hesitate. "By rights, Oksana should have been the one to feed you, but we weren't sure how the poison might affect a newly fledged vampire. None of us were willing to take the chance."

His new instincts rose up, as if to cry, *damn right I should have had Oksana's blood*, but he still asked, "Why should she have been the one to feed me?"

"Because you are her mate," Duchess said.

He resisted the urge to tell her that someone might want to inform Oksana of that fact, since she seemed more interested in running away from him than talking to him. Instead, he focused once more on Duchess's words, trying to piece everything together.

"How were you and Xander injured? Did the bokor have guards watching the children?"

Duchess's body went very, very still.

"In a manner of speaking, he did," she said in a flat, deliberate tone. "Ten of the children had already been turned. They were armed with firearms and blades. Xander and I foolishly tried to overpower them without... damaging them any more than necessary. In doing so, we nearly left Oksana to her death — and you, as well."

Mason closed his eyes against the mental image of the two vampires trying to rescue the living without injuring the already dead. "Your opponents looked like kids, even if they weren't, any more," he said. "Of course you'd try not to hurt them."

Her expression didn't waver. "An ill-advised waste of energy and effort. As soon as the force controlling them was destroyed, they crumbled to ash in front of our eyes." She looked at the small window, but he didn't think she really saw the late-evening dusk beyond.

"If you've had your fill of blood," she continued, "then I will leave you now. The humans know to stay out of this building until you gain better control over your impulses. Feel free to move around, but remain inside. When the hunger pangs return, tell one of us immediately."

She left without a sound. Mason sat on the edge of the bed, staring at nothing and feeling his life slowly unravel around him. He was a doctor whose veins apparently ran with a miracle drug, but he couldn't go out during daylight. And at the moment, he couldn't get near a human being without risking descent into a frenzy of bloodlust.

With a fresh pang, he thought about Jackson.

His brother. What in god's name would he tell Jackson? What would he tell Gita?

And why did Oksana continue to flee from his presence, when every newly raised instinct he possessed screamed that they should be by each other's sides? Yet, the touch of his lips on hers — the very *sight* of him, it seemed — sent her into an emotional breakdown. She'd been trying to get away from him since practically the very first moment they'd met.

The idea of facing this new reality, even with her standing steadfast at his side, was daunting. The idea of doing it alone was…

He hurled himself off the bed and started pacing before he could finish the thought. He needed distraction. After casting his mind about for a few moments, he settled on the only one of the three vampires he hadn't seen since he'd regained his senses.

Apparently, he'd slugged Xander a good one at some point while he was out of his skull — and done so while the other man was already injured *and* poisoned. Plus, he'd sent Oksana running off in tears on not one, but two occasions since being on the receiving end of Xander's less-than-subtle shovel talk.

However you looked at it, Mason almost certainly owed him an apology. Of course, he had no way of knowing whether Xander was more likely to punch him in the face in retaliation, or start quietly searching for likely places to stash a dismembered body. But either way, he supposed it would be an effective distraction from the clusterfuck that was apparently his life now.

He found the other vampire at the back of the building, sitting on the sill of a large window with one foot propped up against its side. The glass—if the window ever had any in the first place—was missing, and Xander stared out across the desolate area that might have housed a garden, once. A bottle of something alcoholic looking hung loosely from his right hand.

"Feeling better now, Ozzie?" he asked, without looking away from the darkness beyond the window.

Mason wasn't sure which he was coming to dislike more—Oksana's open anguish, or the others' flat, exhausted monotones.

"Yes," he said cautiously, approaching until he could look out past Xander and into the night. "And no."

The vampire grunted, the sound offering neither encouragement nor censure.

"Do you mind, mate?" Mason asked, taking the bottle of cheap vodka from Xander's slack grip. "God knows, I could use a drink right now that doesn't contain platelets."

He opened it, and Xander finally turned from his study of the barren ground outside to fix Mason with dull green eyes. The smell coming from the bottle was foul, but alcohol was alcohol, and right now he wasn't in a mood to be picky. Xander watched him throw it back... only to collapse into choking and coughing after the very first swallow. He glared at the bottle, hurling it away as if it was a snake that might bite him if he kept touching it.

"Yeah," Xander said. "I could've warned you about that."

"What the—" Mason managed to wheeze. "What the *fuck* is that shit?"

"Vodka, just like the label says." Xander quirked a sardonic eyebrow. "Apparently, something about being on this island makes people want to dump it on the ground. I still haven't really figured that whole thing out."

Mason stared at him. "That. Was *not*. Vodka."

He swiped a hand across his mouth in disgust, the smell nearly overpowering him. The tiny bit that had made it down his esophagus settled in his gut like a hot brand, curling and twisting angrily.

Xander shrugged and went back to looking out the window. "You're a vampire now, Ozzie. If you want vodka, you're going to need to convince a human to drink it for you first. Either that or follow Oksana's example and learn to live with your body throwing a fit over it."

Mason digested this for a few moments.

"Look," he said, when the silence threatened to stretch too long, "I, uh, just came to apologize for slugging you earlier. I was completely off my head the first few times I woke up... but I gather I've got you and the others to thank for keeping me from turning some poor, random sod from the village into an all-you-can-drink buffet while I was troppo."

Xander lifted a shoulder again, and let it drop. "Don't mention it. It's been a decade or twelve since it happened to me, but I remember how it is… right afterward."

Mason regarded him. "How did it happen to you?"

"How was I turned, you mean?" Xander didn't move to look at him as he spoke. "The same way as Duchess and Oksana. I attracted the wrong kind of attention from the wrong kind of evil power, and someone close to me was stupid enough to sacrifice their life in exchange for my worthless arse."

The words were delivered in the same flat monotone Mason was growing to hate, though the bitterness behind them was clear.

"Was it this… demon, then? Bael?" he asked.

Xander snorted, no humor in the sound. "It still twists you up inside to even say things like that, doesn't it, Ozzie? Yes, it was Bael." He paused, and then continued in a quieter tone, as if musing over the words. "It's starting to frighten me, the level of hatred I feel for that filthy stain on the universe. All day, every day, I'm filled with it. It's in the air around me… I breathe it in; it flows through my veins. I spend half my time plotting new ways to hold it at bay for an hour or two. Sex. Drugs. Alcohol. But it always comes *right* back afterward. Seeing those undead children yesterday…"

He trailed off and shook his head.

"This war you've all talked about," Mason said, just as quietly. "Can we win it?"

"Win it?" Xander's eyes flicked back to meet his. "Mate, I have absolutely no idea."

SIXTEEN

Two days later, the others apparently decided that Mason was no longer a danger to anything warm-blooded that came within his reach. Mama Lovelie entered the building where they'd been sheltering, and plans for returning to the village they'd come from got underway.

Duchess had tasted a few drops of Xander's blood and declared it clear of the poison, before drinking from him to heal the remains of her wounds. Oksana was like a ghost, hovering on the edges of conversations, and disappearing the moment Mason started trying to think of a way to talk to her privately. The cloud of guilt surrounding her was a nearly palpable thing.

In some ways, it was a relief to get back to the comfortable house where Mama Lovelie had first sat them down, fed them sweet *akasan*, and calmly demanded payment in vampire blood for their room and board. In other ways, being here was decidedly uncomfortable since it brought Mason one step closer to the inevitable task of dealing with the toppled ruins of his former life.

The satellite phone on the table next to him had been taunting him for hours now. It sat there, as if daring him to pick it up and dial Jackson's number.

He was on the sleeping porch, where Oksana had kissed him four days ago and turned his life upside down. Odd, he supposed, that he marked the upheaval as starting on that day, and not the day when he'd been turned into a vampire.

Steeling himself, he reached for the damned phone. With a sigh, he pulled out the satellite antenna and checked the battery levels—low, but enough for a call. A flick of the power button called up the menu, and he chose the +65 country code for Singapore before entering Jackson's number from memory. Nerves made his foot jitter against the rough boards of the porch, and he stilled it, irritated.

The cheerful GlobalCom tone let him know the call was being connected. It rang twice, three times, four times... and on the fifth ring, a familiar, gruff voice answered.

"Yes? Who is this?"

"Hello, Jack," Mason said quietly.

"Mason! Sorry—I didn't recognize the number. Are you all right, little brother? I was starting to worry, after what we talked about last time, and then not hearing from you for several days."

Mason opened his mouth, but his brain was stuck fast. *Why the hell hadn't he figured out ahead of time what to say?*

"Mace?" Jackson prompted, real worry entering his voice. *"You still there? Hello?"*

He shook himself free of the momentary vocal paralysis. "Yeah. Sorry. I'm here, Jack. It's just... it's been a rough few days."

"*Yeah.*" His brother's heavy tone seemed out of place, but he continued before Mason could question it. "*So, uh, did you find any new information about those missing kids?*"

"We did. And then we found the kids themselves."

"*No shit!*" Jackson exclaimed. "*Were they okay? Did you get them back?*"

Mason swallowed. "We got… some of them back."

There was a pause, before his brother said, "*Oh, Mason.*"

"No. It's good though," Mason said. "There are twenty-two children who can get the help they need now, and hopefully go back to their families if they have any. Only…"

Another pause.

"*Little brother — the way you sound right now, you are seriously scaring the ever-loving shit out of me. Something else happened. Talk to me. Please.*"

He couldn't tell Jackson about what he'd become over a tinny satellite connection. He just… *couldn't*. But if he didn't unburden some of the weight that was pressing down on him like a boulder, he'd go mad.

"I don't really know where to start, Jack," he said. "The children who didn't make it back… what had been done to them… it was so much worse than what I'd imagined. They weren't… *human*… anymore. This man who took them — he stole everything that they were."

"*Jesus. You don't mean —*"

"What?" Mason prompted.

"You make them sound like those reports coming out of Syria," Jackson said, and even over the poor connection, Mason could hear the same heavy, shell-shocked tone he'd noted earlier.

"What reports out of Syria?" he asked cautiously.

The beat of silence was enough for Mason's stomach to sink.

"Mason... haven't you seen a news broadcast in the past few days?"

The sinking feeling grew worse. "Jack, I'm in the middle of nowhere, in a war torn, third world country that just had its infrastructure shaken by an earthquake."

"Oh, my god. You really haven't heard."

"Heard *what*?" Dread sharpened his tone. "Jackson—"

"They're trying to pass it off as some kind of disease; maybe something to do with radiation exposure after that terrorist nuke went off," Jackson said. *"People acting crazy—just mindless and violent, and they keep coming even when the police or military shoot them. Like what they used to say about PCP users going into a berserker rage."*

"Oh, dear god... no," Mason whispered.

"I mean, it's obvious the news outlets are trying to downplay it," Jackson continued, *"but, Mason, no matter how they spin it, people are starting to freak out, and I can't exactly blame them. This is some serious next-level, horror movie sounding shit."*

It could be nothing, Mason tried to tell himself. Bad reporting, or news organizations looking for ratings. But every fiber in his being told him that this was real, and he'd just been plunged into it, headfirst.

"Jackson," he said, "I can't prove it, of course, but… I think what we ran into with these kids may be connected somehow with what you're describing. Tell me — have there been any reports like this in Singapore, or elsewhere in your region?"

"*No, nothing like that around here,*" his brother said, and Mason's shoulders sagged in relief. "*Just the same bomb threats and killing sprees as always.*"

As if that wasn't bad enough.

"Okay," he said. "Good. That's good. But… do me a favor, Jack. Even if what I'm saying sounds a little crazy. Keep your head down. And if reports like that start popping up near you, grab Yi Ling and the girls and just… *go*. Go on vacation, or something. Go anywhere that those reports *aren't*."

Mason could make out Jack's deep breath before he answered. "*This has really got you freaked, doesn't it.*"

Mason closed his eyes for a moment, rubbing at them. "Yeah. It does. If you'd seen what I've seen in the past few days…"

"*Okay, little brother,*" Jackson said quietly. "*Rest easy. I've got no desire to get sucked into playing a bit part in a bad horror movie. Don't worry about us. We're fine. So's Mum. You worry about you, especially since it sounds like you're the one living in Zombie Central right now.*"

He relaxed a bit, mollified. "Thanks. Yeah, I will. Hopefully I'm just jumping at shadows, and all this will turn out to be nothing." A beep sounded in his ear, indicating a low battery. "Um, look—I had to borrow a satellite phone to call you, and I think it's about out of juice."

"Sure, no problem. Just look after yourself, Mace. Oh, and before you go—how are things going with your disaster zone girlfriend?"

Mason grimaced. *Oh, y'know, not so bad,* he thought. *First she kissed me, then she immediately had a panic attack, and the next day she turned me into a vampire.*

"She still runs for the hills whenever I get within a hundred feet of her, thanks for asking," he replied instead.

Jackson snorted. *"Sorry—I'm having a real hard time picturing that for some reason. I don't suppose you've actually—oh, I don't know—told her how you feel? Just a thought."*

"Well, of course I—" Mason began, only to halt mid-sentence. He thought for a moment. "Oh. Shit."

"Uh-huh," Jackson said patiently. *"Look, Mace. The world's going to hell around us. Listen to your big brother on this one. If we're destined to be sucked into a bad zombie movie, you'll want a kick-arse sheila who loves you at your side. Life was already too short, even before the inmates started taking over the asylum. So get off the damned phone and go tell her you want to be with her."*

Mason was quiet for a long moment, the phone beeping its critical battery warning in the background.

"Yeah. Okay." He squared his shoulders. "Thanks, Jack. We'll talk again soon. Hug Yi Ling and the kids for me."

"Sure. Oh, and don't forget—I'm still waiting on that photo of your mystery woman. Goodbye, little brother."

-o-o-o-

Mason was fully intending to take his brother's advice, and just lay all his cards on the table with Oksana. He would do that... just as soon as he could figure out the best time. And the best place. And the best words to use.

It wasn't the sort of thing you rushed into, he told himself. He only had one shot at this, so he needed to make sure everything was right. That was all.

Then, of course, Mama Lovelie informed them there would be a celebratory feast that evening, to mark the defeat of the bokor and the return of the surviving children. Mason didn't get the impression that the other vampires felt any more like celebrating than he did, but turning down the invitation would be beyond churlish.

The village was decked out with as much of a festive air as could be expected in the middle of nowhere during a war. The food, while not rich, was plentiful—even if the smell of it threatened to turn Mason's stomach whenever he let himself focus on it too closely. The dancing and singing dragged long into the night.

Mason made himself take part. In a way, it was a sort of test, to wander among so many humans and interact with them as *people*, rather than as walking ready-meals. Of course, he'd made a point of topping himself off—courtesy of Duchess, as per usual — before heading outside. Though her injuries had faded soon after she'd been able to drink from Xander and utilize the healing properties of his blood, she still looked haggard — as did Xander.

Mason made a point of speaking at length with Anel and his daughter Emily, who had taken over from him as the village healer. Anel apologized profusely for having fled Savaneaux with the children, rather than coming to Mason and Oksana's aid.

Doing so had been a totally rational decision on the old man's part, though, and Mason hastened to tell him that. Mason had left him alone, and Oksana had screamed shortly afterward. When Duchess brought the surviving children to the peristil and hurried off to help the others, Anel had no way whatsoever of knowing which way the battle would go.

Better to leave with the children than risk the bokor surviving the vampires' attack and coming after them. And he'd sent help back for them as soon as he could, after all.

Since then, Anel and Emily had been caring for the children as best they were able. Mason hated the fact that he'd been in no condition to assist with that. But the last thing a bunch of traumatized children needed was for Mason to lose his composure and terrify them with bared fangs or an unearthly, glowing stare.

Because his eyes, as he had discovered with one of Mama Lovelie's mirrors, now burned with an eerie cobalt-blue light when his hunger was roused. That had been more of a shock than it probably should have, given everything else he'd seen and experienced in the past few days. He supposed he was lucky that he still had a reflection at all.

Tonight, though, he let Anel and Emily take him around to meet the children they had rescued. He wanted to assess their condition for himself, even if he couldn't be as heavily involved in their care as he would have wished. Mama Lovelie and others with clout in the local area were already busy trying to track down the kids' relatives. Those with no family left, he planned to transfer to Port-au-Prince once he had a chance to speak with Gita.

And, oh, yeah—*that* was another conversation Mason wasn't much looking forward to. He suspected there would be several such conversations in his near future.

When the crowd started to feel overwhelming with its warm bodies and pumping blood, he sought out a quieter area. His newly uncanny night vision caught a glimpse of someone seated in the shadows of a mapou tree, leaning back against the trunk. An instant later, his senses said *vampire*. A closer look revealed it to be Xander.

Mason wandered over and draped an arm over one of the low, thick branches, looking down at him.

"Lots of drunk people out there," he said by way of greeting. "Also a group having a choof around the back of the peristil. I've gotta say, mate, you're really not living up to your party animal reputation."

Xander peered up at him. "*Having a choof?* Good god, man, are you even speaking English right now?"

"Smoking marijuana," Mason clarified. "You know… weed? Ganga? Grass? Come on, Xander. I was told you were a man of the world."

Xander just raised a sardonic brow. "I hope you'll understand that I mean this in the most respectful way possible, Ozzie, but unless you've got something to say, please fuck off."

"All right, then," Mason said. "I'll be blunt. You and Duchess think I don't get it. But I do."

"Do you, now." Xander's voice was flat.

"About what you saw in Savaneaux? Yeah. I do. I'm a pediatric doctor who specializes in deprogramming adolescents, and I volunteer in war zones. I'll let you take a moment and do the math on that."

Silence was his only response, so Mason continued, "You tried to save innocent children. You gave it your all—everything you had inside you—but it wasn't enough. And then you watched them die right in front of your eyes. Been there. Done that. It's tattooed into my flesh so deep that I'll never be free of it. Is any of this starting to sound familiar?"

"Surprisingly enough, yeah," Xander muttered.

"So, is there anything I can do to help?" Mason asked.

"Not really. Duchess will do what she always does—go have sex with a bunch of pretty boys until she's able to stop thinking about it for a bit. And

I'll do what I always do — drown my sorrows in the most exotic cocktail of drugs I can find contaminating a human bloodstream." He sighed, tilting his head back to look at the branches waving above them. "Maybe I'll go home for a bit. Just slip away by myself for a week or two."

"Is that wise, with the new reports coming out of Syria?" Mason asked, thinking of Oksana's comment about them staying together recently for safety.

Mason had immediately passed on what Jackson told him over the phone, but none of the vampires had been surprised. They'd been there, after all.

Xander only shrugged.

"On the positive side, Bael's low-level minions can't fly, and they're also painfully stupid." His tone darkened. "It's the higher-level ones you have to watch out for."

Mason pondered that, but let it go for now. "So, where's home for you, then? London?"

"Yeah." They were silent for a bit, though it was a surprisingly companionable silence. Eventually, Xander added, "Actually, there is something you can do for me."

"What's that?" Mason asked.

"You can tell me why the hell you're standing here like an idiot, talking to me, instead of talking to Oksana like you should be."

Mason sighed and firmed his jaw. "Touché, mate. All right. I'm going."

"About bloody time," Xander muttered under his breath as Mason turned around and headed back toward the festivities.

SEVENTEEN

Oksana stared at the plate of honey cakes set on the table in front of her, not truly seeing them. Once, for a little slave girl living on a cane plantation, honey cake had been a coveted treasure. Later, Augustin had indulged her sweet tooth to her heart's desire.

Now, the cakes might as well have been fashioned out of sawdust.

The sounds of late-night revelry drifted in through the windows of Mama Lovelie's house, teasing her sensitive ears as she sat alone in the dark, with only her misery for company. She knew she needed to snap out of it. All of them were suffering in their various ways—holed up here in this little village, licking their wounds.

Realistically, though, they couldn't hide here in the mambo's house forever. Xander had left a terse voicemail for Tré before the battery on their satellite phone completely gave up the ghost. She knew they would travel back to Port-au-Prince soon, so they could communicate more easily with the outside world.

As much as she dreaded it, Oksana needed rather desperately to talk to Eris. He was the one with the most knowledge about the prophecy. Because of her, a ninth vampire had been called into being—but, spirits above! How could she have fucked things up so badly? Had she ruined everything?

Thirteen vampires were supposed to come together, forming a council that could stand against Bael's power. For that, they would need to be united, surely. But if Mason didn't hate them already, he most certainly would once he'd had time to come to terms with what she'd *done* to him without his knowledge or permission.

He would hate her, at the very least. It only remained to be seen whether his hatred would be able to eclipse the burning hatred she felt for herself right now.

A soft noise penetrated her accelerating spiral of self-loathing. Someone had entered the house. Her life force recognized Mason's in the space of a single heartbeat, as though her guilt had somehow called him here to further torment her with her own failures. She pushed away from the table, poised to flee, but it was already too late. He was standing in the doorway, blocking her escape unless she wanted to shove right past him.

He was getting better at moving quickly and silently, it seemed.

"I was just—" she began.

"Oksana," he interrupted. "I've been dreaming, these past few days. I've seen... things. I've seen your husband, Augustin. The man you loved. The man you killed. *I'm not him.*"

Her knees gave way, and she fell back into the chair.

"You are, though," she said. "And I stole your life a few days ago, as surely as I stole it then. I murdered your humanity and condemned you to a life of darkness without your consent."

Mason dragged a chair over to sit in front of her and lowered himself onto it deliberately. His storm-blue eyes met hers, holding them as he spoke. "I told you that I dreamed. And, all right, maybe I am somehow connected to this man from the past. I guess it wouldn't be the maddest thing I've seen or experienced over the past week. But I'm still not him. I'm me, and you need to have this conversation with *me*. Not with a man who's been dead for more than two hundred years."

He was right, of course. She owed him that much. She nodded, not speaking.

"Good," he said. "So. First things first. Do you know what happens when someone on a battlefield or in a disaster zone needs emergency medical care? Let's say... someone's trapped under debris. He's unconscious, and his legs are crushed under tons of concrete."

She stared at him, not sure where he was going with this.

"Without help, that person will die in fairly short order," Mason continued. "But the only way to save him is to amputate his trapped limbs, which will alter his life irrevocably. He's unconscious; he can't give informed consent, and there's no time to try to track down someone with power of attorney. So who decides?"

"It's not the same thing—" she protested.

He cut her off with a shake of his head. "The doctors decide. Two doctors can agree that emergency amputation is the only viable response, and if they do, the patient's consent is unnecessary. Doing nothing would be fatal, so doing *something* is the best available option."

His eyes bored into hers. "If you and the others hadn't turned me, would I be dead now? Yes or no."

"Yes," she said, pain wracking her.

"Then by human reckoning, you did nothing wrong," he said.

She stared into his eyes with the same intensity. "And by your reckoning?"

"By my reckoning? I'm not dead. I'm still here. As far as I can see, that's a win."

A new question clawed its way up her throat. "Why did you come after me when I went to fight the bokor?" she asked. "Why did you leave the peristil, when you *knew* how dangerous it was?"

"Because somehow, I knew you needed me," he said simply.

Mason reached out, covering her hand with one of his. She caught her breath at the low thrum of power emanating outward from the contact—deeper and more insistent than ever, now that he'd left his mortal life behind.

"I came because of *this*," he continued. "You're the one who told me there's an unbreakable bond between us. Looks like you were right."

She was trapped like a fly in amber between his stormy eyes and the magnetic pull of his touch.

"But, Mason," she breathed, "I've done almost nothing but try to push you away."

"True. But I know now that you thought you were doing it to protect me," he said. "And I realized something else, though it took two different people calling me an idiot for it to really penetrate. Gotta say, I've been called a lot of things over the years, but not that."

"You aren't an idiot, Mason," Oksana said. "Far from it."

"On the contrary," Mason insisted, "they were both absolutely right. I've been a Grade A, boneheaded fool."

She shook her head in bewilderment. "Why would you say such a thing?"

A rueful smile tugged at one corner of his lips. "I'm a certified halfwit, because I haven't done this again."

His free hand came up to cradle the side of her face, and he leaned forward, drawing her toward him until his lips brushed hers—soft as the finest silk. She choked down the sob that wanted to rise and reached for him. Oksana could no sooner have stopped herself than she could stop the tide. His tongue teased the seam of her lips, and he made a noise of want that shattered any misconceptions she might still have had about his feelings toward her.

His fangs lengthened, new instincts not yet under his control. The kiss deepened, and one of those razor-sharp points pierced her lower lip with a bright flash of pleasure-pain. Blood welled up—thankfully purged of the bokor's poison now. Mason groaned, low and filthy, as he sucked the coppery drops into his mouth and rolled them over his tongue before swallowing.

He tore himself away from her mouth, breathing hard. "*God*," he said. "Please, Oksana... please, I n-need—" He closed his eyes, which were glowing with a desire and bloodlust that called to her like siren song. "I need more. Nothing Duchess or Xander gave me felt right. It's *your* blood I crave—"

She felt her own fangs lengthen in response and knew her eyes were glowing with violet light. In a flash, she was straddling him on the chair, pressed against him from pelvis to chest, pulling his head down to her throat.

The feral growl he released when his lips and fangs brushed the side of her neck went straight to her sex. When he pierced her skin, she gasped like a drowning woman and rolled her hips against his growing hardness, needing to feel him like this so badly, it hurt.

The sensation as he drew the first mouthful from her vein was completely different from any of the other hundreds of times another vampire had fed from her. It made her freeze in surprise, only to melt against him in ecstasy a moment later. He made low, male noises of pleasure, each swallow echoed by a twitch of the thick length she was mindlessly rocking against.

The mental link between them, which lay nascent until now, flared into life as their essences mixed and swirled together.

Finally... finally... so good... so beautiful and perfect...

His nearly mindless chant as he drank from her neck chased away any lingering doubts about the sincerity of his feelings. When he finished and reluctantly pulled away, she had to fight the wash of disappointment at the loss. He rested his forehead on her shoulder, panting.

"Oksana," he said hoarsely. "I need all of you. Please say yes…"

It was all she could do not to start rending the fabric of his clothing with inhuman strength, right there in Mama Lovelie's sitting room. But… he needed to know what he'd already gotten a glimpse of, the first time they'd kissed.

Mason, she sent along the bond. *You have to know first that something inside me is broken. You saw before, when I lost myself to the past after I kissed you. The feelings you stir in me… they're all tangled up with what Bael did to me, and what I did to you. Or rather, what I did to Augustin.*

Mason straightened so that he could meet her eyes, and she could feel through the link as he dragged his need under control.

"You're not broken," he said aloud, "and did I happen to mention that I'm a doctor who specializes in helping people move beyond traumatic experiences?"

His crooked smile, along with the feel of his emotions through the mental connection, robbed the words of any sting they might have had beyond gentle teasing.

She found an answering smile for him, though it was tremulous. Her voice was wry when she said, "I imagine none of your previous patients have been nursing their post-traumatic stress disorder for more than two centuries."

He raised an eyebrow. "Maybe not. But that only means you already have some pretty damned good coping mechanisms in place." He regarded her for a moment, his eyes fading back to their normal ocean blue. "You're claustrophobic, but moments after I met you, you were crawling through a collapsed building. How did you do that?"

Humiliation rose to her cheeks. "No great feat of psychology there, I'm afraid. I told Xander and Duchess to give me a mental smack upside the head if they felt me start to lose my shit."

He snorted in amusement, but the feeling leaking through the bond was respect. "An elegant and no-nonsense solution," he said, succinctly. "Why am I not surprised in the least?"

He lifted a hand to smooth her hair back, his thumb brushing her temple. "Okay, next question. Do you trust me to listen through the mental link while we make love? I probably still suck at using it, I'm afraid. Duchess tried to show me, but it was only just now that I really started to feel it properly."

Mason, she sent, *if I didn't trust you, I'd be shielding. Being able to sense you like this is one of the most incredible things I've ever felt in my life.*

He made another one of those low noises that played havoc with her senses. *Then let me look after you. Because I have an idea about that.*

His communication was a little clumsy... a little louder than it needed to be. It also made her want to burrow into his aura of protective warmth and never see the light of day again. Could she do this? Could she let go and trust Mason to keep her from falling?

Please, she said. *Help me stay here in the present. With you. I can't do it alone.*

Saying it so bluntly along the bond almost felt... *freeing*. She was still straddling him, but now she was the one burying her face in the crook of his neck, as his muscular arms wrapped around her back and held her close. Utilizing the new strength that came with vampirism, he moved one hand down to cradle her hip and stood up, still holding her against him.

"Does the door on the guest room lock?" he asked, with the barest hint of humor. "I can't really say I'm in the mood to give our hostess—or anyone else—a free show."

"Sorry. You won't find locking doors in a place like this," she said, wrapping her legs around his hips carefully, so as not to accidentally stab him with the Cheetah's epoxy arch. "But the others won't be back for hours yet."

I'm going to hold you to that prediction, he sent, his mental voice already gaining confidence. His tone of delicious promise sent a clench of desire through her belly.

The small guest room only held a single, narrow bed. While it was far from grand; compared to the slave shack in which she'd grown up, it was a palace. And given a choice between being back at the Royal Oasis in Pétionville, or here with Mason—feeling fragile tendrils of hope for the future unfurl behind her ribs—she would choose this simple house in rural Haiti any day of the week.

I'm right there with you, sweetheart, Mason said, setting her down with infinite care. *Luxurious trappings are overrated. Though I'll admit I'm relieved as well — I did warn you I was a poor doctor, not a rich one.*

The mattress was soft beneath her back. She smiled up at him, a feeling growing inside her that she tentatively identified as... *joy.*

"Here's what's going to happen next," he said, his fingers caressing the contours of her face. "I'm going to taste every single square inch of your body."

Her eyes flared as he straightened away from the bed and began matter-of-factly unbuttoning his shirt.

"And the instant I sense that you're starting to drift away from me," he continued, "I'm going to do something to remind you just exactly where you are and who you're with. I'm going to bite you, and I'm going to drink from you."

A rush of heat swept over her cool flesh from the roots of her hair to the toes of her right foot. "*Yes...*" she breathed.

The shirt slid to the ground, and Mason pulled off the black tee he wore underneath. His were not the sculpted muscles of a gym rat, but rather the hard muscles of real use — hauling crates of medical supplies, trekking from village to village to meet with rebel leaders, swinging a hammer to fix and maintain substandard facilities.

He toed off his shoes, his hands dropping to the fastening of his trousers as he went on. "Then, when you're crying out my name, begging me to take you, I'm going to sink my fangs and my cock so deep inside you that all you'll be able to feel is *me*."

Trousers and boxers slid down together. A lust far different than the sweet and tender excitement she'd felt as a girl in Augustin's arms surged up. It was the lust of one dark creature for another — the part of herself that Oksana had spent centuries denying, controlling, and subsuming.

Now... it wanted *out*.

She scrabbled at her top, dragging it off. After a mere moment's frustration with her sports bra, she ripped it down the middle — not really having intended to do so, but not particularly worried about it either. Meanwhile, Mason had crawled onto the foot of the bed, and was now prowling up her body to drag off her shorts and panties.

When he pulled them down to her knees and then paused, it was as though someone had thrown a bucket of ice water on her. He was looking at her prosthesis. Her breath caught in her throat, but Mason only threw her a gently chiding look, and paused in his removal of her shorts to ease her leg free of the Cheetah's molded sleeve.

He set it aside on the floor near the bed, and pulled everything else off, leaving her bare. Despite her best efforts, her mind hummed with uncertainty.

Well, now, sweetheart. Mason's mental tone was wry, but there was a hint of sadness in it, as well. *I think that solves my dilemma of where to start first.*

She watched in amazement — in near disbelief — as he cradled her left leg and pressed an openmouthed kiss below her knee, only inches above where the limb terminated in an ugly stump. It was such an odd feeling, that gentle press of lips. With the exception of the occasional lucky blow by an opponent during a fight, no one had touched her there since—

Since... well... *ever*.

How could he stand to *do* that? It was such a hideous deformity, with the puckered scars and the muscles atrophied—the visual distillation of her monstrous nature. Of the unnatural *thing* she'd become, in those moments when she'd awoken underground and started tearing at the boards of the coffin... at her own flesh and bone...

Fangs sank into her leg, and the twin flashes of pain followed by a deep, drawing heat jerked her back to the present with a gasp.

I did warn you, Mason sent.

He drew another mouthful of her blood from the wound, and the wash of carnal pleasure that flooded the bond from both directions blasted away the unwanted memories under its force.

"M-Mason," she moaned, and received an answering rumble as he pulled out, lapping at the wounds until they closed.

He resumed kissing his way up her leg, awakening every nerve as he passed. It had been *so long*. So long since she'd felt anything more intimate than a chaste kiss on the cheek or a sisterly embrace. And when she had felt something like this, all those long years ago, Augustin had always started at her breasts, cupping and teasing them. Not running his tongue up the inside of her leg, teasing his way slowly upward—

I told you, said the voice twining inside her mind, *I'm not him.*

Fangs slid into the sensitive flesh high on the inside of her thigh, and she cried out, writhing, hands clawing at the bedclothes as he drank again. The dark lust from earlier surged back, swamping thought and leaving only need behind.

Mason pulled his fangs out and caught her wrists, pinning them by her hips when she reached for him. *Fuck, yes,* he thought, *That's it — I don't want you thinking, Oksana. I want you feeling.*

And, oh, was she feeling. She felt every wrinkle in the blanket beneath her as she twisted restlessly against the bed. She felt the addictive jolt of pleasure through the bond as Mason's hips flexed unconsciously against the mattress upon seeing her give herself up to sensation — give herself up to *him*.

She felt the ache of delicious frustration as he continued to kiss up her body, bypassing the place that burned for his touch, in favor of sucking marks onto her belly that faded almost as fast as he could make new ones.

She didn't slide into the past again. Yet he still pierced her with his fangs and drank, over and over, because they were vampires and they both wanted it, and why shouldn't he?

At some point, he released her wrists. By the time he finally kissed his way up her neck to her lips, she was growling and digging furrows into his back with her fingernails. She quieted when his mouth slanted over hers, demanding entrance, teasing her tongue out to duel with his. He coaxed her to invade his mouth in return, sucking on her tongue as his fangs scraped deliciously against her tender flesh.

Her sex throbbed, aching and wet, though he'd barely so much as brushed it with his lips on his way up her body. She tore her mouth away from the kiss, tasting blood, though she wasn't sure whose.

"Take me, damn it!" she nearly snarled. "Take me right now, Mason, or I swear I'll drink you dry, just so I can feed you our mingled blood and then do it all over again!"

Some tiny, quiet part of herself was completely shocked by both the threat, and how very much she meant it. But Mason was a vampire now. She couldn't hurt him by feeding from him. Nothing she could do to him with her fangs would damage him permanently. Quite the opposite. The wall of lust that slammed into her from his side of the mental link proved that if she did get the upper hand on him in such a way, he would go down happy and come back looking forward to the next round.

We might need to work on your begging skills just a bit, sweetheart, he sent, even his mental voice sounding breathless. *But in the mean time, far be it from me to argue.*

A strong thigh forced her legs apart, and teeth sank into her neck, pinning her in place as his cock, large and blunt, slid along the folds of her sex, further enflaming her. She canted her hips, lining him up, and keened as he thrust inside her tight passage.

After so long untouched, the sudden penetration was savage, punishing, and perfect. It was everything she needed, and nothing like *anything* she'd ever had before. It was exactly what her inner darkness craved. She didn't want time to adjust to his girth piercing her. She didn't want tenderness and sweet nothings whispered in her ear. She wanted her mate, all at once, here, now, with nothing held back.

Her fingernails raked down Mason's back and dug into the hard globes of his arse, dragging him into her body over and over as they sweated and writhed together. Her head started to swim as he drained her blood, the room growing dim and hazy around her. Oksana's perception narrowed, all the unimportant things falling away, one by one, until everything was focused on those two incandescent points of contact between them.

She reveled in the feeling of their life force twining together. In the way his pleasure grew and grew, until he jerked his head away from her neck, red liquid dripping down his chin and pleasure coiling at the base of his spine, ready to explode.

She surged up, fangs tearing into his neck, swallowing great mouthfuls of their combined blood as he cried out. He jerked into her, arms holding her tightly to him as his blood and seed filled her at the same time, flooding her with their mingled power. Ecstasy shook free from her center, spreading outward through her awareness in great, rolling waves until she was certain her body would not be able to contain it all.

When the blood red haze across her vision finally faded, it revealed that she and Mason had collapsed into a tangled heap on the narrow bed. He'd rolled to the side just enough not to crush her, but her legs around his hips meant that his length was still nestled intimately inside her.

"Bloody *Christ*," he mumbled against her neck. "Oksana…"

She held him in a tight embrace, something like awe blanketing her mind.

I guess I was a bit overdue when it comes to accepting what I am now, she thought, a bit sheepishly.

A puff of cool breath against her collarbone accompanied Mason's flash of exhausted amusement. *Well, whenever you need a reminder…*

I know exactly where to come, she agreed.

He lifted his head enough to look at her with eyes still lit from within with sparks of cobalt. She smiled, bringing a finger up to swipe a thin trail of red from his lips before sucking it clean. Despite the shattering climax they'd just shared, his cock twitched inside her at the sight. They both shivered in reaction, oversensitive, and she reluctantly let him slip free.

"I don't know how I could possibly have gotten this lucky," she said, the words barely more than a whisper.

His mouth twitched. "Funny, I was thinking very nearly the same thing." He rolled them into a more comfortable position in the cramped space, her head resting on his chest, one arm and one leg flung over him.

"I can't say that I'm not terrified by what's coming," he said truthfully. "But it would still be coming whether we'd found each other or not, Oksana. This way, we have someone to lean on, when times get hard. I'm so glad that we stumbled into each others' lives."

Tears clogged Oksana's throat, and she didn't fight them. Unlike all the bitter ones that had choked her over the past days, these felt cleansing. Freeing.

Mason must have sensed that, because he only held her tighter against him as she let them run their course.

"I was lost," she said, once they'd passed. "I've been lost for *so long*, Mason. But you've showed me the way home."

They kissed, with none of the urgency of lust, and none of the bitterness of the painful past. When Oksana finally pulled away, she settled back against him and traced her fingers over the hard lines of his chest.

"What will you do about the clinic?" she asked, knowing that she would do anything in her power to support whatever he decided.

"I don't know yet. I plan to talk to Gita — she's my partner there." Mason met her eyes, his expression serious. "I intend to tell her the truth, Oksana. I trust her with my life, and something inside me says that it's time for us to stop living in the shadows."

A week ago, Oksana might have protested. But she had felt the same thing in the last few days. "I'll speak with the others," she promised. "But I think you may be right about that. It feels as though something is changing. Something fundamental."

He nodded.

"What about family?" she asked. "Do you have any?"

"My mother is in Australia, at a nursing home in Sydney. She has early-onset Alzheimer's. I'd like to visit her, but it's unlikely she'll recognize me," he said, and she could feel the old pain leaking through the link. "I have a brother, though. In Singapore. His name's Jackson. We're as close as two people can be, who live on opposite sides of the world. So that's another difficult conversation I need to have."

"Then we'll go to Singapore together, if that's what you want," she said.

He smiled. "I'd like that. He's going to go head over heels for you, you know. I bet his wife and their kids will, too."

A faintly sheepish look came over his face, and Oksana looked at him questioningly. "What is it?" she asked.

"As it happens, you've got Jack to thank for us being here right now," he said. "He's one of the two people who called me an idiot."

That strange, unfamiliar feeling of joy crept over Oksana once more. "In that case, I'm even more excited about meeting him. Though he was still wrong."

"You two can argue that one without me," he said with a smile. He paused and gave a short laugh. "Oh. You know what? That just reminded me of something. Stay here for a tick."

He eased out of bed and rummaged through the pockets of his discarded trousers in the dark. When he came back, he held a mobile phone. Oksana looked at him curiously, but didn't protest as he got back into bed and arranged the blanket over them, pulling her back to rest against his chest when they were settled.

"That's not a sat-phone," she pointed out. "You won't be able to get a signal out here."

"I know," he said. "The battery's about dead, anyway. But Jack has been after me since the day you and I met to send him a picture. I assume since I still have a reflection, that means I can take a photo?"

Oksana nodded, amused.

Mason unlocked the screen and pulled up the camera app, before holding the phone out at arm's length and angling it toward their faces. "I think this one will convey all the relevant information, don't you?"

She laughed softly. "I guess it will, at that."

His chest moved beneath her cheek as he chuckled. "Smile for the camera…"

She did, not blinking as the flash went off. He brought the phone down and tapped the screen, bringing the photo up for her to see.

He'd been absolutely right. His incandescent look of happiness, combined her satisfied, cat-with-the-cream smile, would tell anyone who saw it *exactly* what they needed to know.

No question about it.

EPILOGUE

London, two weeks later

Xander's mobile phone buzzed in his trouser pocket, and he ignored it. Like clockwork, some thirty seconds later, it vibrated again to indicate a new voicemail. After debating with himself for the space of a few heartbeats while the pounding bass of the club's music system throbbed through his chest, he pulled it out.

Under the strobing blacklight, his pale skin looked even paler than usual. His hand felt pleasantly and ever so slightly disconnected from the rest of him, after the blood he'd just drunk from a random junkie who'd been skulking around the hallway in the back. He flicked a thumb across the screen lock, unsurprised to see Tré's number at the top of the notification list.

Tré's smooth, Eastern European accent competed with the deep house track rumbling through the club, only vampire hearing allowing Xander to untangle his words from the din around him.

"Xander. Pick up your damned phone. Disappearing like this is foolhardy under the present circumstances, as you well know." A pause. *"Oksana is concerned for you, tovarăş."*

Xander ground his jaw for a moment before opening up a text window.

Fuck off, Tré. You can give me a damned week without breathing down my neck every fifteen minutes.

The reply came almost instantly.

Are you in London?

Of course I'm in bloody London. Now. Fuck. Off.

He powered the phone off and slipped it carelessly back in his pocket. Already, his pleasant buzz was wearing off, his undead metabolism breaking down the drugs in minutes. Just another one of the many, many shitty things about vampirism.

The atmosphere of *Club Cirque* wrapped around him like barbed wire dipped in anesthetic. Hidden under the rails not far off Lambeth Road, the only public access was through an unmarked railway arch that looked like nothing so much as a simple garage.

Lambeth at large had a reputation—not undeserved—of being home to gangs, drugs, and murderers. *Club Cirque* had a reputation of being home to freaks—also, not undeserved. Dressed in a burgundy button-down, black tailored trousers, and polished Berluti Scritto shoes, Xander's only real concession to the unofficial dress code had been to undo a couple of buttons at the top of his shirt, baring a triangle of pale chest and collarbone.

By rights, this should have made him stand out like a sore thumb among the sea of tattoos, piercings, whips, chains, leather, and dyed hair. That was the thing about freaks, though—they always recognized their own.

His black mood settled firmly back around his shoulders, and he scanned the crowd. Alcoholics weren't going to do it for him tonight. Where was a heroin addict when you really needed one?

A small commotion erupted at the entrance to the hallway where Xander had partaken of his second-hand coke hit a little while ago. It was a woman, maybe thirty years of age with waist-length black hair and a light brown complexion with olive undertones. Her dark eyes were wide, and more than a little frantic looking. Like him, she was not decked out for a place like this—indeed, the look she was sporting could best be described as *newly homeless*. Yet something about her made his intuition tingle.

She was stopping people, talking to them urgently, but they brushed her off. She cast around, saw Xander looking, and closed the distance between them. Something odd teased his nose, but it was impossible to place it within the potent cloud of perfume, smoke, and human body odor that choked the atmosphere of the underground venue.

"Please, I need help," she said, a faint accent coloring the words. Indian—probably from the Kashmir region or thereabouts.

He leaned against the bar, regarding her from his advantage of height. "Sorry, luv. I'm off the clock tonight. The bartender can call 999 for you if it's an emergency."

She shook her head. "No, you don't understand. It's my sister. Some... *thing* attacked us in the alley, and she got in front of me. She's hurt—I can't wake her up."

Xander stopped himself before he could say, *A mugging in Lambeth? How shocking*, because there was being brusque, and then there was being unnecessarily arsehole-ish.

"Emergency services can send an ambulance around," he said instead, and started to raise a hand to get the barman's attention.

"But the thing that attacked us!" she said, her voice rising. "It wasn't human!"

He lowered his hand.

Don't get involved, counseled the truncated and badly atrophied remnants of his good sense. *You need this kind of shit right now like you need eight hours inside a full-spectrum tanning booth.*

"What do you mean, not human?" he asked, sounding tired even to his own ears.

"It was a child," she said, her wide brown eyes begging him to believe her. "But he had these eerie, glowing eyes, and he moved so fast he seemed to blur. Right before he leapt at my sister, he sort of snarled at us, and I swear I saw these long, sharp teeth — like fangs!"

Xander's brain crashed to a standstill, thoughts piling up like derailed train cars.

"What." His tone was utterly flat.

"Please — I'm not crazy! I know what I saw!" She gestured the way she'd come. "Just come back with me and help me with my sister... her neck's all torn up and I'm afraid by the time an ambulance gets here it will be too late!"

Had he said *heroin addict*? After this, he'd need to bypass heroin altogether, and go straight for meth. He pushed away from the bar. If nothing else, he could at least open a vein and heal the poor girl's neck, assuming she wasn't already dead.

"Come on, then," he said, "show me." The implications, if this woman had actually seen what she described...

But, no. Implications could wait until he saw the victim and the scene for himself. His companion broke into a run, and he jogged alongside her to keep up. The tradesmen's entrance to the club consisted of a flight of stairs next to a rickety lift designed to ferry freight up and down to street level. They took the stairs two at a time, and the woman pushed through the double doors leading to the dingy alley running behind the railway arches.

"She's just up here," the woman said breathlessly, gesturing toward a darker stretch of shadows that ended in a solid brick wall.

Xander opened his mouth to ask what the hell two women had been doing walking through a dark, dead-end alley at four in the morning, but then the stench of the place assailed him and he snapped it shut again, grimacing. Piss, vomit, rotting garbage, animal droppings, and—

"Over here." She waved him toward a gap between a dumpster and some discarded truck tires.

—and wet dog.

He whirled back toward the mouth of the alley, in time to see around a dozen feral looking men and women melt out of the shadow, blocking the exit. His erstwhile damsel in distress turned and darted past him to join the group. He let her go.

"Oh, you have *got* to be shitting me," Xander said, wondering for a bare instant which god he'd managed to piss off this time, and how big of a charitable donation it would take to get back on that deity's good side.

"Sorry," the dark-haired woman told him, sounding genuinely sheepish. She jerked her chin at the man next to her, who was decked out in chains and ripped camo like some sort of cut-rate Mad Max reject. "He didn't think you'd come if you knew what we really were, vampire."

"Smarter than he looks, then," Xander said blandly. "Good to know."

The man's answering smile was thin and cruel. "You'd be amazed." He cocked his head. "No doubt you're getting ready to fly away home, little vamp, but you should hear what I have to tell you first. I've got something you want."

"You think so?" Xander asked. "What is it? Fleas? Kibbles? A squeaky toy? Maybe a nice, meaty bone?"

That cruel smile never wavered. "I've got that little baby vamp Manisha described to you, all chained up in iron shackles so he can't get away. Interested, now?"

"God, I fucking hate werewolves," Xander told him, tone still conversational. "Have I mentioned that yet?"

"Oh, well. Off you flap, then," the leader said, making a shooing motion with one hand. "Nothing stopping you, is there? Not unless you want us to take you to see Junior first…"

Xander gritted his teeth, wanting nothing more at that moment than the human ability to crawl into a bottle, get blind, falling-down drunk, and never crawl back out.

"Fine, Fluffy," he grated. "You win. Take me to see this alleged vampire, and I won't brandish the rolled-up newspaper."

Fluffy's flat, hard eyes were starting to make Xander's skin crawl, quite honestly. But he held back any further insults as Fluffy shrugged a brawny shoulder.

"That's real magnanimous of you, mate," said the werewolf. "Best follow us, in that case. Dawn's coming soon. You wouldn't want to get a terminal case of sunburn, now would you?"

Actually, mate, Xander thought sourly, *you might be surprised. Lately, that prospect has been growing more appealing by the day.*

finis

The *Circle of Blood* series continues in *Book Four: Lover's Absolution*.

To get the free prequel to the *Circle of Blood* series sent directly to your inbox, visit
www.rasteffan.com/circle

Printed in Great Britain
by Amazon